WILD WALT AND THE ROCK CREEK GANG

Library of Congress Control Number: 2019911499

Oakwood Terrace Publishing

For CV, ETJ and JDJ

WILD WALT *and*

the ROCK CREEK

GANG

a novel by

ANONYMOUS

1

EVERY WORD OF THIS COULD BE TRUE, and certainly the gist of it is. I've held the proof in my hands. To the literary world, to those who will most covet our discoveries, I say this: Forget it. You'll never be able to verify our story. You'll never track us down either, not that you'd bother to try, or it would do you any good to find us. Walt Whitman's secrets are hereby set loose, free from our clutches and beyond the reach of yours. Free as a bird. So tip your hat to Wild Walt and walk on by. Find your salvation elsewhere.

The salvation of Walt and me both began, as the bona fide literati might say, most inauspiciously.

I, a failed wannabe John Keats scholar and the anonymous fellow who lucked upon Walt's deepest secrets, got fired. Three students showed up to register for my class on the fourth of September, open enrollment night at the one-building branch campus of a community college near Washington, D.C. I told them not to bother. They

3

trudged away in silence. Introduction to Literature, in its heyday a top-draw gut course among the inner-suburban, working-class students who valiantly believed attending community college would lessen their struggles, passed away without a whimper.

Without the long-awaited first paycheck of the fall I couldn't cover the upcoming rent on my cheap, suburban, ground-floor garden apartment. Near broke with nowhere else to stay, I had no choice. The backwoods college boy who long ago shunned his hometown with such highfalutin hopes would skulk back home, tail between his legs.

Walt's salvation likewise began with him throwing in the towel, but under much more dire circumstances than those of my little temporary setback. The failed, largely unknown poet, his breakdown complete, poked his way with his umbrella down the long, steep bank to bid farewell to his beloved Rock Creek. It was Wednesday afternoon, the twenty second of June 1864.

Earlier that month Grant had advanced into central Virginia. Sixty-five thousand men were killed or wounded in the gory weeks that followed, overfilling Washington's ramshackle hospitals with torn men from both sides. The wounded died at the rate of one every hour at the big Armory Square Hospital. Walt had spent nearly every day since December 1862 comforting the sick and dying. Melancholy and ill health had transformed him into an old man awaiting death, though he'd turned only forty-five May 31.

He reached the two big rocks gating the entryway to his perch, lifted his round-topped felt hat, wiped his brow and dropped to all fours. He already regretted his sentimental detour and wished he'd walked straight to the train station to begin his retreat home, to his cramped little bedroom in Brooklyn, his refuge of last resort, where his dear mother would leave him be, let him anguish in silence with the dead and be bothered no more by the living.

Whitman scholars say he left Washington for Brooklyn the next day, Thursday the twenty-third of June 1864, a date corroborated irrefutably by our evidence (Exhibits A-E).

Walt crawled halfway out to his seat, the narrowing corner of the rock that angled out over the creek, before he lifted his head and spotted the handsome, bearded man staring at him and the striking young woman with raven-black hair just beginning to cross the creek toward him.

Ezra knew to turn and walk quickly away at the sight of any stranger, particularly a white man. But he recognized this fellow, a hunched-over, wore-out version of the lusty, proud man in the picture, who oddly and abruptly shifted into reverse and crawled ass-backwards fast as he could. Ezra chuckled at the sight—he'd not once been fled from—and hurried up the bank as Walt, still on his knees, stabbed his umbrella in the ground and struggled to his feet.

"I come here for solitude," he declared. "Allow me to have my spot to myself and go on your way." Ezra tried not to bristle at the first command he'd heard since his freedom and glanced back at June, jumping rock to rock, so intent on crossing the creek without touching water that she'd yet to notice they had company.

Ezra well knew it would be more prudent to grant Walt his wish, for June, if she met him, would not be able to resist divulging their secret. But he knew, too, he could never deny her this chance.

He nodded toward June. "I claimed that perch for her and me weeks ago. We claim this big rock down here, too. June wants to meet you, so come on down here."

Walt shot Ezra a mean look, but stymied by the steep climb, started down the bank. Ezra grinned at another first, a white man obeying his command.

Walt hobbled down to the creek, deviled by the idea that in his heyday, before his demise, he would have cherished meeting these two fine American specimens, who appeared as healthy and vibrant as he had once been.

"I remember the first time I met you," June said.

He glared at her. "We've never met."

"I'm from an old New York family of book lovers," she said. "Fell in love with poetry as a young girl. Keats became my favorite. Finer to me than even Shakespeare's sonnets. One morning I saw this little notice in the *New York Tribune* advertising your *Leaves*. Printed with your own hands. I walked down Broadway and went in Fowler and Wells. And there it was, *Leaves of Grass*, on its own table, that strange title embroidered on that fancy, dark green, cloth cover.

"I opened it. Right there on the first page was your picture. But not your name. What a pose you struck." She stood and showed him. "Hand on your hip. Head tilted slightly to the left. The better for you to gaze upon me. As though you already knew me. And dared me to know you. I stood there under your spell gazing back into your eyes for I don't know how long."

Walt looked past her expressionless and sighed. She dropped her pose.

"I bought your book and hurried home and sat in the drawing room."

She recited:

I celebrate myself,
And what I assume you shall assume,
For every atom belonging to me as good belongs to you.

I loafe and invite my soul
I lean and loafe at my ease…observing a spear of summer grass.

"That's as far as I got before I knew we must be alone with each other. I took you up to my room and locked the door. We loafed all day. I read *Leaves* straight through. I bet I'm not the first to confess this to you. I kept going back to the part where you…" She hesitated and blushed. Ezra knew she feigned her innocence but played along.

"Where you celebrate your own self," he blurted out. "That's what I call it. You call it your *villain touch*, your *blind loving wrestling touch*. The one you tell to *unclench your floodgates*."

"That's why I'll never forget the first time we met," June said, "for you inspired me to discover the wonder of celebrating my own self, alongside you, and to induct you, on the spot, into my passionately guarded canon of one. I'd never imagined I'd let anyone join John Keats, least of all an unknown ruffian like you."

Mention of his former audacious self turned Walt's blank look sad-eyed. "I will be on my way down the creek now, since you two won't leave me alone."

2

MY LITTLE PONY PRANCED ACROSS the cover of the giant card slipped under my door to greet me the morning of my dreaded return home. Inside, HAPPY BIRTHDAY was crossed out, GOOD LUCK TEACH! block-printed above.

The first half-dozen inscriptions, off-angled in oversized print in a doomed effort to fill the left-hand page, thanked me for small favors I'd done over the years as life adviser to the stymied, amateur paralegal to the undocumented and lease-cosigner, money-lender and loan-forgiver to the more broke than me.

Then I hit pay dirt. On the otherwise empty right-hand page, "Love always, Teach, and thanks for Emily—the original Goth girl" was black-inked in normal-sized, no-nonsense cursive by a purple-haired Latina, now a blog-published Gurlesque poet, whom the previous spring I'd turned onto Emily Dickinson, Sappho and Edna St. Vincent Millay.

I'd spawned at least one new lover of books and poetry every semester since I'd finagled the job, long ago, to tide me over until I finished a ground-breaking paper on John Keats, which would be published in a notable literary journal, which would get me into a PhD program, which would lead to a proper professorship and, more importantly, possibly put me in contention to win back the heart of the love of my life (who was then earning her doctorate at Harvard and most fittingly has become a renowned scholar of Keats, Dickenson, and Whitman.)

Unlike me, Mrs. Cummings, the elderly, book-loving widow who manned the apartment lobby office, took our parting in stride, unruffled by either my lack of rent money or my imminent departure. My suggestion soon after I moved in that we loan each other our favorite novels had blossomed into a treasured friendship. Every weekday at four we rendezvoused for precisely one hour in her windowless office to banter over writers and poets and the cup of tea I always brought her. "This is for you," I said, and handed her my beloved paperback of E.M. Forster's *Aspects of the Novel*. She gave me a frail hug.

Fernando, my other dear friend, was a book lover too. The reserved, bilingual maintenance man sat on the neatly made bed in his handyman basement apartment rereading Raymond Chandler. We met shortly after five every weekday for cocktail hour, his place one day, mine the next, to swap books and tell tales of our heroes. His was the legendary, blind-at-age-fifty-five storyteller, writer, poet and scholar, Jorge Luis Borges. I handed him his present, *Professor Borges*, a dog-eared treasure trove of unedited transcriptions of miraculously recovered cassette recordings of lectures Borges gave at Buenos Aires University in 1966.

"We'll always have Borges," I said.

"Yes," he said, and stood and politely shook my hand. "Borges was a man of valiant bravery and despair. Be brave, my friend. No despair for you. Stay away from that silent hillside of Keats you speak of so often."

"I will endeavor to be like you," I said, loathe to let go his hand. "Steadfast and undaunted."

I lugged the last crate of books across the dead lawn and weed-sprouting parking lot to my 2003 Charger, christened Black

Beauty years ago by Ademir, a fun-loving El Salvadorian whom I'd granted a gentleman's C five years earlier, during his graffiti period. Thus the eye-catching moniker on Beauty's rear end: her name in loopy, three-inch high, metallic pink cursive, meticulously hand-painted during the last class of spring semester, part prank, part tribute to his teach.

I tucked Little Pony between my only other bona fides: framed diplomas in literary studies, undergrad and grad, from UNC Chapel Hill. I squeezed the crate in the last slot in the trunk and surveyed my hastily relocated library: three plastic crates of poetry and biographies of poets on the left, three of literary criticism in the middle and, on the right, three mixed crates of poetry and novels, all slated to be reincarnated eventually in voice.

Riding shotgun were three fat CD folders of writers already ascended, recorded over the years by students—a few, admittedly, well aware that I should but would not flunk them—who clamored to read for my audio hall of fame, inspired years before by the raptures of my late, book-loving, backwoods grandma, Memaw, when I read her favorites aloud to her during her demented years.

I come from glass-half-full, walk-on-the-sunny side blood, which, along with their sudden crying jags, sustained dear Mom and Memaw through glass-near-empty lives plagued by undependable, make-do men. Their teary anguishing, mostly behind closed doors, tormented me as a child, and as I drove into the city one last time to bid adieu to my favorite poetry-reading spot at the edge of Rock Creek Park, I banished any further thoughts of how terribly sad it was that I would never again see my two best friends or my refuse-to-be-downtrodden students, even those who never read a book.

3

THREE WEEKS PRIOR TO RUNNING into Walt, Ezra broke, for
the very first time, his bedrock rule for survival: never dawdle where
others can see you before you see them.

He sat astride the corner of the rock that overhung the creek
(dynamited long ago to make way for Rock Creek Parkway) and
with a flat-bottom rock hammered on his prized chisel, still able
to distinguish every speckle in its rash of blood stains. He chiseled
out an "E" and paused to exorcise forever from his mind's eye the
spasm of violence that daybreak of his freedom two years ago, for
he believed that evil craved nothing so much as to linger on and on,
to be relived, again and again.

Upon completing the "J", he called forth the spirit of his fre-
quent companion John Keats. Much to his own astonishment, after
living three months with June, he had come to believe, at least in his
least troubled moments, in the Muses and in the ever-lasting spirit

of young John. Ezra looked up into the trees. He pulled forth a vision of the happy, not yet dying young poet and in John's presence, declared himself to be a good-hearted man, despite what he'd done.

He asked John to join him in the closing benediction, the most difficult part of the ceremony for Ezra, who took great pride in never once being so foolish to appeal to god or anyone else for anything. He looked skyward again and mumbled heartfelt thanks to the Muses for the good fortune and absolution he'd found at their creek and in their woods. Before he dissipated, Keats said "amen" and congratulated Ezra for being a favorite of Calliope, whom John declared to be the lustiest of the Muses and his personal favorite.

"I hope you're right." Ezra smiled at himself for conversing out loud with a dead poet, for he considered himself first and foremost a practical-minded man of good common sense. He chiseled the "+" between the E and J and gathered himself to scour the wooded hillsides. A devout student and lover of sightlines, he bored his eyes down each narrowing tunnel in turn and traveled far and leisurely deep into the forest. Barely a leaf fluttered. All clear. He descended greatly satisfied. Time for some creek music and wine-sipping.

That previous spring, in early March, the old man who two years earlier had let Ezra move into a one-room shack in exchange for his full-time labor, both inside and outside the house, had taken his family and fled the Civil War for England. As Ezra hauled out their luggage, the white-suited man, a sad alcoholic from South Carolina low country who demanded Ezra call him master, told him to board up the house. He could stay in his shack. But if Ezra shirked his last duty, or pilfered, he'd find out, and although Ezra could not legally be re-enslaved in the District of Columbia, the man said with a dirty grin, he was well acquainted with slave hunters who combed the city and would consider Ezra a mighty fine catch.

Good thing you don't know there's a rich bounty on my head in Carolina, Ezra thought. Yes master, he said, and smiled to himself, giddy that he'd uttered those words for what he would make certain would be the last time. He finished nailing shut the house, put the tools back under the porch and scooped up his hidden bounty—an armful of books, excluding *Moby Dick* and *Walden*, which he'd already snuck out, read and returned.

The young woman who boarded with the family had caught him that morning eyeing the bookshelves. She'd given him his first ever wink from a white woman, then left with the family to the train station, on her way back home to New York.

He'd headed off across the overgrown pasture and allowed himself to imagine that his stroke of luck was not too good to be true. He worried he might jinx his good fortune if he contemplated its full extent but could not resist. His could now fulfill his only desires—to be free from all indignities and to be self-sufficient and left alone.

As always, he took a slightly different path through the woods and over the ridge, so as not to wear a trail to his one-room home, shrouded in scrawny pines and overgrown with wisteria. He lit a candle and caressed each of his new treasures: *Frankenstein*, *Great Expectations*, *The Woman in White*, *The Scarlet Letter* and *Vanity Fair*. Before deciding which to read first, he would indulge an even greater yearning—to wander freely, unimpeded by the demands of any master, in the solitude of the wooded hills and the creek he'd come to love.

Then came the knock on his door.

4

I ROLLED BEAUTY TO a stop halfway around the empty semi-circle at the trail head and ambled under cover of the big oaks and poplars into the surprising forest that first beckoned me decades ago, when I'd come upon it as I cruised aimless and lost across the city. I'd never seen the park empty and quiet. Minus the steady stream of dog-walkers, stoners and joggers there on every previous visit, always on Sunday, the deserted woods gave off a potent and mysterious vibe.

I plunked down on my regular sitting rock and opened *The Odes of John Keats*. A stout fellow in a cowboy hat, hiking boots, and ancient blue jeans appeared out of nowhere and threw up a friendly hand. He declared it to be his rock and offered to share it with me if I'd scoot over.

I made room. He asked me if it was my first time in the park. I told him I'd spent every Sunday afternoon on his rock for many years. He avoided Sundays and much preferred weekdays, when the park, he said, "shows its true self." I told him this was my last visit—I'd come here to read my favorite poet and say farewell to the gallant oaks that reminded me of him.

"A Keats fan, huh?"

A just-retired poetry professor, I fibbed, on my way back home, way down in the Smoky Mountains.

"Anybody going to be waiting up on you, down home?"

"Nope."

I could already smell the mildew inside the decrepit double-wide trailer. It sits at the bottom of a hollow, deep in the Blue Ridge, a dozen miles outside a once-sleepy town. I could smell the fragrant outside, too, and see the cow shit I would hopscotch through to get from the un-graveled end of the mudhole driveway to the buckling, white plastic front door, where I would be welcomed, I hoped, by my second cousin, my last living kin, whom I'd not been in touch with for years. My bright side reminded me that the view from the concrete-block, jerry-rigged front steps is superb.

The stranger leaned forward to fix me with an up-from-under look and rubbed the brim of his hat between his forefinger and thumb, like it would tell him something.

"They call me Cowboy," he said. "Since this is your last visit to the park, I'll tell you a little secret. What's your name?"

"Jack."

"Jack, these oaks might remind you of Keats, but these woods belong to Walt Whitman."

"Who detested Keats," I said.

"Wrong," he said. "Walt came to admire Keats. Found him to be a kindred spirit, though he never admitted that, not publicly."

I dismissed a burst of naïve glee. I could not be face to face with a fellow who knew something that had been missed by umpteen thousands of Whitman scholars. Everything Walter ever said, and was said to have said, every word he'd ever written—they'd pored over all of it, again and again, and do so to this day, for the elusive allure of Whitman, like Keats, never diminishes. They all agreed Whitman didn't like Keats—he'd said so himself.

"You must be quite the Whitman scholar," I said.

His grin plowed ditches from the corners of his mouth to the sides of his nose. "I'm a retired D.C. firefighter. Made captain, as a matter of fact. But I do know Walt Whitman. Intimately, you could say. The greatest American poet."

"No doubt his mystery looms over the American canon."

"What mystery is that?"

"How an unschooled, common fellow wrote *Leaves of Grass* and fulfilled Emerson's vision of a new breed of American poet."

"Emerson has nothing to do with Walter's greatness," he said. "Greatest American poet, don't you agree?"

I grinned at the funning to be had when strangers abandon chit-chat to tussle on passionately held literary ground.

"The most outlandish," I said. "Rebellious outsider, lover of the common people, defier of the literary kingdom who whipped up, out of nowhere, the most original and revolutionary American poetry ever, still to this day. A sex-worshiping, seemingly bisexual provocateur who reinvented himself as the grandfatherly Good Gray Poet."

The flash that shot through his eyes called for a punch line. "In short, the poet Emerson called for."

I'd set captain firefighter ablaze. He jumped to his feet, put his hands on his hips, blew air out his nose and drew up his meanest look, the one that told me he wished he could wring my neck.

"Listen up, Jack! I know, without a smidgen of doubt, he is *not* a creation of Emerson. Stop dodging my question, professor. Greatest or not!"

"With one caveat," I said. "He can stand center stage. But Emily Dickinson is there, too, just as much a presence, although she prefers being off-stage."

"You so sweet on her because she liked Keats?"

"I'm not quite that simple-minded," I said. "She's every bit as brilliant and strange and puzzling as Whitman. Neither married. Like him, she may have had lovers—men and or women—or not. Doesn't matter. What matters is they're both renegade poets who came out of nowhere to storm the gates of poetry and alter its destiny forever."

"She didn't like Walter," he said.

"She never read him. Her mentor, like most of the intelligentsia, considered *Leaves of Grass* indecent and vulgar. He shooed her away from Whitman. Come on, Cowboy. We can enthrone the perfect odd couple atop the American canon. He pours forth. She burrows in. He's a manic self-promoter. She's a recluse."

He pulled a paper sack from his back pocket and took a hearty pull on a pint bottle.

"Care for a sip of fine bourbon?"

"No thank you." I stood. "Try a taste of this."

Were it to be the last
How infinite would be
What we did not suspect was marked
Our final interview.

"See how Emily packs as much punch as your Walt."

He sipped and plucked from *Leaves* a fine retort.

I have heard what the talkers were talking…the talk of the beginning
*   and the end,*
But I do not talk of the beginning or the end.

I volleyed back.

The thought behind, I strove to join
Unto the thought before—
But Sequence raveled out of Sound—
Like Balls—upon a Floor—

He cocked his head and squinted:

Backward I see in my own days where I sweated through fog with
*   linguists and contenders,*
I have no mockings or arguments…I witness and wait.

"No arguments?" I sat back down. "Good. Our odd couple of free-verse aces are officially enthroned."

"As long as Walter sits front and center and she stays offstage," he grumbled.

"What's the story behind your Whitman fixation?"

He sat down and threw his arm around me like an old chum.

"If we're asking personal questions, I got one for you," he said. "What are you looking for in life?"

"The same things everybody's looking for, if they don't already have them."

"Redemption," he said. "Salvation."

I needed to think in grander, more ecclesiastical terms to better jive with this woodsy Whitmanian priest. All I'd had in mind was a roof over my head and maybe a job at a big-box store back home until I could hustle up some kind of teacher gig.

"And what do you want, at this very moment?" he asked.

That was easy.

"To stay a little longer. Talk more poetry. Put off a long, lonely drive."

"Well this is your lucky day," he said. "You know what I want?"

"Another sip of fine bourbon?"

"For you to meet my two best friends. Come go with me."

I'd not heard that since I was a child, when my granddaddy said it to me, only once that I can recall. Come go with me. We drove beyond Sugarloaf Mountain to the end of a dirt road, then walked in moonlight to a rocky precipice over a sheer drop of thousands of feet and looked out from World's Edge at a sight I never could have imagined: the lights of the big city, faraway Charlotte, hours away, out in the Piedmont, beyond the backwoods.

"I'll come go with you," I said.

5

JUNE DILLYDALLIED BACK ON the west bank—Ezra never allowed her to walk with him in the open—but soon stood transfixed, watching him mumble and chuckle and blow dust from whatever he was chiseling. Him at the tip of the perch exposing himself to the entire creek valley greatly excited her—he must be doing something of great importance.

She waded across and joined him on the island over which they lorded. Ezra had scouted it for weeks without seeing a soul before he brought June there. About twelve feet long and six feet wide, it slanted gently from its northern top end, several feet above the water, down into the creek. More important to Ezra than its size and comfort, it was more or less hidden from the west shoreline by nearby creek boulders, which rose three or four feet above the water, and largely shielded from the east bank by the overhanging

18

rock formation. Most critically, it afforded must-have clear views of the hillsides and up and down the creek and thus satisfied Ezra's rule that they could spot any intruders before being seen, so long as they remained vigilant.

After nights when Ezra woke and fell siege to his worst fear, never mentioned to June, he even preferred the island to their well-hidden shack. It was less susceptible to sudden ambush—trapped and captured with no warning. He began toting enough books and wine and food for the two of them to spend midday to sunset on their rock, taking turns at quick, chilly baths among the boulders before the weather warmed.

June believed their domain extended way beyond their island to the creek valley and woods, for the Muses, moved by their dedication, had anointed them protectors of these sacred grounds.

"What were you doing up there?" she asked.

"Working on a surprise," he grinned. "It's not ready yet." She knew that was a fib.

"Will you chisel my name into our island?" she said, yet more evidence to Ezra that daemon blood ran through her and she could read his mind some of the time, for he was thinking how he wanted to chisel "E+J" right there, where she stood. He wasn't afraid to do so, although it would be a danger, irrefutable evidence of their scandalous coupling. But it would be selfish, would only further detain June from ending her rebellious dalliance with him and reembracing her normal life, to which he knew she would inevitably return, to settle down with a man she could openly love and marry.

"Not right now," he said, his response whenever she cornered him.

She resisted the urge to demand his chisel and do it herself. She believed that this was her island, and her creek, not because she'd moved in with Ezra, but because she had found her chosen place, one she would never give up. And her heirs would lord over this domain in their own right, just as she would, if she had to, without Ezra, although she refused to believe they would ever part.

At the age of thirteen her daddy told her she'd been born with the heart of a poet and the power of a locomotive, and every day since she awoke with that certainty. That's why she and Ezra would always be in love, because unlike any other man she'd ever met—and they'd been plenty in her wild New York days—she could say the same of him.

One day he would ask her to stay forever, and she would tell him all that. And he would carve their initials into their island and wherever else she asked. And the day was young. She stood on her tiptoes, beautiful in an awkward, willowy way in her long, white linen smock, a favorite from her past life, when she would lounge in it to read poetry and await the arrival of her breakfast. She gazed at the distant hilltop and near shouted. "I see it!"

Ezra, ever grateful for how rarely she dwelled on his reticence and often accommodated and even mimicked his preference for routine, smiled at her and took his customary first position, sitting knees up on the top north end, facing downstream.

She would never sit until she'd spotted, on the east ridge top, almost hidden by the other towering tulip trees that sprouted around it in doublets and triplets like humongous celery stalks, the most prodigious one, an outrageous five-stalker. Ezra figured it appealed to her audaciousness and rebellious nature—her determination, which to his astonishment remained absolute, to forsake fancy New York living and wealthy suitors for him and her beloved poets.

She'd so badly wanted to lay hands on her favorite tree, to peer up from its trunk to its tops, that she'd prevailed upon him, in late April, to take her to it. As soon as they reached it, the sight of a gaggle of Union troops trudging north, east of the ridge top, sent them scurrying. They knew that Fort DeRussy, a small outpost among the string of forts built to protect the capitol's northern flank, was about a mile north, but their first sighting of soldiers unnerved Ezra, who insisted she stay put in their shack for the next two days while he patrolled the perimeter, day and night. Unbeknownst to June, he fretted that as the weather turned hotter, it was only a matter of time before the soldiers would seek relief in the creek. If his luck held, they would do so near their little fort, although the best swimming spots were nearby, only two bends up the creek.

She set down her wicker basket, tossed him the wine sack and sat on the south edge of the island, facing upstream, in compliance with his rule that they keep eyes, at all times, upstream and down.

With her properly situated, Ezra, tall and wizened with a hand-some, bearded poker face, moved into his standard second position, taking off his shirt, folding it into a pillow and laying back to savor his downstream view. From an early age he loved creeks, for the relief they provided from fields, and for the sounds they made to muffle shrieking and hollering. Rock Creek was his favorite. Its overabundance of rocks of every shape and size, piled and strewn willy-nilly bank to bank and up the hillsides, helped keep his worries in check when they were not otherwise diverted by John Keats or the Muses or June's powerful imagination and poetic obsessions.

When he ran short of things to say in response to her near constant verse readings and musings about their poets, he enlisted the tunes of the creek. He'd spin long-winded theories of rocks and water to explain their variations, insistent that she either concur, or better yet, offer a differing opinion, which they would ponder until he declared they'd achieved a superior, even more complex theory.

She called theses creations "castles in the air," then took that name for her own game, in which she required Ezra to help her come up with the most fitting musical descriptions for the sounds that enveloped them. Ezra's intuition told him the music of the creek defied words. But he gladly played along and greatly enjoyed repeating later, out of the blue, the new words he learned, particularly "glissando" and "rondoletto."

Ezra's most precious possessions were his surprise revelations to June. They brought her such great delight that he doled them out sparingly, for though he believed June sought and found excessive excitement and happiness, his greatest fear, second only to them being caught together, was the day when he could no longer elicit her wonder. There were hard to come by, too. He'd already unveiled two and sworn to hang onto his last one until he had another well in the works.

He'd begun to shape and polish what would become his first major admission as he lay awake on the floor the first night of her arrival, insisting she take the bed. She'd knocked on his door late that afternoon and offered to buy their food and to teach him to read if he'd let her stay with him. He'd answered with his meanest, coldest stare and admonished her to never come near his cabin again. She was terribly sorry to have insulted him, she'd tell him later. But how was she to know he could already read, when he'd not opened the door far enough for her to see the books piled on his table? Or that he didn't need her to buy food—he could trap more squirrels and catch more fish than he could eat.

On their island on a sunny April afternoon, after she'd apologized yet again for her unintended slights, he offered up his first revelation. The instant he'd opened the door he'd decided she must be setting a trap for him, in cahoots with a white man, and that if he agreed to her forbidden request, he would be taken away and hung or re-enslaved, allowing she and her friend to make immediate use of his well-hidden cabin.

She'd been mistaken, too, about what caused him to relent. It wasn't her desperate plea that she'd fallen in love with the woods and the creek and couldn't bear to go back to New York. And it wasn't her promise that she wouldn't be a burden, or ever let herself be seen. He'd agreed because, even if she wasn't setting a trap, there would be consequences if he defied such clearly stated wishes of any white woman, particularly one well-acquainted with a man who knew slave hunters. He informed her too that he knew at the time he should vacate the shack pronto, let her have it, and head north, but he could not bear to leave the birthplace of his freedom.

She jumped to her feet and wrapped herself around him. "I wouldn't have let you leave" was all she said.

He'd held onto his second revelation until the middle of May, when she needled him again for having taken so long to come around to liking *Leaves of Grass*, which she'd begun reading and reciting to him the first night she moved in.

He told her how he'd became more and more troubled by Whitman's claims, which she repeated over and over in her nightly warm-up recitation: that every bit of Ezra belonged to him, to Walt Whitman; that Whitman was part of Ezra, too; and that he, Whitman, was a spirit force who prowled naked and craved intimacy, not only with those reading his poems, but with the sleeping, and the dead, and even with God himself.

Then came the night she reached the part of *Leaves* where Whitman tells of watching twenty-eight virile, young men swimming naked, not through his own eyes, but through the eyes of a lonely woman, whom he turns into an invisible spirit.

An unseen hand passed over their bodies,
It descended tremblingly from their temples and ribs.

The young men float on their backs, their white bellies swell to the
Sun…they do not ask who seizes fast to them

Those lines, he told her, had thrown him into a waking dream—pulled him into an apparition. Instead of staring into the fire he found himself in the body of a young man with dark hair and innocent eyes, floating in the middle of the twenty-eight. An instant later, he was himself again, but in the same waking dream, still in the water, belly up with all the others. He floated right up against the boy whose skin he'd jumped into and out of and watched him swell from an invisible touch. Ezra would be next. He shivered so violently the apparition released him. He was back staring into the fire but filled with the certain knowledge that he should flee. He stood, determined to head north at once, but hesitated. He had to say goodbye—to let her know he'd never be back. He sat back down and put his head in his hands and tried to clear his mind.

She'd listened spellbound to his confession, then hugged him and whispered that they were destined to always be together—that he wouldn't ever be able to tell her goodbye.

Following her tree-spotting, June always studied the clouds and found shapes in them and forgot all about keeping an eye upstream. Ezra squirted himself more wine. "Any sign of anybody?" he asked.

"Nope," she said. "Never is."

"Don't be surprised the day your daddy comes charging down the hillside with a posse to rescue you."

Her parents Vivian and Samuel and her younger sister Emma Louise, fooled by her letters and satisfied by vague promises of a visit home, believed she remained safely ensconced in the respectable household of Samuel's former business acquaintance.

Whenever Ezra provoked June's zeal to protect him, her pulse quickened and the same memory rushed forward. Early on, when she'd asked Ezra how old he was, he'd told her without a trace of self pity—he'd actually grinned—that he had no idea of when or where he was born, or who his mother or father were. His first memory was as a little boy chained to a mean old woman. An auctioneer—he'd learned later it had been in Charleston—had thrown him in at a bargain price with the experienced housemaid and cook charged with looking after him. Ezra didn't even know how he'd gotten his name. His disclosure had strengthened her resolve that their coupling would never be undone by others. She knew by heart the scolding she would give to anyone who dared try: You will never take me or anything else from this man of an age and birthplace and parentage unknown even to himself.

"I've told you, Daddy's always been an abolitionist," she said.

He smirked. "You know that doesn't mean he'd wants you living with a black man."

"He suspects nothing" she said, "And I would never let anything bad happen to you."

"You don't *want* anything bad to happen to me," he said. "You should not be so naïve as to believe you can prevent it."

"You want me to move away, so it's safe here for you?"

"You know I don't," he said. "But the time will come when you'll want a normal life. And when it does, you'll leave, and I'll understand."

"I don't ever want to leave here," she said. "Ask me to stay here with you, forever."

He would never chain her to such a promise. Time for another revelation, no longer his last, for he had a new one etched in stone right above them.

AS I TRAMPLED AFTER COWBOY, I had no idea of the vast-
ness of the park. The sitting rock, beyond which I'd never ventured,
was near the edge of one small arm that reaches east into a neighborhood called Mount Pleasant. The main body extends north for
miles, at least a mile wide in most places, almost two thousand acres,
twice as big as Central Park.

Nor did I know, even as the clues mounted and the day took me
far beyond where clock time matters, that I'd entered a separate
world, tucked hidden away inside the city, the tens of thousands
who drive and peddle and jog and shuffle through it oblivious to its
true nature.

Someone yelled Cowboy's name. He stopped and scanned the
deep forest and told me to stay close behind him. Three youngish
fellows, with the unmistakable look of having been up all night,

stood inside a circle of rocks and waved frantically for him to join them. He stepped into the ring. The tall one, Zach, threw up his right hand at me like a school crossing guard. "It's against the code for you to enter the circle," he said.

The deranged, even those temporarily so, always think you understand what they're talking about.

Cowboy vouched for me, told them I was a John Keats fan, and, better yet, a fan of Walt Whitman, and guaranteed that I would not repeat anything said in the circle. The shorter, skinny, pugnacious-faced fellow next to Zach glowered at me. With his long, stringy hair and round, wire-rim glasses, he looked like a young Roberto Bolaño, the failed, itinerant poet whose novels, years after his death, earned him worldwide literary fame.

Cowboy told them he could tell they'd been up all night.

"So what?" said Zach, his pupils dilating.

"Poetry does that to us," said the Roberto look-alike. "We were with Louise at Pulpit Rock."

"The false coherence of the insane" came to mind, a phrase coined by a critic to describe the strange quality of Bolaño's stories and their poetry-obsessed characters. Like a ringmaster, Cowboy announced that these three aspiring poets were preeminent members of the Zoo Crew, the most zealous and devoted of all park people.

"If you think we're so devoted, why haven't you ever told us the legend?" Zach snarled.

"What legend?"

"Just before sunrise," Zach said, "when Louise was leaving—she never lets us walk her home—she said there's a legend. About Walt Whitman. Tell us!"

Cowboy snickered. There was no legend, he said, only Louise's flights of fancy.

"She said Whitman spent some unforgettable days here," Zach countered.

"Like I told you before, he liked to walk in the park," Cowboy said. "That's all there is to it. Other than Louise indulging her imagination, which is her favorite pastime, along with getting you three all wound up. End of discussion. Go get some sleep."

No arguing with Captain Cowboy. They bounded away without another word, headed the same way we were.

"Damn it!" Cowboy said. "I've always worried this day might come."

"What day?"

Green and blue speckles flared and rotated around his pupils like a kaleidoscope. "Swear that you won't repeat what I'm about to tell you."

I nodded.

"Say it."

"I swear."

"It's not a legend," he said. "Walt Whitman created a secret world here. A world Louise and I inherited."

"Wow," I said, reminding myself that I'm often naive but, I like to hope, only by choice. "What's the big secret?"

"Don't get your hopes up, friend. You've yet to get okayed by William or Louise."

Don't you worry, you batty old coot, I thought. All I'm hoping for is somewhere to sleep. So I won't have to drive in the dark. So I can rest up and chase tomorrow's sunset into the mountains.

7

JUNE EXPECTED EZRA WOULD once again ignore her desire for him to ask her to stay with him forever. But he did fulfill her other hope, that he would parry her request with another tantalizing secret.

"You remember how you pretended to be surprised, when I told you how Walt Whitman spooked me so?" he said. "You weren't really surprised. That's why the very moment I jumped up to run out the door, you slammed shut *Leaves of Grass*. And that's why, when I sat back down, you told me it was time to meet your first true love."

He chuckled and shook his head in wonder.

"What's so funny?"

"Know what I thought, when you said that?"

"What?"

"Another man has come—no doubt a white man—to take my place."

"No!"

"You'd been biding your time, waiting for your true love to arrive. He'd signaled you—I figured it was that supposed owl hooting we'd heard—and was waiting at the door."

Her mouth dropped open.

"You stood up to go unlatch the door," Ezra said. "I only hoped he'd let me leave rather than shoot me dead. Then you grinned at me and said, 'John Keats wrote his poetry long ago, but he's very much alive in me.'"

"That's why you looked so relieved!" she said.

"That's right. Then you put your hands together and recited, and I could see clear as day that Grecian urn and right into the living souls of those figures on it, frozen in time, and I said to myself, 'This is why she loves poetry so. And she'll treat me to as much of it as I want.'" He hesitated. "I can tell you this now. It was the first time I was glad you'd moved in."

"You were more than glad," she grinned. "I suspected that as soon as you asked me to repeat those four lines."

"Suspected what?"

"That you wanted us to be lovers."

"Your imagination is as potent as Johnny Keats'."

June recited:

> *Bold Lover, never, never canst thou kiss,*
> *Though winning near the goal—yet, do not grieve;*
> *She cannot fade, though thou hast not thy bliss,*
> *For ever wilt thou love, and she be fair!*

"And there was no doubt of your desire when you picked up your Bible and began reading me 'Song of Solomon,'" she said.

"I read it because it was my favorite, because my friend used it to teach me to read, with that very Bible. He and I must have read it to each other a hundred times. But I worried, as soon as I started reading, that old Solomon wasn't as fine to the ear as Keats—that you wouldn't like it."

"Wouldn't like erotic love poetry? How beautiful you found me? My lips like crimson thread, my breasts like two fawns you would suckle all night."

"That was the boy in the Bible talking!"

"Ha! You were casting your magic spell on me."

Ezra chuckled and drank. "So it was my magic made you undress, huh? And made you tell me to keep reading, while you undressed me?"

"I can remember every word you read," she said. "*You have ravished my heart. Your lips distill nectar. Honey and milk are under your tongue. Your channel is an orchard of pomegranates.* Then you had read me the woman's answer! *Blow upon my garden. Let my beloved come to his garden and eat its choicest fruits.*"

"I didn't ask you to read it three times," Ezra said. "Or to shove the Bible back at me and tell me to read the rest of it. Good thing old mister Solomon's song isn't too long."

He stepped down to the low end of their rock and threw water on his face and chest. "So, I can cast magic spells, huh?" he said.

"With help from John Keats you can," she said.

He turned and faced her. "I did learn a blessed lesson that night. Before then, I'd been certain that one person's desire must always be another person's loss."

"I see desire in your face right now."

"No you don't."

"I want the sun all over me."

"Stay dressed," he said.

She moved too quickly for his liking and yanked a linen tablecloth and a satin curtain sash from her basket. She belted her smock with the sash. She ran to the high end of the rock and pulled the straps of her smock off her shoulders and let the top fall below her waist. She spread her feet and stretched her arms out behind her and leaned forward into the breeze.

Ezra imagined her first as a striking figurehead on the prow of a ship, then as a fairy queen about to fly away. He slowly approached and put his hands on her shoulders and whispered. "You've got to get down in the creek."

"You told me last night John lives in your very soul," she said.

"Let his immortal self bud forth in you. Let him come to me, through you."

"You know there's no budding allowed down here," he replied. "Down here, I prefer the calm of your more even keel."

June broke into laughter and scampered around him just out of reach. She rose on her tiptoes and threw her arms in the air, an awkward ballerina's pirouette.

"Please, get in the water," he said.

"Let John Keats speak," she said. "Maybe that'll even my keel."

"*I am certain of nothing*," he said, "*but the holiness of the Heart's affection and the truth of Imagination.*"

"I love to hear you quote his letters," she said, "But I want more. Let him embody you." She commenced showing off, prancing around him hands in air, tightening her circle.

His eyes lighted on a doe, halfway up the west bank. The doe munched and took one unhurried step. "Get in the creek and John will recite to you."

"John wants more than that. He wants to come to me, body and soul, though you." She grabbed Ezra's shoulders and pulled him tight. "I'm not a true sorceress," she whispered. "I just follow the desires of the Muses, and of our forever-young John. You know how much he desires me."

The doe's ears twitched, but she kept her head down. If she startled into a run, Ezra decided, he would grab the tablecloth and throw it over June, then run up the bank to hide from whoever startled the doe and make sure no harm came to her.

"Sit down in the water and I'll see if John has something to say."

She loosened the cord around her waist. Ezra's eyes darted back and forth between her and the doe. June wiggled. The cord fell. The smock dropped to her feet.

"John, will you be my priest?"

She asked that question regularly, always in the privacy of their shack. Green streaks flashed across her eyes. Ezra had seen them only in candlelight, when they made him imagine the wispy beginnings of immortality, in which he did not believe, other than for John Keats and the Muses.

"Answer me, John, and I'll get in the creek."

The doe took another leisurely step and resumed munching. Ezra closed his eyes.

Yes, I will be thy priest, and build a fane
  In some untrodden region of my mind,
Where branched thoughts, new grown with pleasant pain,
  Instead of pines shall murmur in the wind…

His ear well-tuned to the quiet roars and burps of the creek, he was able to distinguish the off-beat splashes of limbs entering water.

"Do you find truth in me?"

"I tell you that every night."

"Is that you, John?"

"Yes."

"Do you find truth in me?"

What the imagination seizes as beauty must be truth—whether it existed before or not—for I have the same idea of all our passions as of Love: they are all, in their sublime, creative of essential beauty.

He opened his eyes to verify her submergence, then rolled on his side and propped his head on his elbow to keep her and the doe in his sightline.

"Are you still there, John?"

"Yes."

"I am the nymph you wrote about, *Fast by the springs where she to bathe was wont, were strewn rich gifts, unknown to any Muse…Ah what a world of love was at her feet.* Do you remember me?"

He took a slug of wine and a slow, deep breath and recited:

Ay, in those days the Muses were nigh cloyed
With honors; nor had any other care
Than to sing out and sooth their wavy hair.

She rocked slowly back and forth, on her knees, chest-high in the water, running her fingers through her long hair, watching it spread in the meandering current.

"I'm flattered you call on me, John, for long ago I dedicated myself to you. And to our love of poetry. And to the Muses who brought you here."

"You're lucky your life allows that."

"I never forget that, not for one moment," she said. "Do you like immortality, John?"

"When I was dying, I feared my poetry would suffer a less kind fate. Death with no death, words abandoned forever on pages of a few hundred dusty, never-opened books."

"Yet you dreamed of poetic immortality."

"A drainless shower Of light is poesy; tis the supreme power."

"Are you happy to be with me?"

"I scarcely remember counting upon any happiness. I look for it not if it be not in the present hour."

"Do you find it, in this present hour?"

He glanced one last time at the doe, still munching, then sighed and rolled on his back and closed his eyes.

"I do, floating high in the oaks, in shady immortality, and then summoned here by you."

"How far behind you've left your awful, early death."

"I feel escaped from a strange and threatening sorrow, and I am thankful for it. There is an awful warmth about my heart like a load of Immortality."

She rose out of the creek and knelt beside him and put the wine sack to his lips. "Taste the beads of mulberry nectar, John," she said. "Do you recall how you once coated your throat with pepper to intensify the cool delight of claret?"

Ezra tasted pepper as he swallowed. "I do," he said.

"Will you stay here with me, forever?"

"Even though I am immortal, sometimes I do imagine growing old here, where *I feel more and more every day, as my imagination strengthens, that I do not live in this world alone but in a thousand worlds.*"

She unfolded the white linen tablecloth and lay next to him and pulled it over them.

She whispered. "It breaks my heart to think of you so madly in love with Fanny Brawne, your young self, ill and dying and broke, a failed poet—of that you were certain. She, so near you, in the other half of the same house. You, forbidden to see her, overcome with passion you were certain could never be fulfilled, scribbling her feverish letters, waiting by the window for a glimpse of her. After enduring that, you must enjoy being such a virile immortal."

"Even immortal poets can be at a loss for words," he said.

She recited in a whisper.

Pillow'd upon my fair love's ripening breast,
To feel for ever its soft fall and swell,
Awake for ever in a sweet unrest,
Still, still to hear her tender-taken breath,
And so live ever—or else swoon to death.

"Will you let me fill your immortal desire?" she asked.

John Keats' delight surged through Ezra, and for the first time ever, June did the reminding. "We must be vigilant, John" she whispered. "You keep an eye downstream. I'll keep one upstream."

WILLIAM CACKLED AND GRINNED and put his hands on his hips like he expected us. The patio where he held court perched at the top of the steep bank overlooking the street where we'd emerged from the woods. Three wine bottles and a tore-open box of chocolate donuts graced a weathered table straddled by a rocking chair.

He radiated spunk. A knotted, worn-out belt held up his stain-speckled, khaki-colored pants. His eyes sparkled the welcoming kindness of someone willing to share your troubles. I bade him a friendly hello and told him I liked how he held the high ground.

"One of my friends travels a lot," he said. "One time she told me she was looking for somebody to house sit, water her house plants and what-not. You homeless, man, you never offer to house sit inside. So I told her, hey, we'll move your plants outside and I'll yard sit. Whenever she's out of town—which be for weeks and weeks at a time—this be my place."

Cowboy told him I had just retired from being a poetry professor. William thrust out his chin and recited in a fine cadence:

I am the poet of commonsense and of the demonstrable and of immortality;
And am not the poet of goodness only…I do not decline to be the poet of wickedness also.

"Tell me who that be, professor," he said.

"Surprise, surprise," I said. "Walt Whitman."

"Me and Cowboy are learning *Leaves of Grass* by heart. Us two together, before we die, we intend to recite it in its entirety."

Cowboy said he needed to go confer with someone named Eli.

"Trouble in the kingdom?" William asked.

"Louise apparently can't keep a secret any longer. I'll leave Jack with you. You know what to do." He hurried off.

Right off the bat William told me that all I'd gotten from Cowboy was the standard teaser. He'd heard it years before, when Cowboy had offered to let him in on the big secret, if he'd do something for him and Louise. Do what, I asked. Put it to rest, for good, is how Cowboy put it, William said. Put what to rest? "The secret story, fool." Put it to rest how? "Write it down for them and never tell anybody." He'd refused them.

"And don't think it was because I can't write. They can't even agree on what their secret is. Cowboy swears it's short and sweet. Louise said it's a saga. Both say the other one tells it all wrong. I wasn't about to take sides between my two best friends.

"There was another reason, too, one I've never told them. Ever since I learned to write, I've never felt right chaining words to paper. I prefer talking. Setting them loose. See what they can do when they fly back and forth between people, like you and me right now."

I confessed to William that I was a just-fired, part-time community-college night teacher, not a retired poetry professor.

"You're a Keats lover, though, and enough of a Whitman fan to suit Cowboy. Word travels fast in the kingdom."

I told him I'd had to give up my apartment, was near broke—down to a two hundred dollars—and was therefore about to head back home.

"Now listen up, fool," he said. "First of all, you're flush. Two hundred is not near broke. Second, why in the world would you pass up a chance to learn the secret story, just because you're homeless and don't have a pot to piss in."

I thanked him for putting it so plainly.

"If I'd high-tailed it home just because of that, I'd be wasting away right now down in the swamplands of Blackwater, Virginia. Look at me." He tucked his thumbs in his armpits and stuck his chest out. "You see how I'm living the high life?"

I'd found a kindred soul, a flighty-minded walk-on-the-sunnysider. I felt better for the first time since my firing. I thanked him for helping me see my promising prospects. He cackled and we were off to the ha-ha races, riding high on the unbridled joys of our unencumbered, free-wheeling futures.

EZRA FIGURED WHY NOT give Walt another order.

"You'll not leave until June is through speaking to you. Might as well get comfortable."

Walt, tired of standing, tired of everything, sat at the bottom of their rock.

"Forgive my confession," June said. "I'm only trying to amuse you. To see if you can smile. Like the joyous man who wrote *Leaves of Grass*."

Walt moaned and put his head in his hands.

"Ezra and I always bring our favorite books here," she said. She reached into her basket and held them up one at a time: two volumes of John Keats poetry, the original *Leaves of Grass* (Exhibit D) and the two subsequent editions.

Walt looked up but didn't bat an eye.

She stepped closer. She opened the original *Leaves* to the picture of him and held it in front of his face.

"I call this your 'ain't-I-something' pose," she said. "You're still handsome. But sad and tired. Is that what makes you look so old? Why are you so sad?"

The sparkle of her blue-green eyes held Walt's glance, despite himself. An inkling that she could be a force of nature, like he once was, rose up in him, but his despondency, ever vigilant, chased it away.

"I am not well," he said. "My ears are ringing. My head is over-filled and heavy. I suffer dizzy spells. My throat is sore. But far worse is the melancholy that bedevils me. A bit of faintness is coming on me. I must rest for another moment before I go."

"We'll show you our cabin," June said. "It's a short walk. We'll get out of the sun. You can rest there and refresh yourself." He dropped his head back in his hands. She pulled a newspaper clipping from the first *Leaves* and read aloud.

"Large, proud, affectionate, eating, drinking and breeding, his posture strong and erect, his voice bringing hope and prophecy to the generous races of young and old…Every move of him has the free play of the muscle of one who never knew what it was to feel that he stood in the presence of a superior. Every word that falls from his mouth shows silent disdain and defiance of old theories and forms…"

"Here's my favorite part," she said. "'If health were not his distinguishing attribute this poet would be the very harlot of persons. Right and left he flings his arms, drawing men and woman with undeniable love to his close embrace.'"

"You must remember those words. They're from the review of *Leaves* you wrote yourself, under another name. Fling open your arms once again. Come with us, and we'll restore you."

Walt snorted and threw his head back. "I have no hope of being restored. Do not mock me, young lady."

"Her name is June," Ezra snapped.

"The great Walt Whitman hopeless?" she said.

"Don't be impetuous! Do not speak of things of which you know nothing. Fetch me some creek water, and give me that wine pouch, and I shall disabuse you of your indulgent fantasy."

Ezra wanted to slap him but instead handed him the wine and

filled a tin cup with creek water. Walt gulped water and squirted himself a long stream of wine.

"Both are foul tasting. But it matters not to me. I look not for even the smallest pleasures. When I began visiting the hospitals, more than two years ago, I comforted those most in need, the worst cases, the ones teetering on death. I witnessed what I believed was the mystery of transcendence. Their souls leaving for the next life. Hundreds and hundreds of them. The loved ones whose hands I held. The beautiful, brave ones whose cheeks I kissed as they took their last breaths. Oh, dear God, how they loved me for sparing them from dying alone.

"That extraordinary love of those beautiful young men blinded me. The idea that comforted me when I felt their hands begin to cool—that I was taking part in their souls transcending death—was a delusion. The entire time death and its never-quenched thirst was fiendishly consuming this foolish, vain old man. Vanquishing my soul. Punishing me for daring to imagine that I could dilute the full strength of its most satisfying moments.

"I wrote to their loved ones that they died in peace. They never found peace. What I witnessed was not the transcendence of the dying. It was the terrifying gleefulness of death. I am certain, with every atom of my being, that I will never escape it. I see it every day, every hour, this very moment. Their faces. One after another. The inescapable despair descending on them. Making itself felt in every bone and fiber and molecule of their helpless bodies and souls. And every time I see the last death I witnessed, the first one returns. How can I deny him, or those who follow? I will dutifully watch them die, over and over, until I can embrace my own death, which I greatly look forward to, but is not yet allowed, for this merciless evil greatly relishes my suffering."

He dropped his head. "The man in that picture is no more, though god knows how long he must wait to be dead and buried."

"Goodness gracious," Ezra said. "You're the saddest-sounding, most suffering man I've ever met who wasn't in the throws of being whipped or hung."

June leaned over and tried to embrace Walt.

He pushed her away. "I cannot stand to be touched."

"We're your redemption," she said. "Your unvanquished spirit is here, with Keats, in our Rock Creek Canon. Here in these woods, and in our hidden temple to the Muses. Let us show you."

"You must be mad," Walt said as he stood and stepped toward the bank.

Ezra jumped to block his way. "Listen up," he said, "and when I'm done, tell me if you still pity yourself so."

10

OUR LAUGHING JAG SIMMERED down and William fished a half-empty, half-gallon jug of red wine out of the fern bed and offered me a swig. I passed. He helped himself. He told me I could stay with him until his friend got back. Then we'd find a new spot. I told him I had a car. That brought a big smile. We couldn't sleep in it. The rich white folks overrunning the neighborhood would have the cops rousting us lickety-split. But it could serve as home base. Everything we wanted to keep dry and safe from pilfering we'd lock in the trunk.

Although he'd turned down Cowboy and Louise, he'd not given up on learning their big secret. He knew he'd meet whoever ended up doing what they wanted—he was Cowboy's "tester."

"Soon as he gets back, he's going to ask me if you passed."

"How many you tested?"

"Good lord, brother. This been going on for years. Boils down to this. You need to be crazy enough about poets and such that Cowboy and Louise like you, and crazy enough to go through all the trouble that comes with learning their secret and writing it down. But not too loony—not more than halfway off your rocker. He's brought me plenty of those. I don't even bother testing them anymore. I just tell them Cowboy is wacko and send them on their way."

"Is he?"

"Nope, he's the real deal."

"If someone did pass the test," I said, "knowing that you'd still like to learn the secrets, if that someone asked you to help them figure out the story, seems to me he'd certainly need to convey the gist of it to you."

He winked, toasted me bottoms up and refilled his cup.

"But it could well turn out to be nothing," I said. "Just some tale Cowboy cooked-up to keep the two of them amused."

"You see if you figure Louise for the type of woman who'd spend years dillydallying around with some fellow's cockamamie fantasy."

"She and Cowboy a couple?"

"Louise nobody's woman but her own."

"Known her long?"

"We been helping each other look out for Cowboy as long as I remember."

"He needs looking out for?"

"Don't we all? Speaking of which, don't be falling for Louise."

"Worried she'll break my heart?"

"You never know with loners." He grinned.

"What's your story?"

"Just another poor boy. Good thing I got good luck. This fine place to stay. All my park buddies." He turned and opened his arms to the woods beyond the street below. "And best of all, my secret kingdom. And now I might finally learn Walt's big secrets. If you play your cards right. But if that doesn't pan out, you'll come back here and stay with me anyway and school me on your boy Keats, right?"

"I'd be honored," I said. "Walt's your favorite though, right?"

"Hell no," he chuckled. "I like him alright because he's Cowboy's salvation. Langston Hughes is tops with me. I like how he talks back to Walt."

He fixed me with a gaze of milky blue wonder.

I, too, sing America.

I am the darker brother.
They sent me to eat in the kitchen
When company comes,
But I laugh,
And eat well,
And grow strong.

Tomorrow,
I'll be at the table
When company comes.
Nobody'll dare
Say to me,
"Eat in the kitchen,"
Then.

Besides,
They'll see how beautiful I am
And be ashamed—

I, too, am America.

William had already won my heart. With that, he won my soul.

Cowboy rounded the corner, plunked down a bag full of sandwiches and asked if I'd passed the test.

"With flying colors," William said. "Best one yet. By far."

Cowboy, as I suspected he would, wanted to hear for himself the answer to the burning question. He dropped the "American" after "greatest." I'd had a hunch he might do that, too.

"Yes or no?"

"Yes," I said. "Greatest among any poet ever born after 1800.

That's as far back as I know enough about. But Emily stays put, like we agreed, right there with Walt."

"Backstage only," he said. "And Walt tops anybody born after 1800, plus those yet to come."

No use quibbling over great unborn poets. "Yep."

He pulled out his pint, saluted us with it and drank.

"Yes indeed. Jack passes the test."

I'd thrown a few of my favorite dark horses under his Whitman bandwagon: Elizabeth Barrett Browning, Swinburne (the young, pagan version, not the aged reactionary, living under virtual house arrest), and Baudelaire. I'm fine with Walt topping them. But Emily remained in place. And Keats, Homer, Sappho, Virgil, Dante, and Shakespeare would never have to do battle with Cowboy's greatest-ever fetish.

11

FINDING FOR THE FIRST time in his life his path blocked by a black man, Walt, all six feet and two hundred pounds of him, took another step and went chest to chest with Ezra, who was about the same size. Ezra grabbed his shoulders.

"As I told you, you'll not leave until you hear this." Walt sighed and sat and told himself he would grant this pair one last indulgence.

Ezra stood over him and burnt his eyes into Walt's so he wouldn't dare look away. "When I was younger, me and another fellow were field slaves for two North Carolina dirt farmers," he said. "They saw my friend glance longer than they liked at one of their scantily dressed kin folk. I suspected they were both already having their way with her, for she had reached the tender age they like. He was going lame and sickly, worth less and less to them, so they tied him to a tree in front of their run-down farm house that afternoon and stripped him and whipped him bloody.

46

"Before they locked me in the shed where he and I slept they walked me past him. They told me if I as much as went near him, I'd be chained to the other side of that oak. They gathered dozens of kin and neighbors that night. They filled the front porch and stood in the yard. Some were quiet, not much entertained by his suffering. Others hollered and hooted as they heard the lies about how wide-eyed and desirous he looked upon that girl. The most excited and talkative began arguing how long it would take the vultures and wolves to sniff him out and wagered how long he would anguish before he died, and he desperately drank the water offered to him by those who bet he'd last the night.

"The six or eight most enjoying their cruelty finally got bored. 'No more water now,' one said, 'or it ain't a fair bet.' The crowd quieted. The wolves began howling. My friend called for me.

"'Ezra, come finish me,' he pleaded. 'Put a pitchfork right through my heart. Don't leave me to be ripped apart. Send me to the Lord.'"

"His begging brought the party back to life. 'Get the other nigger out here watching,' somebody yelled. Four of them dragged me out of the shed and leashed me on a long rope tied to the front porch.

"'Come send me home, Ezra. I beg you. I'm ready. Ezra, you hear me?'

"'Oh, he hears you,' the drunkest of the kin said. 'He's right here. But it don't look like he wants to help you. He ain't even pulling on his leash.'"

"I yelled out loud and clear. 'Don't say another word, brother. Don't give them the satisfaction. I can't help you. You're with the Lord already. On the cross with him. Until your soul is taken home, sing to yourself, brother, sing this.'

"I've never been a believer in the white man's god, but I sang for him, as believing and deep-voiced as I could. 'Swing low, sweet chariot, coming for to carry me home. Swing low…'"

"The drunker brother whacked me with a shovel. But I kept singing, for my friend had taken up the tune. The other brother kicked me in my stomach and left me gasping for air. Bless my friend's soul, he kept singing. He didn't say another word. He only sang that song, real quiet, over and over. Soon as I caught my breath, I got out the first line again before a kick to the head quieted me. With no water, he got soon too dried out to sing. But as dry as he was, he kept humming, real quiet. The show was over.

"They dragged me back into the shed. In the middle of the night, when his humming stopped and his screams began—something had begun tearing on him—I recalled how that poor boy, such a strong believer, would ask me, during our long nights locked in that shed, what I thought it was like for Jesus after they drove the nails through him, and as I covered my ears I couldn't help but think, you poor soul, those nails were kind compared to your crucifixion.

"I did not look at him the next morning when they took me out to the field. I worked as far away from that oak tree as I could. Kept my back to it so as not to see the crows coming and going. I hummed the first lines of that song to myself, but it brought me no comfort, for though his humming was done, he was not dead. I heard each weak cry of torment and hoped it was his last, but I could see the vultures flying in take over from the crows, to finish picking him over. The young kin out in the field kept their backs turned to him and stayed quiet all day. I wished mightily for them to feel shame for what the older folks had done, but I do not believe they did. I did not want to look at him when I came in from the fields, but I had no choice, for I walked close enough to vow this to him: 'I will avenge all your suffering.' I hoped he was dead and couldn't hear me.

"After that, no one paid him one bit of attention. He might as well have been a scarecrow. On the second morning, the two brothers dragged me out and made me look at what was left before they untied his carcass and dragged it far enough from the house and fields so as not to smell it, for they refused him a burial.

"Unlike you, who give leave to those dying faces to haunt you, I forbid what I saw from conjuring up itself. I do not countenance those images. Believe me, they do try to come up in me from time to time. I refuse them substantiation. Keep my mind's eye shut tight for as long as need be. The reach of those people's evil, alive in those images, is smothered in me, never to be looked upon by me or others, and I will take it to my grave, to be buried, dead, with me.

Ezra had never told June. She wept.

"My god, man," Walt said. "What a brave, resolute soul you are. Unlike me."

"My name is Ezra. My aim is not to belittle your suffering, or what you've been through. I tell this account, for the first and last time, to return a favor to you. In hopes that my words might help you fight off the evil that shrouds you, for your *Leaves* is a great help to me in keeping my own evil hauntings at bay."

Ezra walked slowly back up to the top of their island and spread his arms turned his hands palm up.

Have you reckoned a thousand acres much? Have you
    Reckoned the earth much?
Have you practiced so long to learn to read?
Have you felt so proud to get at the meaning of poems?

Stop this day and night with me and you shall possess the origin of
    all poems,
You shall possess the good of the earth and sun...

June would recall forevermore that moment, when Ezra became the Homer of Rock Creek, a teller of terrible tales and a timeless keeper of verse.

"Don't you see, Walt?" Ezra said. "June and I are living proof of your words. We explore the origin of all poems, and we embrace the good of the earth and the sun. And just as you tell us, we are not afraid of the merge."

"You know my *Leaves* very well," Walt said

"You bet we do. You said the known universe has one complete lover—the greatest poet. No matter how many men you've seen die, you are still the greatest...one of the two greatest poets ever. Repeat after me your own words. The ones I tell myself every day. Every hour."

I believe in you my soul.

"I am deeply touched by your kindness," Walt said. "And by your love of my *Leaves*. But my poetic soul left me barren long ago. Long before death clasped me to its evil breast, I was no longer the poet in that picture. I could no longer take flight. I will be on my way."

12

LIFE FLINGS CLUES LIKE meteor showers, whenever and wherever it pleases. Most go unseen. The few we do glimpse disintegrate in a flash and leave infinitesimal bits that conjure up a snippet no more telling than a dissipated dream. A rare few land intact, burn hot in memory, and become forever re-decipherable in light of later events.

Cowboy and I backtracked the trail and crossed the bridge I'd parked near. We climbed a steep hill on a twisting path back into the forest and reached deeper woods along the flattened-out ridge.

A pale-faced woman sat back against a huge tulip tree and cried dutifully, her legs splayed out, her hands clasped in her lap. She rocked and bowed to a precarious three-foot-high stack of flattish stones inside a small circle of rocks.

An unsheathed hunting knife lie next to her. Right above her head, so deeply and freshly carved that the sap still bled, the big block letters read like a crazed, two-deck headline:

iDEATH NIGHT
HAIL inBOIL

Memories fought their way up in me like wisps of smoke from a firecracker muffled under a clump of moss.

In Watermelon Sugar, a novel by Richard Brautigan, the destitute 1950s beat poet suddenly turned famous hippie writer, people lived in quaint, little shacks in a mind-bending forest full of magical creeks. At the age of sixteen it tantalized me with vague, trippy notions of the farthest frontier of back-to-nature hippiedom.

On a quest to spice up my night class syllabus, I reread it decades later. It floored me. Brautigan's whimsical telling had mesmerized me to such a shocking degree that somehow that I'd wiped clean from my memory all the horror and tragedy in his bizarre story.

The bad guy, named inBOIL, and the gang he leads believe that the contented residents are reality-defying frauds. He and his followers barge into iDEATH, the communal gathering place, pull out jack knives, and proceed to methodically cut off their thumbs, noses and ears in a bloody, mass suicide that is witnessed, nonchalantly, by the narrator and his friends. The narrator subsequently looks into a magic mirror and watches with no reaction as the ex-girlfriend he left heartbroken climbs an apple tree and hangs herself.

Above the block letters the woman had sliced out of the bark a sap-beaded heart and pierced it with a thick, elaborately spiked, even more deeply carved arrow. She reached with her right hand and clasped the knife. I gasped and stepped toward her. Cowboy stopped me and crouched and moved toward her. "I see you've made another shrine," he smiled. "You don't need this anymore, not just now. I'll keep it for you. You can find me at my rock the next time you want to carve." He sheathed the knife and tucked it in his waistband.

She never looked at him. Her eyes blazed into mine through the salty tribute she still poured forth. She pulled out from under her shirt the amulet that hung round her neck and bandied at me a figurine of a child, head bowed and hands together in prayer. "Get him away," she snarled.

An ugly shiver crawled down from the top of my head, took me by the throat and froze me. Cowboy put his hand to my cheek and turned my head away from her, grabbed my arm and yanked me back along the path.

"Heartbroken," was all he said. "We all do our best to look out for her. But you let her be. She doesn't take to strangers."

"I'm not a retired poetry professor," I confessed.

"I figured," he said. We spoke no more until we crested another hill and neared an eight-foot-high, razor-wire-topped, chain-link fence. Several hundred feet beyond, in thick woods atop the next rise, a cottage sat on stilts. A side staircase rose to a front porch that overlooked a steep ravine with a stream crossed by an arched stone bridge. It could have been the cover of a book of fairy tales.

13

EZRA WOULD HAVE GLADLY let Walt go on his way. The cranky old man peeved him, giving up without a fight even after hearing his most-painful-to-tell story.

"I am not mad," June yelled at Walt. "You're the one going mad. With melancholy. You allow it to blind you. All we need do is rid you of your demons. Maybe you're right. Maybe we can't resurrect the man in the picture. But I can envision your next rebirth."

No wonder I can't help loving her, Ezra through. She never relents, no matter how far-fetched her cause. "Tell us June," he said. "Tell us what you see."

"Your new poet will be wiser and more serious. No longer wild and scandalous. Heroic. Made so by his brave, tireless service in the hospitals. Solemn and resolute, the poet who will memorialize this war, this great tragedy.

"The three of us can birth that new poet. The one the children and their children and their children's children will come to know. And *Leaves of Grass*, rather than forgotten, will be widely comprehended and treasured, as you've always dreamed."

"I do fear that *Leaves* will never be accepted in my own time," Walt said.

"No one else need ever know of this moment, or any of our time together," June said. "Just the three of us. And the Muses, the divine infusers of poets, who have brought us together to resurrect you. To offer you immortality."

"Don't let that evil melancholy rob you of your place among the greatest poets," Ezra said. "Not without a fight. See if me and June can help you chase it away."

"What...compels you?" Walt asked.

Ezra showered Walt for the first time with a heartfelt smile. "How could we ever allow evil melancholy to keep its grip on the man who declared this:

I am the poet of the body,
And I am the poet of the soul.

I am the poet of the woman as same as the man,
And I say it is as great to be a woman as a man,
And I say there is nothing greater than the mother of men.

"Or this, which tickles me to this day, and still brings me pure glee:

I am less the reminder of properties or qualities, and more the
*   reminder of life,*
And go on the square for my own sake and for other's sake,
And make short account of neuters and geldings, and favor men
*   and women fully equipped.*

June gathered their things and stood by Walt's side, careful not to touch him. Ezra slung his arm around Walt's waist. "Come go with us," he said, and kept Walt hip to hip as they broke into step.

"Put your arms around us, just as you foresaw," June said and recited.

Wandering the same afternoon with my face turned up to the clouds
My right and left arms around the sides of two friends and I in the middle.

Walt grew more and more perturbed with himself as they entered the shack. His wretchedness was toying with him, flexing its grip yet again, in this instance exercising the cruelty of false hope—the absurdity that these two could resurrect him.

Most galling, he'd let himself be lured farther away from the train station, from his only desire, to get home to his cramped little room, where his dear mother would leave him be, let him live out his days in solitude. He would sit in this uncomfortable chair only until he regained enough strength to leave.

Ezra, out of devotion to June, decided he'd help this cantankerous, sweat-dripping has-been cool down. He'd be happy to give Walt one more shaming, followed by a pep talk, and send him on his way. He knew that that wouldn't be near enough for June. He put a half-filled wash basin at Walt's feet.

June knew they both doubted her. She could care less. They had no notion of what she really intended to prove. She handed each of them a cup of Ezra's homemade wine. Ezra sat cross-legged on the floor and splashed water on Walt's ankles and legs. She stepped behind Walt and rubbed his neck and shoulders. He snapped at her to stop. She went and stood behind Ezra. Seeing her ready to resume her badgering, Walt closed his eyes on the slim chance she'd take the hint and let him doze off.

"Just because we love your *Leaves*, don't mistake us for zealots," she said. "Like that little group that swoons over you, wants to believe you're a prophet or a demigod. I've met some of them. I know poetry lovers all over. New York, Boston, Philadelphia, even London."

"As do I," he said, refusing to open his eyes.

"The first *Leaves* excited them, and Emerson too, because of their fervent wish—their belief that souls transmigrate," she said. "What a funny word. They saw in *Leaves* their own visions of reincarnation. Their first love is mysticism. Our first love is poetry."

Since he couldn't be allowed to doze, Walt's only want was to hear from this man at his feet, so he could better remember him for the rest of his lonely, loveless days. He eyed Ezra. "Surely though, you both believe in the life of the soul."

"We nourish our souls with poetry," Ezra said.

"Matters of the spirit are profoundly personal," Walt said. "Mine once had its private ecstasies. They sprang from my epiphany, when I first felt the sheer wonder of being part of everything, everything connected, infinite and wondrous."

June circled back behind Walt and winked at Ezra to remind him of her conjecture regarding Walt's pre-*Leaves* awakening.

Over Walt's shoulder she recited:

I believe in the flesh and the appetites,
Seeing hearing and feeling are miracles, and each part and tag of me is a
miracle.

"I used to find exhilaration so easily," Walt said. "The sights of the city or the woods would spark me so. I could envision all things out across this great country, and even take flight into the endless universes. All born from that epiphany. It would go dormant, of course, drown in my everyday fears and longings. But then it would birth sudden wisps of astonishment, and my senses would come back fully alive, and my imagination would soar, and I would compose my *Leaves*."

"That was the Muses," June said. "They will return. Like moths to the flame."

"There is no fire left in me," he said.

"They'll reignite you," she said. "Make you their daemon again. Surely you believe in the Muses."

"That's Old World," he said. "Very Greek. The kind of thing Keats liked to write about. My poetic ambition, my dreams, were of the New World, freed from the Old World."

"But some say all you did in *Leaves* was to take Emerson's ideas— the country is a poem, every man is a poet, break from the past, don't worry if you contradict yourself—and turn them into a poem."

"No!" he shouted. "Those were my visions. I could take flight!"

"Well then, you certainly are not a child of Emerson," June said. "We'll make that abundantly clear when your next poet emerges."

"I was the new breed of poet Emerson called for. But not the version he wanted. He's not at ease with the body. Can't admit that its appetites are as true and genuine as the aspirations of the soul, the intellect. He wants to separate them—the inseparable."

"You are the indeed the first original American poet," she said. "We'll make that very clear—you'll have no predecessor, no forerunner."

"That was my essence," Walt said. He shut his eyes again and leaned his head back, tired of her and wishing Ezra would speak.

14

A WILLOWY WOMAN IN white floated out the cottage door. She sashayed back and forth in a floor-length gown and held an open book in both hands and mouthed words we could not hear. She bounced up and down on her toes and grinned when she saw us.

The stream under the fairy-tale bridge narrowed to a trickle under a gate chained with a rusty padlock. Cowboy pulled out a key ring and opened it. I followed him up the stairs.

"Louise, meet Jack," he said. "A just-retired poetry professor. Jack is a strong believer in the Muses." I didn't recall mentioning the Muses. "And he's big fan of both Whitman and Keats."

He gave her arm a little squeeze and disappeared into the cottage.

She relished me so earnestly that I stopped three steps short of the porch. She stepped down and led me by the hand onto the porch.

"I'm so thrilled that you've come," she said.

"Why?"

Her wide mouth and slightly plump lower lip spread into an infectious grin. Her eyebrows arched into hyper-inquisitive mode. "Why wouldn't I be?"

"When I first saw you, I thought you might be an apparition," I said. "Are you learning something by heart?"

"By heart," she said wistfully. "So much more romantic than memorizing." She was barefoot. She threw her right foot out to the side and let it rest it on her heel. She put her hands on her hips and parodied what I guess was meant to be a 1920s flapper or a shoeless 1930s Hollywood starlet. "Your conjecture, darling," she winked, "is spot on. I endeavor to emulate the miraculous Edna St. Vincent Millay. She could learn anything by heart so she could speak to the Muses the very poetry they inspired. It helped her weather the blues."

"The greatest living American poet of her time," I said. "So says A.E. Housman, considered by some the leading critic of his day. And Harriet Monroe, an accomplished poet in her right, declared Edna to be the greatest woman poet since Sappho."

"I know all that, you silly-willy," she giggled. "And she preferred her friends call her Vincent." She pointed to the table between the two rocking chairs: *The Complete Poems and Selected Letters of John Keats*. "Vincent could recite all of Keats' odes, and the entirety of the 'Eve of St. Agnes.'"

Maybe this was my lucky day. I knew one small bit of that 500-plus-line poem, bounty from my Keats death-pale-warrior obsession. I recited for her:

Awakening up, he took her hollow lute,—
Tumultuous,—and, in chords that tenderest be,
He play'd an ancient ditty, long since mute,
In Provence call'd "La belle dame sans mercy"

She threw her right leg up on the railing and her left arm high in the air. "I must be dreaming!" she exclaimed. "Better yet..."

She took her leg down, raised her chin to the sky and threw her other arm into the air.

"I have awoken and found it true…"

She was a real live wire. And she was feeding me lines.

"As Keats said of Adam's dream In *Paradise Lost*," I replied.

Cowboy carried out a tray with two cocktails and a forlorn glass of water. Now that I'd passed the test, he wanted me sober.

"How'd you find Jack?" she asked him.

"We ran into each other at my sitting rock."

She stared me down, fiercely, searching for something only she could see. "The story's come back alive," she said. "You are the proof of its resurrection."

"Glad to hear that," I said. "I could use a little resurrecting."

"The story can do that for you," she said.

She couldn't stay still. She clapped her hands in tiny claps, then wrapped herself around Cowboy. "Isn't this wonderful!"

"It might be," he replied, then held her at arm's length and winked at both of us. What the hell was that supposed to mean?

"Have you told him why he's here?"

"Only that we inherited the secrets."

"The secrets of the story that's come back to life?" I asked.

Cowboy nodded.

Her Joni Mitchell mouth stretched big and wide into a toothy smile. "Keats is in our secret canon—the Rock Creek Canon," she said. "He and the Muses brought you to us."

Cowboy put on a resigned face. "I figured you'd turn this into divine intervention."

They sat down in their rocking chairs, leaving me to lean against the railing and face them.

"Can you assure immortal John that you can be trusted with the secrets of the canon?" she asked.

"She means to say trusted with Walt Whitman's secrets," Cowboy said.

She ignored him. "What sayeth ye?" She titled her head and looked into my eyes like she was trying to put a spell on me. I stared right back. I figure by my age you ought to be pretty well spell-proof. But she did dazzle me, and I proceeded to strip bare my poetic soul.

"Keats is how I came to love poetry," I said. For an instant I pictured the three of us rehearsing a scene in a doomed little-theatre production, but her eyes reignited me. "I've pursued him my entire adult life. With great satisfaction and pleasure. But also with an abiding fear that I'm failing him. Not living up to his hopes. That I'll will end up bereft on that cold hillside."

She looked away. Her face turned bleak. "I've been on that hillside," she said. Cowboy looked alarmed. He stopped rocking. She closed her eyes and recited, but she wasn't speaking to us.

> *I saw pale kings, and princes too,*
> > *Pale warriors, death-pale were they all*
> *Who cried, La Belle Dame sans merzy*
> > *Hath thee in thrall!*
>
> *I saw their starv'd lips in the gloom*
> > *With horrid warning gaped wide,*
> *And I awoke, and found me here,*
> > *On the cold hill side.*

Her words and the ensuing closed-eyed silence made my teeth clench. Finally, she blinked. "I'm not kidding," she said. "The story really did rescue me." She looked into me again like she could read my mind.

Cowboy crunched an ice cube. "What's your point, Jack?"

"Keats is giving me another chance."

"What's in God's name are you talking about?" he said.

"He's led me to two poetry lovers and maybe a chance at salvation—a way, finally, to a true Keatsian life."

Louise let out a little moan marinated in pleasure.

Cowboy looked at me alarmed. "Are you off your rocker?"

15

JUNE YANKED A CHAIR away from the table and reconnoitered it so she sat looking straight at Ezra and next to Walt, where he couldn't see her face. She was fine with winging it, confident that they would, one way or another, overpower his melancholy, so long as Ezra stuck with her. It wouldn't be easy. They needed to get him talking, to remember the unquenchable man he'd once been, so fearless and exuberant, then to confront him with what he wouldn't want to admit, to prime him for his rebirth.

"Tell us of your flights, when you were writing *Leaves*," she said, and shot Ezra a help-me-out look.

"Whatever was in me, when I could take flight, is long gone," he said.

"Tell us anyway," Ezra said.

Walt sipped more wine. "After my epiphany," he said, "I could stop thinking, make my mind negative—that's how I envisioned it. I could see everything purely on its own terms, without imposing my thrashing thoughts on it."

"I would stroll aimlessly all day. My undistracted spirit could pour itself into any living miracle I came upon. I could inhabit ordinary working people, the pit of a peach, a powerful sunrise—anything. The soul, once truly aware that it is connected to everything, can do that. It can feel itself being a rock, the sea, an oak tree, an animal, a horse, a fish or a bird, or even the earth, and feel the very motions of the suns and the stars."

June slipped off her chair and tiptoed behind Walt to the table and perused the original *Leaves*.

"I loved opera, how the singers could send me soaring. When I started writing *Leaves* I found I could hear my own music, a primeval tune, a chanting, and as I kept writing, I heard a finer chant, and it would send me soaring, and more visions and words would pour forth."

Her timing perfect, her timbre just right, June let loose with Walt's verse, a Greek chorus to dramatize his recounting.

> *Now the performer launches his nerve…he has passed*
> *His prelude on the reeds within.*
> *Easily written loosefingered chords! I feel the thrum of their climax and close.*
> *Music rolls, but not from the organ…*

She glanced at Walt, his cue to resume his performance, now focused solely on his preferred audience of one, the man who sat studiously at his feet.

"As the words spilled forward—a line or a spurt of lines—only the freest verse could accommodate them. Sometimes I wouldn't tinker at all. Other times I would rework. But I didn't mind—working the words and hearing the music would keep me in flight until another wisp would come up in me and send me flying even farther."

June's voice took wing on the quickening rhythm of Walt's words:

> *I am afoot with my vision.*
> *Speeding through space….speeding through heaven*
> *   and the stars,*

Speeding amid the seven satellites and the broad ring and
*   the diameter of eight thousand miles,*
Speeding with tailed meteors….throwing fire-balls like
*   the rest,*
I fly the flight of the fluid and swallowing soul

Ezra loved how Walt's eyes lit up and stayed sparkly through that whole verse. He might come to like this strange fellow after all. But not before Walt had answered for some things.

"That epiphany of oneness would light me up like the brightest sun. Fill me to the very brim, and the words and the music would spill over in perfect synch, and I would spew forth my yawps."

June slipped in without missing a beat.

The spotted hawk swoops by and accuses me, he complains
*   of my gab and my loitering.*

I too am not a bit tamed, I too am untranslatable
I sound my barbaric yawp over the roofs of the world.

"My chanted hymn—all its tremendous sentiment—uncaged in my breast a thousand wide-winged strengths, and unknown ardors, and terrible ecstasies. The most powerful exuberance I'll ever know—my poem infusing me, and me infusing it, my very own creation, my beloved *Leaves*. I was astonished when I read the final proofs to find myself capable of feeling so much."

"You will take flight again," June said, "for you've given us the missing clues we needed to cure you."

"Do tell, for I am near rested enough to be on my way."

June glanced at Ezra, certain he'd not missed the opening they needed.

"The first one is that you and Keats are very much alike."

"I don't care for Keats," Walt said. "His poetry is sweet and lush, in praise of deities of thousands of years ago. He's polished and ornate. I'm rough and tumble. I write of ordinary humanity. His poetry has no more of normal people, of life in this century, than the Greek statues have. No, Keats and I are not at all alike."

Walt had finally gotten comfortable, titling the chair back, angling it just right, the front legs a few inches off the ground. He emptied his cup and held it up to be refilled.

Ezra stood and put his hands on his hips. "Not too foul tasting, huh? Better sip the next one. I know full well you and Keats write about different things. That's not what I'm talking about. You said your poetry comes best when you stop thinking, when your mind goes quiet and you can inhabit things. That could be Keats himself talking. He was pondering the genius of Shakespeare when he came up with his notion of negative capability."

He went to the table and opened his notebook. "Listen up to what he wrote in one of his letters."

At once it struck me, what quality went to form a Man of Achievement, especially in Literature and which Shakespeare possessed so enormously—I mean "Negative Capability," that is when man is capable of being in uncertainties, Mysteries, doubts, without any irritable reaching after fact and reason.

"Ceasing to thrash about is one thing," Walt said. "I went way beyond that, to become whatever I saw or imagined, as I said."

"I know what you said," Ezra replied. "Keats said the same thing, long before you."

A Poet is the most unpoetical of anything in existence because he has no identity, he is continually in for and filling some other Body.

"You say you can inhabit a peach pit, or a sunrise, or feel yourself being a rock, or the ocean, or the stars, while Keats says he can feel the delight a billiard ball takes in its own roundness and its smooth, fast rolling. Or inhabit a sparrow.

If a sparrow comes before my window, I take part in its existence and pick about the gravel."

"I never heard of Keats saying these things, in which, I admit, I do see some small degree of likeness between us."

"A child asked you, *What is the grass? How could I answer the child?* you said. *I do not know what it is anymore than he.* Then you become the grass, and make a whole book, 128 pages—128 leaves, of grass. Keats inhabits his Greek urn, or his beloved autumn. But he doesn't go on and on like you. He chisels them down into odes—*load every rift with ore,* he told Shelley."

Walt sat up straight.

"You speak of him as though he's alive."

"Immortal John lingers here and down at the creek" June said. "On occasion, he inhabits Ezra."

"The dead live in me, too," Walt said. "The dead, the dead, the dead—our dead. The young, dead, cold soldiers, whose lifeless faces torment me."

"Their souls are all departed," June said. "Let us lift your wretchedness, and they'll torment you no more."

"I'm afraid that is not to be, no matter how alike Ezra finds me and Keats."

"You're alike, too, in the woes you must bear—so much death and loss," Ezra said. "You should follow his example."

"I hope my death is quicker—not so terrible as his," Walt said.

"Not his death," Ezra said. "His life. Marked by death of loved ones from boyhood on. But unlike you, he refused to give into despondency, not until tuberculosis had him in its final, agonizing grip. Even then, he was brave. You're nowhere near that sick."

Walt hunched over and put his head in his hands.

"Listen up to what John says.

Call the world if you please 'The vale of Soul-making.' A place where the heart must feel and suffer in a thousand diverse ways! How necessary a World of Pains and troubles is to school an Intelligence and make it a soul.

"Don't you find virtue in that? In living a difficult, death-filled life, yet not letting it rob your spirit? Destroy your poetic soul?"

"Of course I do," Walt said. "You speak to me as though I haven't tried everything in my power to shake this. As though my nature has always been weak-willed—unable to surmount life's difficulties. Don't you see, Ezra? I was as strong and determined as any man, ever. Until death and evil made me like this."

"I'm sure you were," Ezra said.

"My melancholy torments me, not only with the faces of the dead, but with memories of my old self. I will speak no more of my once soaring self. And I will not speak harshly to you again, my friend. For you do bring me comfort, how you speak of me and Keats, the sensations and marvels you find in our poetry. You make a profound impression on this sick old man. Your knowledge of poetry, what you have told me, is rarely perceived, even among my most ardent followers."

"Well thank you kindly," Ezra said. "That doesn't surprise you, I'm sure. For a man as receptive and free-thinking as you would never, for one moment, think me dumb, an ignorant, former slave content to wash the feet of white men. Even though you are the man who wrote,

Through me many long, dumb voices, Voices of the interminable generations of slaves."

"I wanted to speak for those voices too," Walt said. "I should be washing your feet. I'm a failed ne'er-do-well who once dreamed of being a great poet. You're a brave man, fearless and insightful, who has suffered greatly, yet endures and lives joyfully."

Ezra stepped back around the table and stood over Walt. "You're wrong. On both counts. You are a great poet. And if I was brave, I'd enlist in the Union Army. Which I will not do. I hide from the war. I stay put right here, in June's army of poetry lovers. An army of two. Celebrating ourselves and our poets. We fight for nothing more than our own happiness, and for the well-being of the immortal John Keats, and now, for you."

He leaned down in Walt's face. "And if we're found out, I don't believe that will be considered proper service, do you? A black man living hid away with a young, white woman? You better never tell anyone."

"Never," Walt said.

"Look me in the eye and swear to it."

"I swear."

16

LOUISE SPRUNG TO HER feet and dashed to lean backward over the porch rail. She closed her eyes and parted her lips in longing, like Bernini's "Saint Teresa in Ecstasy," sparing me a reply to Cowboy's "off-your-rocker" query.

"Thanks be to you, John Keats, for bringing Jack to us," she whispered. Her power of imagination so defied the mundane gravity that grounds most of us that I knew she could transport both of us beyond the do-not-cross, half-loony line demarcated by William. At least we'd outnumber Cowboy.

The first time I'd felt Keats' actual presence was the summer after graduate school, stretched out in the grass on the top of the most sacred mountain in his beloved Arcadia, amidst the ruins of Apollo's ancient temple, the Temple of Apollo Epicurius, gazing through the still-standing columns to the Adriatic Sea, the first and last woman who fell in love with me at my side. John watched over us as we wandered off and made love.

Louise switched off St. Teresa and returned to her drink and toasted. "To the three of us—detectives in poetic ecstasy."

I raised my glass of water. "To the Whitman mystery."

"We've been over that—there is no mystery," Cowboy said.

Louise shushed him. "So, mister private-eye professor," she said in her sassy voice, "how about partnering with us and your buddy Keats to solve that mystery?"

Cowboy slammed down his drink down and jumped out of his rocker. "Damn it! This is not about Keats. This is Walt Whitman's story."

The red surged up from her chest and neck and flooded the Milky Ways of freckles on her cheeks. "Don't you scold me like a school girl. I didn't gin up our disagreements. We inherited them. From the founders of our dynasties. I believe—I'll not speak for you—that's why Jack is here, to sort those out."

"Agreed," Cowboy said. "One of two reasons."

"What's the other one?" I said.

"Those who inherit the story can pass it down only once—to a single inheritor," he said.

"The sacred oath of the single tell," she said.

"I'm the last in my line, and Louise is the last in hers," he said. "The third line—the one started by Whitman himself—disappeared from the get-go. Never been heard from."

"We tried everything," Louise said. "Never found any trace of it."

"Walt's line must have died out," he said. "It's down to just the two of us."

"Why would either of you choose me, a stranger?" I asked.

Louise looked at Cowboy.

"We both missed our chance," she said. "The only ones we wanted to tell are gone. We're destined to be the end of our lines. The end of our dynasties. We helped each other came to terms with that. But all is not lost. We came up with a brilliant idea."

"To do the story one better," he said.

"To make certain it will endure, forever," she said.

I played dumb. "Endure through whoever inherits it from me?"
She grimaced.

"No," he said. "You wouldn't get to tell anyone."

"That's okay," I said. "I don't have anyone to tell either."

"No need to," he said. "The three of us are going to make the story immortal."

"And the Rock Creek Canon, too" she said.

"It will be written down," he smiled. "The first and only recorded tell. You get to do that for us."

"Will you?" she said.

I reminded myself this had to be an elaborate myth they'd concocted, an enchanting madness they'd perfected over many years. So what.

"Can I put my name on the tell?"

"I don't see why not," Cowboy said. "But before we decide that, let's get her done—get the story written down."

They were playing cagey. I played hard to get. I cocked my head and made a face like I was full of troubling doubts. Cowboy stood and pulverized an ice cube. "We're offering you the best story a poet-lover could ever know. All we're asking is to sort out our differences and jot it down." He walked inside and let the screen door slam. She hooked her arm through mine and pulled me to the railing to look into the forest.

"We've waited many years for you, our knight in shining armor. Won't you do this for us? We'll have a glorious time."

"I gather it's your Keats against his Whitman?"

"Cowboy wishes it was that simple. Wait until Vincent shows up. Will you do it, please?"

"I will, if you promise me we'll see each other again tomorrow, maybe even offer me a cocktail."

"Tomorrow?" she giggled.

Cowboy walked out.

"Jack's ready! We can do it tonight!" she said, then ran inside.

He squeezed both my arms and looked as happy as I ever saw him.

"I have to go prepare the sanctuary," she yelled. "I'll be waiting there for you two."

"Don't haul too much stuff though the woods," he said to the screen door. "It'll look suspicious. And promise me you'll make sure your Zoo Crew fans aren't following you."

"Bring everything you need," she shouted back. "It could take all night."

He threw his arm around my shoulder. "Come on, friend. We're going back by my place and get you moved in. I got a nice bed for you in the basement."

17

STEAMED-UP EZRA NEEDED to cool down. He pulled the two boards from the heavy-duty brackets that held them fast across the door and walked outside. He surveyed the perimeter and left the door open for the breeze, then dumped the dirty water and clanged the empty wash basin at Walt's feet, sat across the table from him and refilled their cups.

"Ezra, my friend, do you recall in my first *Leaves* when my poet takes in the runaway slave and nurses and feeds him for a week and then beholds him and loves him?"

"I do," Ezra said. *When the sun falls on the black of his polish'd and perfect limbs.* Right before you declare equal love for the dumb animals there with the slave—the horses and the oxen. I recall your entire list of dumb voices:

Voices of the interminable generations of slaves,
Voices of prostitutes and of deformed persons,
Voices of the diseased and despairing, and of thieves and dwarfs.

"Please forgive me, and my long-ago poet. I thought you found my poetry inspiring."

"I do."

"How so?"

"You are a wild, free-thinking man. I do admire that in your verse."

"And the great power of imagination you find in my poetry, you find traces of such powers in Keats, too. I must reconsider him, given our similarities."

"There are more similarities," June said. "He was a common man, like you, not someone you'd expect to become a poet."

"And a renegade poet," Ezra said. "As scandalous as you in revealing his desires. In his case, for breasts and kisses and seductions."

"Self-taught, like you," June said. "A hunger for books. A compulsive thinker about everything he saw, and a scribbler, too, like you, writing long letters and filling notebooks. Although not a list-maker like you, with your long lists of stagecoach drivers and dock workers. The ones you liked to bring home to spend the night with you."

Walt harrumphed, sipped wine, folded his hands on his belly and closed his eyes. June winked at Ezra. "In '55, you sent Emerson your first *Leaves* and were thrilled by his letter. 'I greet you at the beginning of a great career.' By the summer of '56, you had put together the next edition. So much fancier than your first *Leaves*. Emerson's quote gold-stamped on the spine. His entire letter in the back with your long response, in which you declare yourself unifier, sage and preacher to the nation on all matters—personal, physical, spiritual."

She opened the book and thumbed to the back. "'A profound person,'" you brag, "'can easily know more of the people than they know of themselves.' You call Emerson 'master.' It made me cringe. I feared your rebel poet had vanished."

"Made me cringe too," Ezra said. "Talk about too big for your britches. Sounded like an egotistical preacher had taken over the original wild man."

Walt snorted.

"But then we read your new poems," June said. "You'd birthed a new poet, even more wild and explicit. She read:

A WOMAN waits for me—she contains all,
nothing is lacking,
Yet all were lacking, if sex were lacking, or if
the moisture of the right man were lacking.

Sex contains all,
Bodies, souls, meanings, proofs, purities, delicacies...

All the passions, loves, beauties, delights of the
earth...

Without shame the man I like knows and avows
the deliciousness of his sex,
Without shame the woman I like knows and
avows hers.

"You vowed to write thousands of more poems," she said, "to make *Leaves* the American bible, to tour the country and be more than a great poet—to be a preacher and a unifier, to instruct us how to live, in all our greatness, as free and happy as you."

"That was my dream," Walt said. "Though I did not awake to find it so, like your daydreamer Keats."

Ezra laughed. "He never dreamed that people would flock to him, like Jesus reincarnated, wandering the countryside."

"I know too well my sad story. Why do you taunt me with these long-dead dreams?"

"Let her speak," Ezra said.

"You kept writing poetry at a fevered pitch, nearing a hundred poems, looking for a new publisher for a third version of *Leaves*. Then it all crashed down. The '56 edition sold even fewer copies than the original. Reviewers liked it even less than the first *Leaves*. Readers were embarrassed by the sexual poems. Didn't like your brazen self-promotion. You were broke. You had to ask for loans. You couldn't pay back the two hundred dollars you borrowed from Sara Parton."

"Dear god, child," Walt said. "Have I no secrets?"

"Secrets never leave here," Ezra said. "But out there, nothing is secret."

"Her lawyer seized whatever you had worth taking," June said. "You were humiliated."

"Just like Keats," Ezra said, "when he had no money, no place to live, and his friends had to take him in."

"Your dream of being a wandering poet-priest was dead," June said. "You went back to work as a newspaperman."

"Like the destitute Keats gave up his great lyric poem to write magazine articles," Ezra said. "Except you didn't have a deadly disease."

"Stop!" Walt banged his fist on the table. "Is this how you fulfill your promise to restore me, by reminding me what I already know too well, that I am a failure?"

June danced like a sprite behind Walt and kissed him on the top of his head to see if she could make his shoulders twitch. His whole body jerked. "Not a failure," she said. "A pure poet, who must overcome his trials. You got fired in '59 from your newspaper job. You wrote poetry again. Your third coming. A publisher who admired you printed your new book. You went to Boston. You were welcomed by a small but devout following and better yet, your new *Leaves*."

She picked it up from the table. "Four hundred and fifty-six pages, brimming over with new poems from the next poet you'd birthed."

"I become more indirect in the '60 *Leaves*. More personal. The meaning more decipherable the more times you read it, not the words alone, but the directions they take together."

"I see that," Ezra said. "Your first poet traveled the universe. Your second poet returned to earth with dreams of being immortal, a savoir preaching free love. Your third poet is a mere mortal. But more courageous, I'd say. More revealing of his true self. And most amazing, he's humble, like when he stands on the beach and sees what washes up."

June flipped near the front of the '60 *Leaves* and read.

O baffled, balk'd, bent to the very earth,
Opress'd with myself that I have dared to open my mouth,
Aware now that amid all that blab whose echoes recoil upon me I have not once had
*   the least idea who or what I am,*
But that before all my arrogant poems the real Me stands untouched, untold,
*   altogether unreached…*

"Then come those *Children of Adam* poems," Ezra said. "My goodness. Such blatant celebration of sex between men and women."

"You thumbed your nose at the gentlemen poets and critics," June said. "You must have known they would dismiss you as notorious and distasteful. But you did it anyway."

"Emerson pleaded with me to take them out. Told me I could become widely read if I did. Needless to say, I refused. To take away from *Leaves* the celebration of the body and the soul, and procreation and love and sex of all sorts, what would be left of my *Leaves*?

"My aim was never to succeed at so-called literature. No one will ever get at my verses who views them as a literary performance, an attempt to reach what the reviewers would see as some level of art or aestheticism."

Ezra decided he truly did like Walt. "Damn right! And you, wild man, were just warming up with all that loving between men and woman. Then came your *Calamus* poems, all about manly, brotherly love, which you believed could hold the country together. You dreaded so much what you saw coming that you had to imagine how it could turn out different. A year after your new *Leaves*, men began slaughtering each other."

"Foolish man that I am, I did believe that love and affection could unify us," Walt said.

"Not foolish, this third poet," June said. "Mysterious. Torn, like Keats, between poetry and the one you love.

For I can be your singer of songs no longer—One
*   who loves me is jealous of me, and withdraws me*
*   from all but love …*
I am indifferent to my own songs—I will go with
*   him I love.*

"You end up lonely and heartbroken. The 'Hours Continuing Long' poem is so sad—the sullen and suffering hours—and so painful—*I am ashamed—but it is useless—I am what I am.* Then we found the last clue we needed, in the next *Calamus* poem.

> *You bards of ages hence! when you refer to me, mind*
>   *not so much my poems....*
>
> *Publish my name and hang up my picture as that of*
>   *the tenderest lover,*
> *The friend, the lover's portrait, of whom his friend, his*
>   *lover, was fondest,*
> *Who was not proud of his songs, but of the measure-*
>   *less ocean of love within him—and freely poured*
>   *it forth....*
>
> *Who pensive, away from the one he loved, often lay sleep-*
>   *less and dissatisfied at night,*
> *Who knew too well the sick, sick dread lest the one*
>   *He loved might secretly be indifferent to him."*

"Proud not of your poems, but of being the tenderest lover. So alone and heavy-hearted, like Shakespeare in his 'Sonnet 29.' Did that inspire your 'Hours Continuing Long?'"

"Of course not," Walt said. "I am nothing if not original."

"Shakespeare and Whitman," June said. "Your *Calamus* poems and his sonnets. Both of you recall a man he loves and misses terribly. In your case, a young Irish man, a stage coach driver who got married and stopped spending the night with you."

"You do know everything about me," Walt said.

"The first thousand copies printed of the '60 *Leaves* sold, many more than the two earlier editions," she said. "Some traditional critics loathed it, as you knew they would. But some liked it. You were more notorious than renowned—an eccentric poet repudiated for blatantly celebrating sex. Still, you were gaining readership. Your dream came back to life. Then, just like in '56, it all turned sour. The sales weren't enough. Your publisher went out of business.

You returned to New York, even more broke that before. You spent day after day at your favorite bar. And found new friends among the stage-coach drivers."

"My New York stagnation," Walt said. "Before the war brought me here."

"I became acquainted with two nurses who worked in a hospital you visit," June said. "One has a great dislike for you because of your love and affection for the younger men. It so disturbs her she tried to have you barred from visiting."

"A mean woman," Walt said. "Unkind to the boys."

"She told me about the two young men you grew so fond of. One let you give him a long kiss. The one you fell in love with. You pleaded with him to live with you, his friend too, all together in blissful, brotherly love. She said when he ignored you, you badgered him with so many letters that finally, last winter, he had to rebuff you in writing, to stop your unwanted pursuit."

Walt dropped his head. "You're right, Ezra. There are no secrets out there. Tom and Lew, both dear boys. Tom, I'm afraid, didn't comprehend manly adhesiveness. He found my love for him as a comrade strange and unusual, though I assured him I didn't expect him to return to me the same degree of love I have for him."

June filled Walt's cup and sat on the floor cross-ankled in front of him.

"The soldiers you comforted in death did break your heart. But so did those you nursed back to health, the ones you fell in love with, only for them to leave you. And they weren't the first to break your heart, as your *Calamus* poet makes clear."

"You're suffering from terrible love melancholy, just like Keats did," Ezra said.

"If your conjecture were true," Walt said, "what is this cure you claim to have for me?"

"For the first part," Ezra said, "I go back to you and Keats and the obvious way you're most surely not like him."

"There are more than one, certainly," Walt declared.

"Stop arguing," Ezra said. "Keats preferred humbleness to pride. Oh, he was a proud man, but never so full of himself as you. His notion of negative capability came to him when he got fed up with the petty arguing of his most egotistical friends. Unlike them, pride did not compel him to believe he was right and others wrong. Listen to this."

The only means of strengthening one's intellect is to make up one's mind about nothing—to let the mind be a thoroughfare for all thoughts.

"I assure you that my poetic mind could wander more freely than Keats," Walt said. "My poetry, as you said yourself, is nothing if not free-minded, and disdains any need to pin down trifling matters."

"This has nothing to do with your poetry," Ezra said. "I'm talking about your great ego. How it's turned on you. How you take such great pride in how well-deserved your melancholy is. You need to make better use of your pride and stubbornness. Send it into battle, to fight for the soul of a pure poet."

"How so?" Walt said.

"Buck up!" Ezra said. "Find your courage. You ever read Keats' letter that compares life to a mansion of many apartments?"

"Why would I?"

"Listen up."

We no sooner get into the second Chamber, which I shall call the Chamber of Maiden-Thought, than we become intoxicated with the light and the atmosphere, we see nothing but pleasant wonders and think of delaying there forever in delight.

"That was your first, high-flying, happy-as-a-lark poet," Ezra said.

However, among the effects this breathing is father of is that tremendous one of sharpening one's vision into the heart and the nature of Man, of convincing one's nerves that the World is full of Misery and Heartbreak, Pains, Sickness and oppression, whereby this Chamber of Maiden-Thought becomes gradually darken'd and at the same time on all sides of it many doors are set open, but all dark, all leading to dark passages. Now if we live, and go on thinking, we too shall explore them.

"That's where you stand now. Steel yourself. Charge through

the darkness. Find what awaits you. Which in your case, could be immortality."

"You do provoke me, brother" Walt said. "Not even these fiend-ish spirits in me can dilute my affection for you. Or your affection for me, which I can tell comes from the depths of your poetic soul. I pray I have a place there, alongside your beloved Keats."

"Keats believes the purpose of poetry is to relieve our maladies and suffering—to lift us, to cheer us, and if not, at least to *lift a little time* from our shoulders," Ezra said. "Deep down, you believe that, too. That's why I hope you'll rise again."

"Now you see in me what you would not see before," Walt said. "Like your dear Keats, I do strive, above all else, to be a friend to men, women, and children of every kind, including slaves and other unfortunates, the list in *Leaves* you found insulting."

"Despite your arguing self, I do see that," Ezra said. "In May of 1819, during his great run of poetry writing, with some of his great-est work yet to come, Keats was exhausted, much sicker than you, besieged by critics, broke, and madly in love with a woman he knew he'd never be fit to marry.

"Hear him, Walt, one last time.

I must take my stand upon some vantage ground and begin to fight. I must choose between despair and Energy. I choose the latter."

18

I CAN PICTURE GRANDPA clear as day in the overalls he wore every day after he lost his floor-sweeper job at the paper mill. He sat contently on the lone front step of the dilapidated wood-frame house, way out in the country, hemmed in by unfarmed fields and rusted-out junkers, Memaw pestering him for a proper porch, where she could sit and read her books.

He paid her no mind, for he preferred to sit alone, his somehow never-empty bottle of Jim Beam hidden between the cinder blocks that held up the splintery, bowed barn plank.

That summer I turned eight I came home at the end of another hot afternoon, a memorable one at the swimming hole a mile or so down the gravel road. "Settle in, boy," he said, making just enough room for me, a little grin on his saggy face. "Look at that holly tree way yonder, between them pines, way up the field, past the lone oak." He put his arm around my shoulder. "Tell me what you see."

There was no breeze, but the limbs in the holly jostled. Distant dots zoomed at it. Those slow-moving, ground-walking worm-eating robins were making themselves into jet planes and disappearing full speed into that tree. Every wave of sudden arrivals triggered matched departures—robins fired back out of the holly like rockets. More robin squadrons swept and circled, the sky filled with their fleeting, careening formations that would put the Blue Angels to shame, eventually landing in the trees surrounding the holly and waiting their turn to launch their attacks on the holly berries.

I jumped up and shrieked in glee. "I see 'em! I see 'em!"

"I knew you had it!" he slapped his knee.

"What?"

"The keen eye. You and me boy, we're the only ones I ever come across who's got it. Your mama and your Memaw, they ain't got it. Your daddy, he don't have it neither. I suspected you might have— you got that special twinkle in your eye."

"You really believe so?"

"We better make sure," he said. "Now usins with keen eye always take a true gander, a long look upon those sights that catch our eye. And cause we got the keen eye, we pay heed to what we see, unlike most others who got lazy eyes. Now tell me more what you see, boy. If you do got the keen eye, make it work for you!"

"A huge number of them robins, hundreds and hundreds I would say—I can count every one if need be—is having a berry-eating frenzy," I said. "Lazy eyes would take a glance and see a plain old holly. But us keen eyes can see it's chocked full of robins, and that they're in all the trees, taking turns feasting in the holly."

He was so happy at my excitement I feared for an instant he would cry. A touch of bright promise and great cheerfulness descended upon us, and like a breeze can rev up into a sudden whirlwind, it cleared out the grimy fog of decay and discord that overhung the homestead even when the sun shined.

I hugged him, the only hug I know of he ever got. "I can see every one of them robins and exactly what they're doing, Granddaddy, cause I got the keen eye, like you!"

"Now don't be bragging about it," he smiled. "It ain't nothing to be cutting up about. Don't flaunt it. Keep it a secret, just between us. We don't want nobody to be jealous."

Memaw turned off the radio. He gave me the quiet sign and whispered how lucky I was, how the keen eye would turn out to be a greater gift than even the one my mamma desperately wanted to provide me—moving us into town so I could graduate city high school. For when keen eyes grow up, he said, they can see the stories in people that they never say out loud—the ones they only tell themselves. And if you keep working your keen eye, making it stronger, he said, you'll get to where you can decipher stories in people that they can't even see in themselves, stories they don't even know is in them.

He had me raise my hand, no fingers crossed, and whisper a swear in his ear to never tell anyone of our secret power.

19

TIME FOR THE REAL fun, Ezra thought, for he was certain June would easily top, somehow, his straightforward, buck-it-up fix for Walt. He delivered Walt a friendly slap on both shoulders. "Now for the rest of your cure," he said.

"The Muses direct me to carry out their own remedy—a proper enshrinement of Walt Whitman into the Rock Creek Canon," she said.

"Oh course," Ezra grinned at her.

"And what would that entail?" Walt said.

"The deities," June said, "as is their wont before they grace us with their presence, wish us first to call them forth. Their desire is to descend upon us at the creek. There, they will touch you again, re-infuse you. By bringing forth the spirit of your first happy poet, and of Keats himself—your one and only Rock Creek Canon brethren."

"June's a daemon, pure and simple" Ezra said.

Walt threw him a worried glance.

"We should ready ourselves," she said. She stepped toward the back wall and stood aside the bed, lost in thought, splotched in sunlight from the lone window.

"I've been with her when the Muses possess her, make her their priestess," Ezra whispered to Walt. "You've never seen anything like it."

June took off her linen smock. She leaned across the bed, her backside to them, to retrieve a silk nightgown hung on a nail. She leaned over again to reach her favorite amulet, a tiny silver figure of a yearning female embracing the air above her. Ezra couldn't help but grin at riveted Walt, already halfway to spellbound.

She hung the amulet around her neck and pulled on the gown, then twined a long braid down the right side of her face.

She took a spray of blue wild flowers from the vase on the table and made it into garland she placed on her head. She turned and stared out the window, her hands palm to palm and fingers to fingers, like a child in prayer.

"June dear," Walt said, "please tell me more of the ceremony, how it cures."

She ignored him.

"We're not going to hear anymore from her until the Muses come to her at the creek," Ezra said.

June pointed to the things to be carried. She picked up her original *Leaves* and held it in both hands, like a churchwoman's *Book of Common Prayer*.

"Lordy be, June," Ezra said, "I hope no one sees you." He yanked a sheet off the bed and draped it over her shoulders and tied it like a cape. Walt picked up the basket. Ezra gathered towels and soap. June clutched her precious book to her bosom and headed out. Walt looked befuddled. Ezra shoved him out the door and they followed June out into the hot, still bright day.

Walt seized Ezra's arm and forced him to halt. "I've never met a woman like her," he said.

"Me neither," Ezra said. "And I've never been the same since. And never will be."

"You've witnessed her possessed," Walt said. "A daemon, you say. How so?"

"The first time she threw a spirit into me, I flew into an inspired trance. Profoundly wakeful. Like your flights, I imagine."

"What happened then?"

"She called forth Keats, through me. That's when I realized he'd truly become part of me—as much a presence in me as my own soul."

Ezra scanned the woods. June's ghostly figure drifted further down the hill. "I'd never known such a state," he said. "So wide awake, yet calmly trance-bound. There's no telling what'll happen. It's different every time. But if the spirits come into you, you'll know. It's the highest my soul has ever soared."

"What happened after Keats came forth in you?"

"Don't worry. If the Muses get her fired up and she conjures up spirits in you, you won't be fretting about what comes next. You'll be flying high, like you used to.

"I mean it when I say this, Walt. I do love you. Like I love Keats. Like I'll love any other pure poet who touches my soul. But this, whatever happens, this is between you and her. This is her part of the cure. You already heard mine."

"You bore into me the need to accept the unhappiness of life," Walt said, "But you are a very happy man."

"No luckier man alive," Ezra said.

"With no necessity to surrender to life's misery."

"I prefer not to ponder my current good fortune one iota," Ezra said. "And I never dare count on it lasting beyond the present moment."

"If she tries to touch me, I don't know that I could stand it."

"Not even to birth that next poet? The one she's got such big plans for? This is spiritual for her. It might show itself physically. But with her it's purer than that. Intimacy serves her deeper desires. To ascend."

"To a state of grace, body and soul," Walt said.

"That's the spirit. From what she's told me, her deepest desires are connected somehow to those newfangled, spiritual-scientific theories you like so much, the ones that link everything together.

She told me that you believe semen—what do you call it? the father-stuff?—is the purest, finest nectar of the brain and the spine and the soul."

"You'll be right there with us though, won't you?"

"For her calling forth the Muses? For your invocation? For what I hope is your reincarnation? Wouldn't miss it for the world. I'll be there, spellbound like you, if my luck holds."

"For you, it's a spell of enchantment. Natural white magic. For me, it's an exorcism."

Ezra wrapped his left arm around the mound of towels he carried and threw his right arm around Walt.

"Brother, best to stop thrashing about in your thoughts. Let's see if June and the Muses can stir your soul."

20

COWBOY AND I STRODE through the night woods, deeper into the park, well past Louise's playhouse.

We took a narrow trail up along a ridge side to a huge rock formation. Hundreds of feet straight down the wide creek wound its way. Cowboy sat down and dangled his feet over the edge.

"Pulpit Rock, Louise's favorite night-time haunt," he said. "We'll wait here for a minute. In case anyone's following us, they'll think this is where we were headed."

I sat next to him and asked to whom he'd wanted to tell the story. He stood without a word and nodded for me to follow him. The trail led to a bridge over the creek. Another trail took us to a deer path we followed up the other side of the creek valley. It turned into a bushy, narrow, uphill tunnel that wound through tall rhododendrons.

Room-sized loaves of granite, stacked two and three high, separated by a table-sized slices sticking out like balconies, rose out of a steep hillside.

Cowboy picked up a rock and climbed up the moonlit side of the edifice and pounded three times. He waited three beats, pounded twice more, then returned. He led me half way up the front of the helter-skelter formation into one of the bigger nooks. Dropping to his knees, he crawled four or five feet into Little Bear Cave—they had names for everything—until he reached what appeared to be a solid back wall.

"There's only one way to go. It gets kind of tight before it opens up."

"How tight?"

"Big enough for me. So big enough for you."

He dropped over the top of the back wall. I hoisted myself over and fell into a pile of leaves.

I could hear him scraping the pebbly ground. Into the pitch black I shimmied on my belly, shoving our bag of supplies in front of me. The ceiling and sides closed like a sieve. I tucked my elbows together under my ribs and grasped my hands together under my chin and snaked on, my head forcing the bag forward. One mighty thrust gained me a foot or more. The back of my head was flush against the ceiling and my shoulders squished too tight against the sides. I tried to stick my right hand out. I couldn't. I'd wedged my folded-under arms so tight under me they were stuck and going numb. I tried to thrust my hips but they were jammed fast. I tried to wiggle backwards but I couldn't get traction with my feet or my shoulders to dislodge my hips.

A grizzly memory materialized in the pure dark. Richard Brautigan, broke and unpublishable despite his earlier fame and book sales in the millions, had shot himself in the head with a .44 magnum. He body, undiscovered for six weeks, etched an indelible death image into the wooden floor of his cabin, a phantom that future owners never could remove. Would the stain I'd leave after wedging myself intractably in this horrid rock be equally indelible?

"Stop screaming!" Cowboy hissed. "You're scaring the hell out of Louise."

"I'm stuck!"

He reentered the tunnel and crawled back to me. He slid his right hand under my chin, grabbed my left wrist and yanked my arm free. I could tilt just enough to free my right arm and wiggle my shoulders forward and shimmy through the final curve and I shot myself out head first. He caught me under my armpits and almost tumbled but held fast and righted me.

I looked with the greatest relief at a room-sized, five-sided cave lit with candles everywhere on the floor and wedged in the odd-angled recesses that pocked the fissured walls. Oriental rugs plied the floor, surrounding a circle of pebbles in the middle. Stacks of blankets and books and an old metal bookcase that housed an impressive array of wine, liquor and snacks lined the walls.

Cowboy handed me a blanket. "Welcome to Hideaway. That's Hideaway Loft."

Louise dangled her legs off a deep, roomy ledge, with space behind her under the curving ceiling, about seven feet high in the middle of the cave.

She was clad in a heavy, full-length cape, purple with fury cuffs and borders, held closed at her waist by a red silk sash, an outfit you'd find only at a serious costume store.

"Quite a dramatic entrance," she snickered, "I'll tell you the true names of our most sacred place, to be spoken only in here. Never, ever out there."

"Holy of holies? Sanctum Sanctorum?"

She vaulted down and stood queen-like, her hands joined in front of her. "You're warm. We stand in the underground temple of the Telesterion, where the secret initiation rites—including the anointments—are given. Then the most sacred objects are brought out from the Anaktoron"—she pointed at the dark space in the loft—"by the priestess."

"Like the Eleusinian Mysteries," I said.

"Bingo," she said.

Accounts and speculations I'd pored over during an obsession with the top-secret Eleusinian Rites—wild dancing and all-night carrying on followed by the most sacred and serious rites—danced in my head. For Greek and Roman initiates, including Plutarch and

Hadrian, my favorite, the rites were profoundly life altering, in a good way, in part because they drank a potion of barley infested with the hallucinogenic fungoid Claviceps.

"Do you concoct a magic potion, like the kykeon brewed by your Eleusinian counterpart?"

Cowboy chuckled. "She's been working on this batch for a long time. Dip your fingers in it if you want. Maybe you'll grow wings on your feet."

Where had I heard that before?

I weaned myself long ago from psychedelic pleasures, but the whimsy of one last, unsought and therefore innocent, mind-altering adventure had a naughty, nostalgic shine to it.

"Cowboy must think it's trance-inducing, like Walt's calamus," she said.

He shook his head at her in disappointment. She stepped on a footstool and pulled herself back up into her lair, out of the light. A minute later she jumped back down, an urn in one hand—a miniature replica of Keats' Greek one—and a leather-bound journal in the other.

I hailed the urn by reciting my favorite lines from Keats' ode:

Heard melodies are sweet, but those unheard
  Are sweeter; therefore, ye soft pipes, play on;
Not to the sensual ear, but, more endear'd,
  Pipe to the spirit ditties of no tone;

"Quit dithering and set your butt down in that circle," Cowboy said.

Louise folded her legs under herself and we sat face to face, the urn pressed between her thighs. She dipped the first two fingers of her right hand in it and sucked on them, test tasting, then dipped one finger and applied a sheen of bubbly, light blonde amber the consistency of honey to her lips.

"Ready?" she said.

I nodded. She re-dipped and rubbed two fingertips on my forehead in slow circles, her mystery mix less sticky that I expected, more like hash oil than pancake syrup.

"I anoint you with the essence of the secret-keepers, the sacred sacrament of Calliope and Erato, and their sister Muses, and the Rock Creek Canon."

She finger-dipped again and held her concoction under my nose: pure Mother Earth, dominant whiffs of pine-needley forest floor followed by a woodsy, slightly sweet aroma of sawdust and small-town-carnival cotton candy.

"I do want to taste it," I said on a whim.

I puckered my lips out to be braised. She bypassed them and pressed two fingertips on my tongue. They felt like a pair of sticky communion wafers. She re-dapped me, then wiped her fingers on my lips. The goo on my tongue hardened into a mossy brittle, then melted away and gave me a wicked case of cotton mouth.

Cowboy opened the journal and took his time, leafing through page after page.

The candle flickers got flashier.

"We've been rewriting this new version of the oath for years, ever since we decided to do this," he said.

The candles definitely were burning brighter. There was no breeze, that was for sure.

"After all that," he said to Louise, "I'd rather just wing it."

Would that unmistakable brain tingle, that sure sign you're getting off, be next?

"Fine with me," she said.

My head prickled from the inside out. I gasped. Cowboy pretended not to notice. She locked me down with her eyes, to help me ground myself, I figured, for knew what she knew awaited me.

"I'd like to have him swear on my *Leaves*," Cowboy said.

I tried to come to grips with the most flagrantly stupid thing I'd done in my entire life.

From somewhere deep in her lair she retrieved his book.

He held an old *Leaves* in front of me like a Bible. I put my hand on it. He covered my hand with his. She put hers on top.

I had ingested psychedelics trapped in a cave at the end of a tunnel too tight for me.

"You go," he said to her.

"Do you swear, with your heart and soul, to me and to Cowboy, and to the Muses, and to Walt Whitman and John Keats, that you will never reveal the story, other than to record it in the first written tell?"

"To be written without delay," Cowboy said, "and turned over to us immediately upon completion."

I dug my fingernails into my palms and deployed in quick succession every other means in my once trusty but now ragged anti-panic, keep-your-wits-about you tool kit, forged, fittingly enough, in a long-ago day-tripping era. This time, for the first time ever, I failed. I had to squeeze my way back through the tunnel. Once I got outside, I'd be fine, no matter what she'd laced the potion with. I panted and jumped to my feet. She jumped up and jammed her hand against my chest and kissed me on the forehead. "Don't worry," she smiled. "There's nothing mind-altering in that mix. I promise. I wouldn't let you taste it if there was. I'd worry you might get claustrophobic."

Glory be. Relief saturated me. It truly was my lucky day. Who could ever ask for more than that?

She hopped on the stool and back up on her ledge. I scooted backwards and propped myself against the wall so I could sort of see her. She scooted further back, completely out of view.

Her words flowed like a shady river on a hot, lazy day. At some point—I lost all notion of clock time—I stood on tiptoes and peeked. She was stretched out, her hands folded on her stomach, her head propped up on pillows. Her eyes glittered, looking where I could not say.

21

WALT STRIPPED NAKED, CAJOLED by Ezra. He covered himself with a towel and lowered himself into the throne, a five-foot
high, once oval boulder smoothly hollowed out on one side that sat
off the low end of the island. A long string of hot, rainless days made
for a dry, warmed-by-the-sun seat that brought forth a wiggle from
Walt when his bottom hit home.

June planted herself close in front of him, nestling her toes into
the creek bed. "I'm a bashful soul at heart, almost timid in your presence," she said, then lifted her gown and tied it above her tummy.
"All I have is my faith in the Muses."

She lowered herself on her haunches, the water not quite up
to her belly button. She cupped her hands, doused his chest three
times, then plunged both hands to the creek bottom. "I feel among
the tiny, time-worn stones and press the chosen one in my palm."
She raised her closed hand from the water and held it over her heart.

"Oh Muses, I have never called upon you in such great need. You have touched before the gentle soul of Walt Whitman. He is a pure poet. Dedicated to all the daughters of Zeus and Mnemosyne. And especially to you, the most beautifully voiced Calliope, the inspirer of epic poetry.

"He has lost his way and fears he will never again hear your joyful music, or feel your blissful touch, or be carried by your breath into the heavenly realms of poesy."

Her flat voice and Walt's disinterested eyes alarmed Ezra. His pontificating caused the three of them to fritter away too much of themselves and this precious day in the cabin. Where was June's enchantress self? Ezra scooted down the rock double-time and hovered close to the throne. June stood and swayed and her amulet swung back and forth.

"Please forgive him for doubting you," she said. "He suffers greatly. In the spirit of Psyche, forgiven by Zeus in an assembly of the gods attended by the Muses, please hear his vow to rededicate himself to you."

She stopped swaying. The figurine hung at the tip of Walt's nose and he blinked to avoid looking cross-eyed.

"Psyche and Cupid enraged Venus by falling in love. Yet the deities forgave her. The mortal lover of Cupid was made immortal, and gave birth to an immortal daughter, Pleasure. You see how Psyche poses? Her head leaned back, her arms circled above? She is imagining her arms wrapped above Cupid's head, as he prepares to kiss her.

"The stone I hold is your soul, Walt Whitman. The creek water, creator of the stone, is the Castalian Spring on Mount Parnassus, the sacred ground of the Muses."

She unfisted her hand and lowered Psyche to lounge on the creamy brown stone, the size of an oblong penny.

She told Walt to take off his hat. He frowned. Ezra yanked it off his head.

"Welcome Psyche to your soul," June said. She leaned closer. "Kiss her."

Walt squeezed his big head between June's chin and her open palm and found little Psyche with his lips.

June's eyes came alive with delight. "A long kiss!" she commanded in her fired-up enchantress voice and held Walt's head to his kiss. Ezra hailed the Muses and recalled the clamorous night June recited Keats' "Ode to Psyche" to him in the pitch blackness.

"John Keats' spirit now descends and declares his everlasting devotion to Psyche and to Calliope," June declared. "Do you, Walt Whitman, equally devote yourself?"

He muffled a yes in June's palm.

"Do you acknowledge the presence of John Keats and ask him to join us in this ceremony?"

Silence.

"Walt!" Ezra said.

"Yes," he murmured.

June slid Psyche from under his lips and stepped up on the rock. She kissed the stone and placed it on a slight hump that marked the middle of their island.

"Muses, I lay upon your altar this divine symbol of Walt Whitman's poetic soul, now dedicated to you. I beseech you come forth and exorcise the evil spirits who infest him with unending memories of the dying men he so loved."

"Rid me too," Walt blurted out, "of those wicked spirits in me who relish the killing, the spirits from those men who take great glee in the butchery of war."

June glanced at Ezra as though she didn't recognize him and jerked her head back, her wide eyes so unfocused that Ezra jumped to his feet. "June?"

Her arms hung stiffly. Her hands trembled.

"June," Ezra said softly.

She didn't hear him.

"Look at me," he whispered. She began, with great effort, to lower her gaze, not at him, but back across the creek.

"Do you hear that swishing?" she said. "Those whispers from the water?"

Ezra put his finger to his lips. "Don't spook them." He fetched the soap and lifted her quivering hand and pressed the bar in it. She grasped it and froze. A strange grin forced itself on her mouth.

Ezra held her by the waist and walked her in front of Walt, whose face grimaced in stoic panic.

"Quiet your mind," Ezra said, and patted him on the knee. "The spirits are here."

"They're coming closer," June said, her body far too stiff for Ezra's liking. She kneeled face to face with Walt, a good sign, Ezra thought. But then, to keep her eyes on the creek, twisted her head so far around it made him cringe. She was more revved up than he'd ever seen her, and, by god, she was right, it was true: the creek stirred louder. She stayed strangely twisted, but what troubled Ezra more was the ghoulish grin that pained her face, so unlike the previous spells he'd witnessed, when she'd transformed into a joyfully possessed enchantress, a charming, clever presiding priestess, still somewhat herself.

A breeze near blew Walt's hat into the creek. Ezra grabbed it and pulled in down tight on his head for safe keeping. June's hair lifted from her twisted head and made her look even further bewitched. She blindly slapped the soap against Walt's chest without turning to face him and began washing in helter-skelter motions, as if someone else controlled her arm.

Ezra gulped and licked and bit his lips. He feared he'd underestimated the evil that obsessed Walt—freshly sowed evil, which Walt had warned them was more pernicious than they realized. Maybe the evil was using Walt to spread itself, to this creek, even to their shack. June had said John had come, but Ezra could not sense his presence. Where was he?

Walt's gaze went from worry to blank. He took no notice of the now unmoving bar of soap plastered into his chest hair. His eyes rolled back in his head.

Ezra's strength waned. He waded out into the creek, his cohorts oblivious to him and, more worrisome, unaware of each other and even their own selves. New fears pierced him. The batch of wine he'd broken out at the cabin had aged too long, turned bad, and robbed them all of themselves. Maybe June had mischievously fiddled with it, seasoned it with unknown roots and herbs and mushrooms that were turning June and Walt half mad and listless in what should be their finest hour. He would be next, stranded helpless in the creek, leaving all three of them easy prey to whoever happened upon them.

Terror seized him: His bragging to Walt of his good luck had jinxed everything. Such prideful boasting could surely account for this wretched reversal in their fortunes.

He nestled his behind into the malleable, thick frosting of pebbles on the creek bottom and put his head in his hands and grieved. A cool shiver ran down his spine. A sad, depleted breeze blew over him and made his shoulders rise and fall. Guppies nibbled the hairs of his legs and he couldn't help but grin at the tickles. When the monstrous beating in his ears quieted slightly, he took a deep breath and confronted his darkest worry. It wasn't the wine. It was June's madness. He'd blinded himself to it. It must have finally wormed its way too far inside her and in a final, evil siege conquered her happy willfulness, which, until now—now that his bragging had turned luck against them—had managed to hold her wild spirit and imagination on the right side, the joyous side of the fine line of lunacy. He'd one seen the same fate befall an irrepressible young slave woman who one day turned sullen and vacant.

Minnows in great numbers weaved round him like their sea-worthy brethren through sunken ships. Their puckering and sucking spread up his thighs, a leg hair as succulent to them, he imagined, as a gravy-dipped finger. His voice surprised him when it boomed over the creek.

. . . o'er their pebbly beds,
Where swarms of minnows show their little heads,
Staying their wavy bodies 'gainst the streams,
To taste the luxury of sunny beams
Temper'ed with coolness.

June heard the untitled Keats closed-couplet she'd read to Ezra the morning after their first love-making and unswiveled. Delight loosened her frightful grin. The bar of soap in her hand startled her. "Your friend Keats comes to you," she bellowed. "You two make me swoon, and the Muses too."

For once, Ezra relished her boisterousness. "I do my best to please the Muses," he shouted. "You know what they most desire?"

"What?"

"For you to be their calm priestess."

"They wish me to bathe Walt," she said. "And for you and John to finish the minnow verses, then service us with wine and water."

The return of June's confident conjurer brought Ezra an electric shiver of gratefulness and a half-formed tear in each eye, gone with a blink. He smiled at the minnows.

How they ever wrestle
With their own sweet delight, and ever nestle
Their silver bellies on the pebbly sand.

He lowered his hand and the wavy, gold-streaked fish scattered like silver arrows.

If you but scantily hold out the hand,
That very instant not one will remain:

He lifted his hand and the guppy horde darted back to resume their harvest.

But turn your eye, and they are there again.

June threw open her arms and he ran splashing to her. They pondered the state of Walt. His reddened face tilted up at the afternoon sun. The slits in his eyes showed only white. Ezra put Walt's hat back on his head. June circled her soapy hand gently over his chest. He blinked rapidly and sucked in air. She made a show of letting the soap slip from her hand and fall to the towel that covered him. He jiggled his cheeks and lips and his eyes widened on her as if he faced an apparition.

"Taken by a trance?" Ezra chuckled.

Walt took on a grave countenance.

"This blasted heat has me dazed. My head is swimming."

They splashed and showered him from head to knee and he howled in coolness.

Ezra poured him swallows of water and squirted him wine. June gulped water from their jug and had Ezra fetch her the linen cloth. She gingerly retrieved the soap from Walt's lap.

"Bold Calliope infuses me and guides my hands to cleanse you. She touches you and penetrate your soul."

"I don't detect her presence," Walt said.

"You'd better believe she and John are here," Ezra said. "They just had me recite a Keats poem I've never learned by heart."

June lifted Walt's arms and washed down his sides, re-soaped her cloth and patted his tummy and thighs. His face doured and his eyes squinted shut.

"The dead, the dead, the dead still gather around me," he lamented. "Faces so pale. Such dreaded sorrow in their eyes."

"Every atom of those men is part of something else now," Ezra said. "That's what you tell us in *Leaves*. The Muses command you to let them go."

"Oh, I try, I try. Seeing them is such sad madness."

"Calliope enters you," June said. "She confronts the evil spirits who parade the innocent before you. She commands you to speak your first poet."

She and Ezra waited.

Walt opened his eyes.

"I fail, again. He will not come forth in me." He squeezed his eyes shut.

"Then he will speak through me," June said. Eyes on fire, she tossed her head in languid circles and sent her braid swinging.

Read these leaves in the open air every season of every year of your life, re-examine all you have been told at school or church or in any book, dismiss whatever insults your own soul and your very flesh shall be a great poem and have the richest fluency not only in its words but in the silent lines of its lips and between the lashes of your eyes and in every motion and joint of your body.

She slid the straps off her shoulders and her gown slid down and fell around the gathered-up bottom half knotted around her middle. She spread her arms. "I make my flesh a great poem. Consider it at your leisure. The divine sisters speak to me of their favorite features of each other. And of us, as well."

"Yes they do," Ezra said. "Calliope greatly admires June's bottom half. She calls it Junoesque. Calliope has a fine shape herself. You ever heard the word Callipygian, Walt? It means having a shapely bottom. Treat herself to a peek, Walt." The old poet stared open-mouthed at June.

"The Muses blow breath on me and my poem comes alive," June said. "Your first poet takes me in his thrall." Her voice dropped a half-octave.

> *Loafe with me on the grass...*
> *loose the stop from your throat,*
> *Not words, not music or rhyme I want....not custom or lecture, not*
> *even the best,*
> *Only the lull I like, the hum of your valved voice.*

She suckled the drops lingering on Walt's breasts, then kneeled aside his throne and laid her head sideways on his belly. With her right hand she raised his leg, and with her left seized his foot, then reached her right to his beard and settled her head into him like a pillow.

> *I mind how we lay in June, such a transparent summer morning*
> *You settled your head athwart my hips and gently turned upon me*
> *And parted my shirt from my bosom bone and, and plunged your tongue*
> *to my barestrip heart,*
> *And reached till you felt my beard, and reached till you held feet.*

June rubbed tender circles around his lips with her fingertip. Ezra glanced at his undisturbed lap towel. June lifted her head and took Walt's hand and held it to her breast.

> *I merely stir, press, feel with my fingers and am happy,*
> *To touch my person to someone else's is about as much as I can stand.*

She made his fingers gently strum her and emitted little chirps, then took his hand away and stood. Bright red streamed up her neck and into her face. Ezra splashed her. She raised her leg and propped her foot up in the throne seat aside Walt and went perfectly still.

Not about to abide her slipping back into a daze, Ezra tried to divert her with a sip of wine. She took no notice, would not part her lips. Ezra was about to lick the drops that shimmied off her chin to her breasts and beyond when her pupils dilated and she slipped back into priestess gear and let loose a rumbly, manlier voice.

This is the female form,
A divine nimbus exhales from it from head to foot,
It attracts with fierce undeniable attraction,
I am drawn by its breath as if I were no more than a helpless vapor....
    all falls aside but myself and it,

Ezra took three steps and leaned against the side of the throne to observe June and wondered if Walt's expression changed when June's two fingers found their destination.

Mad filaments, ungovernable shoots play out of it...the response
    likewise ungovernable,
Hair, bosom, hips, bend of legs, negligent falling hands

Is this then a touch? ...quivering me to a new identity,
Flames and ether making a rush for my veins,
Treacherous tip of me reaching and crowding to help them,
My flesh and blood playing out lightning, to strike what is hardly
    different from myself,

Without warning Walt shot into a dither. His head quivered. His shoulders jerked up and down. June kept on in her odd, low voice:

I am given up by traitors;
I talk wildly...I have lost my wits...I and nobody else am the
    greatest traitor,
I went myself first to the headland...my own hands carried me there.

"Hush!" Walt commanded and threw his hands up, palms to the sky. "My poet is with me now! All my poets come back to me. I am them. I contain them all. I am...

Walt Whitman, an American, one of the roughs, a kosmos,

Disorderly fleshy and sensual...eating drinking and breeding,
No sentimentalist...no stander above men and woman or apart
*   from them ...no more modest than immodest.*

June extracted her foot from under Walt's bottom and stepped
away. Walt thundered.

Unscrew the locks from the doors!
Unscrew the doors themselves from their jambs!

Through me the afflatus surging and surging...through me the
*   current and index.*

I speak the password primeval...I give the sign of democracy;
By God! I will accept nothing which all cannot have their counterpoint
*   Of on the same terms.*

I sound triumphal drums for the dead...I fling through my
*   embouchures the loudest and gayest music for them.*

"Hallelujah," Ezra muttered, wishing Walt to be less resounding, imaging his words echoing up and down Rock Creek valley.

Do you guess I have some intricate purpose?
Well I have...for the April rain has, and the mica on the side of
*   a rock has.*

Do you take it I would astonish?
Does the daylight astonish? Do the early redstart twittering through
*   the woods?*
Do I astonish more than they?

This hour I tell you things in confidence,
I might not tell everybody but I will tell you.

He sucked deep breaths and gripped his throne as if preparing
to jump up and lead a charge. Instead, he shook his big bottom,

resettled in his seat and thrust out his chest, then leaned over and scooped creek water into his mouth.

> *Through me forbidden voices,*
> *Voices of sexes and lust...voices veiled, and I will remove the veil,*
> *Voices indecent by me clarified and transfigured.*

> *I do not press my finger across my mouth,*
> *I keep as delicate around the bowels as around the head and heart,*
> *Copulation is no more rank to me than death is.*

> *I believe in the flesh and the appetites,*
> *Seeing hearing and feeling are miracles, and each part and tag of me is*
> *   a miracle.*

Ezra grinned at the sight of Walt's towel rising, the center beam of a miniature circus tent being shoved into place under a draping canvas. Walt lifted his arms higher.

> *Divine am I inside and out, and I make holy whatever I touch or am*
> *   touched from;*
> *The scent of these arm-pits is aroma finer than prayer,*
> *This head is more than churches or bibles or creeds.*

"His poetry infuses him," June giggled. Ezra well knew Walt's lines, but was stunned nonetheless by how this strange man infused them with unrepentant power and glory.

> *If I worship any particular thing it shall be the spread of*
> *   my body;*
> *Translucent mould of me it shall be you,*
> *Shaded ledges and rests, firm masculine coulter, it shall be you,*
> *You my rich blood, your milky stream pale strippings of my life;*
> *Breast that presses against other breasts it shall be you*
> *My brain it shall be your occult convolutions,*
> *Root of washed sweet-flag, timorous pond-snipe, nest of guarded*
> *   duplicate eggs, it shall be you,*

A storm came upon the tent. It swayed, precarious, then snapped back to upright.

Mixed tussled hay of head and beard and brawn it shall be you,
Tickling sap of maple, fibre of manly wheat, it shall be you;
Sun so generous it shall be you,
Vapors lightning and shading my face it shall be you,
You sweaty brooks and dews it shall be you,
Winds whose soft-tickling genitals rub against me it shall be you,
Broad muscular fields, branches of liveoak, loving lounger in my
*   winding paths, it shall be you,*
Hands I have taken, face I have kissed, mortal I have ever touched, it
*   shall be you.*

Walt paused to pant. Embers in his eyes, he slapped his hands together and looked straight to the sky. "Devine Calliope," he shouted. "I welcome you."

June untangled the garment tied around her middle and tossed it on the rock. "She revels in us!"

The day's trepidations flew from Ezra. He closed his eyes and ascended into the overhanging trees. The leaves brushed his face. He and John were in the presence of all nine Muses. Plump-bottomed, curly-haired Calliope floated frontward. Ezra exalted her and told her his gratitude would be eternal, that no matter who else shaped his fate, it would be her and her immortal band in these very trees he would recall in his last breaths.

"I will remove the veil," June declared, and whipped off Walt's towel and flung it in the creek.

Walt began rocking and poeticizing on the fly, sprinkling in a few lines of his earlier verse.

I rush through Keats dark passages and beyond.
My vision is restored; I see beyond far-ago flights to new vistas.
The Muses cleanse me; they stand by in wonder, where will this
*   relit misfit fly next?*
Calliope dares me; Look up to the divinities with me,
My earthbound friends, for I will show her.

No worshiping she dare expect from his one…it is the twirl of my tongue
  she desires.
To hear through me all true voices…to extract from me the threads of the stars
  and of wombs, and of the fatherstuff.
She and her band dare me to prove the truth of my visions.
Their eyes reach forever, and wait there, like mine."

His rhythmic preaching danced though Ezra like a shaman's chants.

I take up her dare! Not under the weight of oath …but to quench the endless
thirst of my visions, past and yet to come, intermingling anew.
Witness she will! With divine eyes and ears, coming forth from me
those sacred threads of my deepest being.
With which she and her Muses can drape the universes,
  and all wombs and fissures.

My god, Ezra muttered to himself, he really does believe his juice is divine.

The what's-next wonder in June's eyes grew superabundant and launched her into her own spur-of-the-moment free-versing, jerry-rigged, like Walt's, around some of his original *Leaves* lines.

You stir the divinities; you gather in yourself their audacious dare.
You distill it, undisguised and naked, by the bank by the wood.
They are wild to witness your proud, potent enactment.

You are in love with it, the distillation, how it enlivens Calliope to
Urge and urge and urge you.
To let seep through the procreant urge of the world.

You hurdle me into your visions with the promise
  of the fruits of your distillation.

She astonished Ezra, the way she double-spiced her poetry-on-the-fly with Walt's lines and her own blatant desire. She squirmed against Walt's legs and inched her chin up his thigh. Unperturbed, his hands behind his head, his eyes cast gently into the distance, he resumed his spontaneous versifying.

The absolute beauty of all bodies is perceived again by this cleansed soul,
Intertwined always with this preposterous body, refilling, stronger, always
*   replenishing, never not to be replenished.*

All bodies, this body, and yours, woman, and yours, man, all glorious
*   in their particular beauty,*
Eminent and almighty gorgeous, as is every glory of all earths and universes.

I over fill! I become the surplus
*   of these woods and this creek…of all places, and all desires.*
Visions and threads amass in me.

I am pristine and pure light and fire and stone,
As are you, man, and as are you, woman,
*   like all nature itself, part of the miracle.*
Of that I am sure.

June seemed to be blooming in ecstasy and let go a satisfied sigh that warmed Ezra's heart.

Walter picked up his pace, plucking verse from *Leaves.*

Sure as the most certain sure…plumb in the uprights, well entretied,
*   braced in the beams,*
Stout as a horse, affectionate, haughty, electrical
I and this mystery here we stand.
Clear and sweet is my soul…and clear and sweet is all
*   that is not my soul.*

June jumped up and erupted in playful laughter to go eye to eye with Walt, but he looked right through her and poured forth.

Welcome is every organ and attribute of me, and of any man hearty
*   and clean,*
Nor an inch nor a particle of an inch is vile, and none shall be less
*   familiar than the rest.*

She threw her head back and highjacked his verse:

*The atmosphere is not a perfume, it has no tastes of the
    distillation, it is odorless,
It is for my mouth forever, I am in love with it,
I will go to the bank by the wood and become undisguised
    and naked,
I am made for it to be in contact with me.*

Walt broke back in with a bellow:

*The smoke of my own breath,
Echoes, ripples, buzz'd whispers, love-root, silk-thread,
crotch and vine*

"Walt!" June shouted.

"What?"

"The Muses dispatch me. To go with you to the headland."

Now he looked her in the eye.

"Calliope cares not with whom or how I come forth."

"Oh yes I do," June declared in a gravelly voice, rare but not unknown to Ezra.

She kneeled athwart Walt and engulfed him. He growled like a bear.

"Quiet, Walt! For god's sake!" Ezra said.

Walt's hands shot up as if being robbed at gun point. "I must know that no one will ever know of this day."

So full of himself, Ezra thought, he can't abide anyone knowing how the spirits and us rescued his sad ass.

"We'll put your worries to rest," June said.

"How?"

"Tell me first, the parts of a woman you describe in *Leaves of Grass*, have you ever touched them, or only imagined?"

She took his left hand and placed his forefinger and thumb. He moaned. She raised herself and pushed against the tip of him and held him there.

"You will write a sacred vow. The three of us will swear to never betray our secrets, from this day, or any day."

"Good," he mumbled.

"I have a fresh diary you'll use," she said. "You will memorialize your resurrection.

"Good," he said.

"You'll sign it and date it and we'll hide away forever, won't we Ezra?"

"Yep," said Ezra. "Hurry up."

"Can we show Walt where we'll keep it?"

"Yes," he said, and scanned the hillsides and pleaded for good luck.

Walt tossed his head side to side and slung mouthy rumbles, then threw his head back: "Witness us, Calliope and all divinities! I have sworn to never doubt you again. Now witness how I fulfill your divine dare, and you will never doubt me again!"

He chanted his canticle to June's rocking rhythm.

Built of the common stock, having room for far and near,
Used to dispense with other lands, incarnating this land,
Attracting it body and soul to himself, hanging on its neck with
*   incomparable love,*
Plunging his seminal muscle into its merits and demerits.

June quieted him with a kiss and took over.

This is the touch of my lips to yours...this is the murmur of
*   yearning,*
This is the far-off depth and height reflecting my own face,
This is the thoughtful merge of myself and the outlet again.

Ezra stood on the high corner of bed rock. He turned his back and scanned the northern flank.

He wanted to think he'd done right. That on this occasion—which after all the improvising and trials and tribulations had turned out to be the nearest thing to a miracle he'd ever witnessed—it would have been unwise, hypocritical, to deny, or try to deny, June, to pretend he had say over her, like his masters once had say over him.

What settled his mind and soothed his jealously was the

knowledge that John, too, saw what he saw, and had come to the same conclusion. Yes, Walter had proven himself a pure poet, one of only two adored by June. But no, he would never be a man to steal June's heart, not from John, in the immortal realm, or from Ezra, here, in this world.

John agreed with him, too, that if today kept panning out, if no one came strolling down the hillsides, if Walter's resurrection held, if his new poet came to fruition and made Walter immortal, June would love Ezra, not just this day, but until his dying day, long after he'd run out of surprises.

He turned back and surveyed the southerly vista. He considered all the ruckus they'd made, the long moments he'd paid no attention, how lucky they'd been so far. In tribute, he promised that if they made it through this final act, made it back to the cabin without being caught, not only would there never be a June-Walter encore, there would never again be any such risky celebration at the creek.

He couldn't help but grin at how a man, on this very day reluctant to be touched at all, was now enthralled, and decided it would be better to witness June's joint triumph with the Muses rather than turn his back on her.

June swayed and Walt's voice built its boisterousness.

To think how much pleasure there is!
Have you pleasure from looking at the sky? Have you pleasure
*   from poems?*

The sky continues beautiful…the pleasure of men with women
*   shall never be sated . . nor the pleasure of women with men . .*
*   nor the pleasure from poems…*

"Walt!" Ezra said. "Keep it down!"
June quieted Walt with her right breast and spoke his lines for him.

Mine is no callous shell
I have instant conductors all over me whether I pass or stop,
They seize every object and lead it harmlessly through me.

She kept him happily mum and continued:

My lovers suffocate me!
Crowding my lips, and thick in the pores of my skin,
Jostling me through streets and public halls...coming naked to me
at night

Walt pulled his head back and chanted:

Push close my lovers and take the best I posess,
Yield closer and closer and give me the best you possess.

This is unfinished business with me...how is it with you?
I was chilled with the cold types and the cylinder and the wet paper between us.

I pass so poorly with paper and types...I must pass with the
*   contact of bodies and souls.*

I do not thank you for liking me as I am, and liking the touch of me
*   ...I know that is good for you to do so.*

He gulped air and shouted to the sky:

On all sides prurient provokers stiffening my limbs,
Straining the udder of my heart for its withheld drop
Behaving licentious toward me, taking no denial

The sentries desert every other part of me,
They have left me helpless to a red marauder,
They all come to the headland to witness and assist against me.

Quick Walt was not to be, Ezra lamented. The sun had sunk
behind the tall trees on the western hilltop. He envisioned their
homey cabin. The moon was up and rising in the east. He fretted that June was turning duty-driven, like him, and pined for the
simple pleasure of returning home. Less vulnerable in the dusk, he

wrapped his arms around his knees and let his head loll forward. His heavy eyes excluded Walt. He saw only beautiful June as he heard Walt's chanting:

Long I was hugged close...long and long.

Immense have been the preparations for me,
Faithful and friendly the arms that have helped me.

Sleepy vapors of thankfulness for how John had settled his mind overtook Ezra. Dream seeds closed his eyes and gathered into hazy strands—a moon-drenched, fairy-tale vision of his proud shack. He knocked on the door. His modest paradise floated up into invisible mist. Words formed up in the air above him, appearing not letter by letter but whole lines at a time, slightly too small to read from the ground.

He could not fly but he could bound. On his first try he floated, not entirely weightless, for if he went perfectly still, he was happy to learn, he headed gently back toward ground.

The second time, by fluttering his arms, he floated even with the stacking-up lines, pleased there was no breeze to disturb them. He read the nearest lines, which he spoke out unaware, for Ezra, when at ease, had taken to the habit of speaking out loud to himself.

Those lips, O slippery blisses, twinkling eyes,
And by these tenderest, milky sovereignties—
And by the nectar wine,
The passion—

June stopped and savored the early Keats verse that Ezra wove through Walt's *Leaves.*

But what is this to love? Oh I could fly
With thee into the ken of heavenly powers,
So that wouldst thus, for many sequent hours,
Press me so sweetly.

June moved quickly and decisively.
Walt superimposed his verse:

Be not ashamed woman . . your privilege encloses the rest . . it is the
exit of the rest,
You are the gates of the body you are the gates of the soul.

June heard only Ezra and John.

Why linger you so, the wild labyrinth strolling,
Why breathless, unable your bliss to declare?
Ah! You list to the nightingale's tender condoling,
Responsive to sylphs, in the moon-beamy air.

'Tis morn, and the flowers with dew are yet drooping,
I see you are trading on the verge of the sea;
And now! ah, I see it—you just now are stooping
To pick up the keepsake intended for me.

June stretched mightily and finally sighed and went still. "Ezra!"
she cried. "Ezra!"

He bolted to his feet and ran to her. She clutched his arm and
leaned her shoulder against him. "Calliope praises you and John
and I, for she is satisfied."

In the corner of her left eye, three tears, each in turn, formed,
hesitated, then glided down her scarlet red cheek. Ezra raised his
right forefinger, June still clutching his arm, and dabbed and gathered each one, and put his fingertip between his lips. She smiled at
him, raised her eyebrows and turned back to Walt, who warbled on
in his own world.

The bodies of men and woman engirth me,
and I engirth them,
They will not let me off nor I them till I go with them and respond
To them and love them.

"All evil in this man's soul, hear me!" June proclaimed in a voice that Ezra identified as an incensed Greek priestess. "You cannot abide the gathering by the sacred Muses of the very sap of this pure poet. For Calliope and her sisters and my own soul, in her service, and the souls of Ezra and John, also in her service, now celebrate the resurrection of Walt Whitman, which you cannot abide. Depart. Be gone!"

"They vanish into the ether," Ezra declared. "They are gone, long gone."

"Gather and surge, Walt," June commanded. "Awe the Muses! Ascend to the immortal Rock Creek Canon! Who need be afraid of the merge?"

"The ocean—I am in the ocean. It is full of life. It engulfs me," Walt thundered.

You must habit yourself to the dazzle of the light and of every
  moment of your life.
    I tramp a perpetual journey,

Undulating into the willing and yielding day,
    Lost in the cleave of the clasping and sweet-flesh'd day.

"Walt!" Ezra said. "Now or never, friend."
"Hear me Calliope!" Walt cried and versified on the fly.

I call home all the ineffable, disparate bits of my soul
from all the universes.
They scatter and rejoin through me like leaves in a gusty wind,
blown across gentle slopes of open grass.
They join ranks to savor this inevitable ascension
to the homecoming, the one we three incite.
They gather, to be welcomed, to be glorified by Calliope.
Who stirs them and kneads them with her divine hands.

"She better send 'em on out, right now," Ezra said.
Walt wailed a high-pitched coyote cry and then growled:

You villain touch! what are you doing?... my breath is tight in

its throat;
Unclench your floodgates! you are too much for me.

Ebb stung by the flow, and flow stung by the ebb…loveflesh
  swelling and deliciously aching,
Limitless limpid jets of love hot and enormous…quivering jelly
  of love…white-blow and delicious juice

Something I cannot see put upward libidinous prongs!

June leaped up so the Muses could witness. Walt threw up his arms and shouted, *Seas of bright juice suffuse heaven*! then quivered all over and curled into a ball. June hugged Ezra. They sprawled on the still warm rock. He could finally hear the creek again. Marveling at its overture, so relieved that the three of them were finally at peace, he checked his sleepy descent and got to his feet.

"Time to go. Up and at 'em, Walt," he said.

Walt un-balled himself and got halfway sitting. "Call me Walter. Like my lovers and family. Lay me in the creek, so I can wash."

They slid him off his throne and set him in the creek. Minnows converged and tickled his hanging parts and turned him into squirming, hapless giggles.

"It's the hairs they like," Ezra said.

"And the drippings of your long-stewing juice," June said.

"I hope I can reach the stars when I'm white-bearded, mister shooting-to-the-heavens poet," Ezra said. "Let's go."

"Let the fishes feast," June giggled, fascinated by the unruly schools taking turns tasting Walter.

"They'll spread those seeds far and wide," Ezra declared. "Down the creek, to the Potomac, to the deep blue seas, where they'll be sun-baked and vaporized and spread across all the universes."

He lifted still-dazed Walter to his feet. "Come on, old Rock Creek poet, come wading in the water."

Ezra led him by the hand. They sat down and put on their sandals. Walter stood first.

There was never any more inception that there is now. And will never be anymore perfection than there is now.

"My strength regained, I climb this hill, my friends once again at my side."

22

LOUISE REEMERGED FROM HER lair beaming, redeemed by how well she'd spun the opening act of the story she'd waited too long to tell.

I roused myself, taken away for I know not how long by storytelling more powerful than the finest, most engrossing dreams. Cowboy stood and beamed back at her. She launched herself from the jittery shadows and embraced him. "I know my story troubles you," she said. "But I've given a true recounting."

"Congratulations," he declared, holding her tight. "Your tell is superb, despite the parts I differ with."

I smiled too, both at the pure joy in her face and at the thought of how her account, which I did not believe at the time, would send Whitman fans and scholars spinning topsy-turvy.

"Who told you?" I said.

She swigged Irish whiskey straight from the bottle, chased it with thermos coffee and wiped her mouth on her royal sleeve.

"Aunt Alberta. Aunty was born and raised in the big house—the one you can see from the playhouse—and moved back there when I was still young. We were very close. She never married. I was like a daughter to her. After I graduated Vassar, I came back to DC to pursue my dream, to become a poet. Got my own apartment. Lived the wild life. Then came my downfall.

"I hadn't seen Aunty for months when I showed up, unannounced. She opened the door and I broke down and wept, so wasted from burning the candle at both ends that I'd lost all hope. Her first words were, 'Child, the time has come.' She never asked what had happened to me. She parked me on the living room couch and made us tea and read me 'Renascence,' Vincent's first great poem. The story of her soul escaping the grave to be reborn. Then she gave me the oath, and assured me that, like her, I would know when the time came to use my single tell. I thought she'd gone batty.

"She begun to blush before she even started, when she told me how proud June made her, what 'a force of nature' she was. Aunty called her 'fearless June,' and teared up and said she'd always done her best to live as fearlessly as June, whose only fear was being forced to leave the park.

"She began her tell, and then told me she must take me there, and dragged me up Pulpit Rock trial, past Boulder Bridge, holding my hand the whole time. I swear her voice grew younger as she led me down the steep hill to the creek. She was in her seventies, but she threw off her shoes and socks and took me by the hand out to the rock and sat me in the throne. 'You sit where June and Walt frolicked naked in poetic intimacies,' she said, the biggest grin I ever saw on her face, then told me what happened there, moment by moment, just as I told you.

"I can still see her when she finished, standing in front of the throne, right where June stood. She took my hands. 'June saved Walt Whitman's very soul,' she said. 'Yanked it from the clutches of perpetual, death-drenched wakefulness, of death without death, of the death pale knight.'

"Then she recited Keats—the death pale knight poem. She said

Keats and that image, in the hands of June and Ezra, made Walt Whitman realize he must escape that tragic fate."

Louise took my hands in hers. "Keats was there," she said. "He pulled Ezra and June back from the abyss. So important to the story, our dear immortal John, to whom you've dedicated your career, whose poetic wonders you've spread among all those lucky souls you've taught."

I squeezed her hands in thanks, her words the most charitable view of my career I could ever imagine.

"The last thing Aunty told before we left the creek was that among all the wondrous things the secret would do for me, one would be most lasting. My imagination, from that day on, would be as powerful as June's. 'That's what it did for me,' Aunty said, 'My imagination roams free as a lark, and will do so until the day I die. So will yours.'"

"Hearing that, the immense joy Aunty took in saying those words, the thrill she took in telling the story—which I naively assumed to be a wonderful family fable—made me hug her and cry in sheer gratitude."

"Who was it you wanted to pass the story to?" I said.

"I met a young woman who loved the park as much as me, who had her own secret places, like I do," Louise said. "Esther was an artist, a sculptress. Her boyfriend was the founder of what became the Zoo Crew."

"Eli the Elder," Cowboy said.

"I first ran into them sharing a joint on the hill overlooking Park Road."

"Where we saw the crying woman," Cowboy said.

"We began chatting about the park. I could tell she loved it as much as I did, so I invited them back to the playhouse, and we drank wine and told tales of the wonders of the park.

"As they were leaving, Esther ran back up the steps and whispered in my ear. Did I want to see her most secret place? Would I meet her there that night?

"There's a vault like a cavern inside the base of the Park Street Bridge. She'd claimed it—put her own paddle lock on the big metal door. Her secret bower. A little oriental rug on the dirt floor and a couple of crates to sit on. She'd sneak off there by herself to get away from Eli and the Zoo Crew craziness.

"I brought Vincent poetry that night. Esther loved to draw by candlelight. She sketched ideas for a sculpture to show me. I told her Vincent's life story and read her verse. We put ourselves very much at ease with each other.

"She began to spend afternoons with me at the playhouse. It was her second oasis. She realized that the wild living and partying was turning from fun into madness and was trying to break clear of it. One afternoon, I convinced her to stay for dinner. I'd gotten drawing supplies and clay for her, and after we ate, she made an elaborate model of a sculpture while I practiced my reciting of Keats and Whitman. She loved their poetry. She fell asleep on the coach and spent the night. We'd become dear friends.

"I knew by then I wouldn't have children, that she'd be my perfect choice to inherit the story. She would be thrilled by it, like I was, and it would help her, like it helped me.

"She and Eli always were always on the verge of going their separate ways. I fretted that if I told her, the thrill of sharing the secrets would be too tempting, that she would tell him right away. She could be impulsive. Then they'd break up, and I feared she'd regret squandering her single tell for the rest of her life.

"One day we were at our favorite, very secluded spot. A strong urge came over me to tell her the story. But I reminded myself there was no rush, it would be better to wait. I missed my chance."

The sadness in her eyes forbid me to ask what happened.

She smiled. "But it all turned out fine, didn't it? Because now I get to tell you the story. Ready to hear more?"

I nodded.

Cowboy grabbed a spiral notebook from next to a bottle of gin on the shelf and tossed it to me, followed by a pen. "Better start taking notes so you can get the tell written quicker," he grinned.

Louise chased one more shot of Irish with coffee and hoisted herself back up on her shelf.

"Part two," she said. "Then Cowboy gets his turn."

23

THE THREE SPENT CELEBRANTS safety in the cabin, Ezra barred the door and the window and curled up on the floor in the corner. Walter insisted they could all fit in the bed. Ezra doubted that but dragged the mattress onto the floor. They stripped near naked in the breezeless heat and Walt sprawled in the middle and June and Ezra straddled the edges and they all slept like tuckered-out babies.

Walter rose first and sat out on the stoop, writing. Ezra sat down next to him and pretended to read *Leaves* while keeping watch. Louise brought them a plate and they ravaged cured squirrel and fish. Ezra led the way to the hidden place, through the woods south along the top of the ridge.

"The female divine, I called her dare, didn't I?" Walt gloated. "And she loves me for that. That's why she opened me up and cleansed me. He chanted as they walked:

"She is the…
Santa Spirita, breather, life,
Beyond the light, lighter than light,
Beyond the flames of hell, joyous, leaping easily above hell,
Beyond paradise, perfumed solely with mine own perfume,
Including all life on earth, touching, including God,
   Including Savoir and Satan,

"Sounds like you two hit it off," Ezra said.

"You better write that down before you forget it," June said.

"No need," Walter said. "The female divine now speaks directly to me. She tells me at this very moment to further unburden myself."

"Go right ahead then," Ezra said.

"The suffering and dying in the hospitals are an unfathomable, dreadful, monumental tragedy. Hard to believe I once found hope in that. I believed the mass butchering our own inflicted on each other to be so unimaginable, so utterly shocking, that in this modern age it would make the insanity of war undeniable to all. Some good, therefore, would come of it, for civilization would never again abide it.

"When I could no longer bear to sit only with the worst cases, the ones facing death, I took fellowship with others not as bad off, finding solace in conversation and refreshment, sometimes slipping away to a room away from the near dead and the slowly dying. Last month, when the casualties from the awful battle at the Wilderness flooded the hospitals, I took solace almost nightly with the regular group of men who gathered there and began to talk more freely in my presence.

"Two days ago, after supper, their tongues much loosened by the very drink I snuck past the nurses for them, some revealed their true selves.

"There is a youngish, blond-haired man from western Pennsylvania. His arm was shattered by shrapnel at Wilderness in early May and amputated after gangrene set in. I was drawn to him by his natural shyness, and became quite fond of him, of his exuberance, the direct, honest style of speaking he displayed.

"The night before last, after several others spoke of how they missed being in battle, the exuberance that drew me to him came into full view. He perked up and spoke excitedly of the rampage of killing he'd gone on at Wilderness. Of the thrill of butchering and slicing through man after man with his bayonet, many of them already wounded and lying begging at his feet. He smiled with the purest delight at his favorite memory—the anguished man he impaled and left squirming in death at sunset—his last act, the last day of his last battle.

"I had been suffering the melancholy for months. But the way that man savored the gleeful savagery washed over me in pure horror. It drowned the only thing that still fortified me—the gallant bravery of the dying men I tended. Evil mocked my dream, that ordinary people like him would find inspiration in *Leaves of Grass*. Instead, they find their grandest moments in bloodthirsty killing. The only thing that saddens that one-armed man is how dearly he misses the killing.

"When I stopped yesterday morning at Campbell Hospital, and then at nearby Harewood, I could not enter. I emptied my satchel and left my last gifts at the door. For months, I have persevered through deepening melancholy to give comfort. But I can no longer. For I can not bear, even for one minute, to sit again with one dying or suffering soldier for the fear that they, too, miss the savagery, that I will discover that more of my beloved boys and men crave the killing.

"That's why I wrote my dear mother to tell her I'm coming home. That's why I abandoned the men who so eagerly await my visits and instead walked into these woods."

They reached the pinnacle of the ridge. Ezra signaled Walt to go quiet and helped him down the rocky slope. June crawled in first. Ezra prevailed on Walter to follow him into the dark crevice. Ezra dropped into the cave, then helped down Walter, who grinned like a surprised child at the size and coolness of their candle-lit hideaway. He sprawled out on the blankets June had spread on the floor and turned on his side, his chin in one hand, propped up on his elbow.

"You were naive," Ezra said. "All that poor, one-armed man did was open your eyes. War and killing are evil. There is evil aplenty in this world—in all of us. Some of your beloved men came to savor killing. Judge them not. They give themselves, in the name of duty, to the unholy nature in all of us."

"You're right, Ezra. It is cowardly of me to abhor them. For I could not do what we call on them to do. Yet that does not dilute the evil. Nor does it excuse my deserting the men who lay dying and waiting for me, wondering why I come no more."

"You've served long and gallantly," June said.

"In my tally, I've made four or five hundred hospital visits, in New York and here, and gone among fifty thousand of the sick and wounded."

"No wonder you're so wore out," Ezra said. "You need a break. A long one. Let your soul return to its true calling."

"You're not turning your back on the war," June said. "Your new poet will bear down upon it."

"Not the war the politicians and newspapers tell of," Walter said. "I will not glorify it. It will be a little book, containing night's darkness, and blood-dripping wounds, and psalms of the dead."

"And of bravery and sacrifice," June said. "These men and boys you've comforted and loved, the living and the dead, poems that tell us, as only you can, of the ordinary men, Union and Rebel."

"But not those like one-armed," Ezra said.

"No," Walter said. "The evil in those poor, lost souls will never live through my book, which I believe I shall call *Drum-Taps*."

"Brave, somber poems by a wholesome, grandfatherly poet, with an even longer white beard, who will put to rest any notion that the audacious creator of *Leaves* is a frivolous, scandalous poet," June said. "Perhaps we'll call him the Noble Gray Poet."

"The Good Gray Poet would be better," Walter said.

"That does sound better," she said.

"So all you got to do now is turn yourself into that Mister Good Gray Poet," Ezra smiled.

"I need not transform myself. That is who I am."

"That, plus all your wildness and private desires."

"You mean our secrets."

"Yes," June said. "But until the Good Gray Poet is widely known, you will not add to *Leaves* any more celebrations of bodies and sex. Nor flaunt your affection and lust for men, or women."

Walter stood and glared down at her.

"My *Leaves* will remain my life's work. I will keep adding to it, refining it, regardless of how it's received. I must, for the taste for myself to grow."

June rose and glared right back at him. "You will be discrete. In your poetry and your carryings-on. Only those who can be trusted to keep secrets like us can know. If need be, you can return here."

Walter glanced at Ezra. "You need make no promises, my dear."

Ezra stood. "Your spirit will be here, even when you're not."

"I'll get one of your devout followers to hail the arrival of the Good Gray Poet," June said.

"Unnecessary advice, my dear woman. I was already thinking of that."

"I know the perfect one to do it," she said, and held out a cloth-covered journal. "Now, as you promised, leave us some immoral words."

Walter pulled a small notebook from his pocket.

"Our joint vow is here," he said. "As is another secret. One I found new hope by recounting this morning, knowing it will never be read, except by you two. I shall leave now and resume my journey home to New York."

With a boost from Ezra, he scrambled into the tunnel. Outside, June insisted on a long hug; Walter insisted on the same with Ezra. Without another word, Walter walked away. "Good luck," Ezra shouted. Walter did not glance back but did throw up his arm in farewell.

June embraced Ezra. "You're much more of a miracle than he is," she said. "What magic we make. You're so indulgent of me. And so receptive of him and his reluctant ways."

"More than you know," Ezra laughed. "He was being adhesive all night, right up against the back of me. I woke up and he had his arm over me. And Lordy be, not long before sunrise, if I didn't come half awake feeling him stiff against me."

"So the cure stuck!"

"I whispered to him that if he was all pent up again, he could relieve himself, not to mind me. I'm used to that—boys used to have to do it chained together in our sleeping quarters. Walter said no, that was a private indulgence. So I told him, maybe you can wake up June with that."

"You didn't!"

"You're right. I did not. I hope to never know if you are ever again intimate with another."

"You needn't worry. That was the very aroused Calliope, not me." She squeezed his hand. "And I will always believe it was for a worthy cause."

"I will always believe that, too," Ezra said, and returned her squeeze.

June would not tell Ezra until their waning days that the worthy cause was not the one he'd always assumed it was. Sure, serving the Muses by saving Walter was a worthwhile pleasure, but she'd proved something even more dear to her: Her power of imagination, fired by her closeness to the Muses, was every bit as potent as Walter's, and her flights of fancy, her instantaneous verse, every bit as sublime and inspired as his.

"You had me so worried, that terrible trance you went into" he said.

"A nightmare took me," she said. "I walked into the crowd at a big party at home, happy to be there, happy for the fresh glass of champagne I found myself carrying as I approached my mother and father and their closest friends. They looked at me with pity and alarm and everyone went silent. It was clear they all thought me mad.

"I'm not mad, I laughed, certain they'd believe me. My father smiled. 'Of course you're not. You're touched!' Everyone roared in laughter. Their fun gave way to pity when they saw me fight back tears. 'You don't need to cry,' father told me. 'Just laugh along with us, sweetie.' He threw his arm in the air and the laughter roared again. I began to shiver and tried to scream, but I couldn't. Did I scream at the creek?"

"You were dead quiet. But you looked so terribly vacant."

"Above the uproar of laughter in the dream, I heard Keats speak of minnows. He knew I wasn't mad. My shivering terror turned to happy goose bumps."

Ezra held her by the shoulders and took a step back to admire her. "Now tell me true," he grinned. "You'd never discovered your mad filaments until that first time you read *Leaves?*"

"Only a slight embellishment," she said. "It was your cure that set the stage for me. Your frank talk made him see he was cowering to his melancholy. You know how potent you were?"

"All I know is that the Muses and John were there, at full strength. And I will live happily with that mystery of that."

June took Ezra's hand and led him to their favorite perch near the entrance to Hideaway. They sat and read Walter's letter sanctifying their vow (Exhibit A) and, on separate pages, the promised recounting (Exhibit B):

June 23, 1864

My dearest Ezra and June,
I sit as I write these words in enchanted woods above a wondrous creek.

Thou I continue to suffer ailments the doctors falsely ascribe to hospital fever or hospital fatigue, a strong spark of rejuvenation flows through me this morn. The sun rises in front of me. The day calls me forth with hope that my soul is renewed.

How prophetic I am! Last year I described Washington with these words, as I best recall them, in a letter to Emerson: A new world here I find, a world full of its separate action, play, suggestiveness—surely a medium world, between our well-known one of body and mind, and one somewhere beyond we dream of, of the soul.

My first deed this new day, which I undertake with a purity of purpose appropriate to and inspired by the eternal wonder of these woods and this Rock Creek, is to record our sacred oath. By writing these words, I, Walt Whitman, sanctify our vow: That every word and deed that has occurred in the short time I have diffused myself here with my two new comrades— fine comprehenders of me and my poetry—will remain forever unrevealed. My loving friends whom I leave this with, by reading these words, you also solemnly pledge yourselves to this oath.

The purpose of our secret-keeping is noble and bonds us with all others who with kindness and generosity counter the evil and hopelessness that batter bodies and souls in this bloody war. My melancholy-soaked self rediscovered in these woods and waters the transcendence of body and soul, a flash of blinding internal light that pierced the darkness that had descended upon me.

In gratitude of your dear fellowship, I leave you, my two most dear and receptive confidants, on the pages that follow, a recounting of my most private and exquisite experience, from years ago, one I have never divulged and intend never to be divulged. By reading it you swear that it too falls under the solemn vow above.

Walt Whitman

June 23, 1864

For the eyes only of Ezra and June:

Long ago, before I found my true self in the voice of a poet, I was too prideful and disdainful of others, and I suffered periods of extreme loneliness and unhappiness. One Saturday in June, my sadness overwhelmed me. I sought solace in the woods and on the beaches of Long Island, where I spent my happiest times as a boy, in the wilds where the Indians roamed, looking for arrowheads, floating in the water, and observing with wonder the plants and the creatures.

I came upon a trail I recalled led to the shore. As a boy it had taken me to a field on the edge of a pond that one particular day I remembered had overflowed with blooming plants and wildflowers. I followed the trail for some time through the woods. Lo and behold there it was, this living beauty of earth, bigger and fuller of more ripeness and blooms than in my fond memory. I was overcome by a wave of simple gratitude. I fell to my knees, carefully, so as not to harm these budding miracles of nature. I began touching them, caressing and kissing the flowers in my sudden happiness, making my way slowly on my hands and knees, diffusing my gratitude to one species after another. Most amazing to me was calamus, the sweet flag that grew along the edge of the pond. One drew me to it with the sweet, lemony scent and alluring swaying of its proudest part, its fleshy cattail, and welcomed me to uproot it. I lovingly did so, and lay back and examined its plentiful flower head, its skin of minute flowers each stuffed with stamens. I kneaded clean and spotless the dangly root. I squeezed and comforted it, this gnarly, life-giving miracle, so enamored with its liberation that it quivered in my grasp, beseeching me to nimble it, to make every atom belonging to it belong as well to me. We celebrated our sacred communion and joined for eternity our blessed existence.

The sun made me nicely hot. I can remember becoming very still, no muscle desiring to move, an ideal state of full loafing.

The next thing I recall I awoke. I could see and hear so finely I wondered if I was in a dream. In the grassy shadow I lie in, I could see the colors changing on the blades of grass as they moved ever so slightly. I could hear them swaying. Closer to me I looked into the very eyes of an ant I studied in calm amazement, and it, me. My eyes rose to the traveling clouds. I was newly confounded such that I sat up, for the sky beyond the clouds was expanding, waves of deeper and darker blue breaking like waves in the ocean, farther and farther away. The waves of the outwardly undulating sky moved in the same slow rhythm as the tiny streaks of departing clouds. I imagined wings on my feet, for I could see beyond the farthest universe.

For the first time in my life, I became fully aware of my own self, in my entirety, this amazing being, this infinitesimal yet boundless creature living in the same eternity that I watched grow without limit, this very self, myself, adhering in that instant to every other creature and plant and atom in every moment ever.

I lay back, my thirsty eyes wide open, so at ease that it mattered not if I was awake or dreaming. I admired the grass. I came to love it so, to feel it exploring my face, to see one blade so clearly, to smile at its slight shimmerings. I pulled off my shirt and lay sideways, so my proud belly could know each blade. How it tickled me! I turned over on my back, and I could see and hear the sky still spreading out like the outgoing tide. My body felt so powerful and marvelous, I began to touch myself. That's the last I remember until I woke in the dark.

From as early in my life as I can remember I've been blessed with elevated senses, with high sensitivity and receptivity. That afternoon I learned just how elevated, how incited, all my senses could become. I discovered my high susceptivity could be diffused through the entirety of my body and mind and soul, all at once, in the same moment, the present moment, which I found could become any moment anywhere, past or future.

I found to my delight that I had acquired enough of a taste of my true self in those timeless moments of mystical ecstasy that I could recall the feel of it—that altered state of calm rapture. That very day I began to work at drawing it up in myself in the hope that I could nurture it.

I discovered I could. I could incite myself. My enchantment had further heightened my receptivity and made still thirstier the already advanced seeking of my senses—seeing, hearing, touching, even smelling. I could quench that thirst and incite my senses and imagination almost to the heights they reached that afternoon (I don't know that I ever quite reached the pure calm joy of that first time) by being in crowds, by watching and studying one lone stranger, by attending a play or an opera or a speech by a fine orator, by seeing a painting inspired by an eye as thirsty as mine. (One night in the opera, highly incited, I realized I could chant my poetry—it did not have to be rhymed or metrical—those things only stifled the rhythm and the breathing of my chanting voice.)

Finding new experiences and performances and art that woke my thirst and gave me the ecstatic quenching of it became an obsession. As long as I could reach some semblance of that quenching, I was greatly inspired. I filled notebooks and scraps of papers—my big trunk is still full of them— with thoughts and observations and revelations.

I knew the next thing was to bring the voice of my full being to a poem, and to maintain it through a whole book—to be poet who reinvented poetry with one great poem. It took years and years from when I first truly awoke, but I did birth Leaves of Grass. Even the name, as you may now have guessed, comes from that afternoon, from the simple realization of the profound miracle of grass.

I became so practiced at reaching that state, Leaves of Grass came so natural to me during those years, I came to believe my inspiration and the poetry to express it had become second nature to me. I envisioned writing thousands of poems and expanding my book like the sky had expanded in front of me.

When I arrived here yesterday, my spirits were profoundly low. My sadness mounts for our valiant soldiers, both Union and Secession, who suffer and die so bravely. That terrible melancholy had enveloped me in many ways. It has affected my thinking regarding even my most selfish concerns—thus the doubts I voiced for the plans I still harbor for Leaves of Grass.

The woods and creek I found here, and the kindness and truth and love and encouragement you gave so freely to me, take me back to that blade of grass. For like that day I first took flight, my short time here inspires me, and I leave with renewed hope and determination. I am resolved not only to expand my beloved Leaves to the poem it should be, but to honor with poetry, as the Good Gray Poet, the courageous men and boys I have done my best to comfort.

Walter

"I was right!" June grinned. "His epiphany didn't come out of the blue. It was the roots of the sweet flag that gave him visions."

"Sweet flag?" Ezra said.

"Calamus. Once in New York some fellows I met at a bar were getting their courage up to try it. The one boy I kind of liked told me it's an aphrodisiac and gives you hallucinations. I was tempted but I'd had too much to drink and was already too late getting home."

"I'll be," Ezra said. "He did tell us a secret."

"Look at the *Calamus* poems," she said.

He pulled the '60 *Leaves* from his bag and read. "Here it is. He did go back to that pond. Maybe he's going back home to visit it again. Listen to this. He's talking about handing out laurel leaves and lilacs and such, and then he mentions calamus root:

> *But what I drew from the water by the pond-side, that*
> *I reserve*
> *I will give of it—but only to them that love, as*
> *I myself am capable of loving.*

"After we proved our love for him, he gave us—not the root itself—but his secret of it," June said. "Let's put our treasures away, light the candles and cavort away the day."

"Walt Whitman can turn wild at times," Ezra grinned. "But you're the truly wild one."

24

AFTER LOUISE'S TELLING OF the morning-after episode, Cowboy reached into a crevice and tossed her a leather key holder. She ripped the lid off a big plastic bin, unlocked the lock box and pulled out something triple-sealed in freezer baggies.

She wiped her hands down the long sides of her robe and gingerly pulled out a notebook with an aged, black leather cover, which she cradled with both hands in her lap.

"It's too delicate to be passed around. But you can look at it as closely as you want as I read it to you."

"Walt Whitman wrote that, in his own hand?"

"Yes indeed," Cowboy said. "And other than Louise and me, you're the only living person in the whole wide world who has ever laid eyes on it."

The pages were ruled with roomy lines, the cursive large and readable, as few as four words on some lines, six, at most, on others. Exhibit A took the first four or five pages; Exhibit B many more.

Her breathing picked up as she read. She trembled in silence when she finished.

"Incredible," was all my reeling mind could muster. "I need a break." Lickety-split I climbed into the dreaded tunnel and without incident shimmied through.

I tucked myself away underneath the rhododendrons. I could recall only one time I witnessed mother as happy and proud as Louise reading that notebook. Daddy had finally submitted to leaving the homestead and had snagged a janitor job at the General Electric outdoor lighting plant way the other side of town. We'd moved into town, albeit the wrong side, two blocks from the train tracks. That Saturday morning dear Mom dragged me shopping for new school clothes. Her face, as we paraded down Main Street, beamed as bright and proud as Louise's, for she was sure, every bit as certain as Louise about her story and notebook, that her dream had come true. Now that I would attend city schools, I would break the long family tradition and become a resounding success in life, probably a doctor or a lawyer.

That moment of greatest happiness and satisfaction turned out, for mother, to be a moment of make-believe.

Cowboy yanked me from my reverie. He plunked down, lit a little cigar and told me to never mention his smoking.

"You ever wonder," I said, "if some earlier secret-keepers, to embellish the family lore, forged that notebook, wrote what Walt would have written to fit the family tale?"

"Of course," he said. "Go the library, left at the corner before the liquor store. Take William. He likes going there. I went the day after Pops told me the story and showed me the treasures. I figured it wouldn't take any time to debunk it, which would not have disappointed me one bit. Like Louise, I was thrilled that my family had its own elaborate tale of a famous poet way back when.

"Go dig deep, into Whitman and the Civil War. You'll find the kicker for yourself. It all fits perfectly, down to the very dates the entries were written by Walt."

"That doesn't mean they're authentic."

"That's true. Decide for yourself. Like I did. It's much easier now to find images of originals of Walt's handwriting and his actual notebooks. Print a couple out. Bring them to Hideaway. It's his handwriting. The notebook is just like the ones he used.

"Now it's finally my turn. Once I get started, I don't stop. So go take a piss if you need to."

I came late to Whitman. Why is he such a big deal, a student asked me my second semester teaching. That night I read all of *Leaves* straight through, the 1921 edition I snagged from Memaw's bookcase during her wake.

I cribbed Carl Sandberg's introduction to that edition in my report back to the student. *Leaves* stands alone, the most revolutionary and peculiar work of American literature, the most highly praised and the most fervently damned. I foisted a fresh paperback of the original *Leaves* on bespectacled Josh and promised him this: like it or not, it'll perk up your ears and set your head spinning.

I never saw him again. He quit his barista gig to head out on an open-ended road trip. I was subsumed by Whitman for months. Read everything he wrote and everything about him. He did in fact have a breakdown in D.C. and go home to mama.

Still, I was dubious. I doubted the authenticity of exhibits A and B, and figured the story more likely than not make-believe.

But real or fake, authenticated or not, the document could probably fetch a small fortune among Whitman fanatics, particularly if accompanied by a written account of the long-held family secrets that would explain Whitman's impetus for recording it and how Cowboy and Louise ended up with it. My skeptical self, hell bent on keeping my naiveté at bay, told me that Cowboy and Louise were planning to cash out.

25

"EZRA! JUNE! EZRA! JUNE! Are you there?"

Ezra jumped out of bed and unbarred the door. Walter rushed in breathless and sweat-covered. It was early Monday the eleventh of July 1864.

"The Confederates are coming! Right at us. Federals are headed this way, too, finding every man they can to defend the forts. You need to get to the hideaway!"

"The Rebels can't be coming from the north," Ezra said.

"Twelve thousand of them," Walter said. "Jubal Early's army. They came up the Shenandoah Valley and crossed the Potomac at Harper's Ferry. Wallace brought his troops from Baltimore and slowed them at Monocacy, but the Secesh broke through. They camped along Rockville Pike and they're marching on the city, coming down the creek valley. There's fierce fighting to come."

June thrust jugs at Ezra and Walter to be filled at the creek, grabbed the fullest wine sack and stuffed vittles into a bag.

Ezra was the first to spot the skinny, barefoot, long-bearded white man in ragged pants and a wool shirt who lay motionless on the beach of pebbles, his head face down in the shallow water. Ezra splashed across the creek and flipped him over.

"He's alive!" Ezra threw him over his shoulder and pounded his back and he gushed out water. He couldn't stand so Ezra set him against a tree. "Please boy," the man said to Ezra. "I'm begging you. Put me back so I can get my head under that creek water. Or smash my skull flat with one of them big rocks."

"You crazy," Ezra said.

"I'm begging you. Do your rightful duty. Kill a rebel. Don't leave me alive for Early's boys to find. They done know I deserted."

Walter kneeled, pulled out a flask of brandy and poured a swig into the runaway. He swallowed and drooled into his filthy beard. "I've tended to thousands of soldiers, both sides. I've seen many like you, half out of their minds, and in a day or two, they're back to their normal selves." He poured more brandy into the runaway, who stared at him.

"What the hell you doing out here, old man?"

"When I heard that Early's army is invading, I walked up this way to see the preparations. I happened upon this young woman, and later on, ran into this fellow here. They kindly offered to share a safe hiding place. You're coming with us."

"Ain't you a kind old nosy fellow," the runaway said. "I'm begging, since that one is too coward to kill a white man, release me from my suffering. From what I've seen and done. Please old man, have a heart. All I want is to put my head under that cool creek water. I won't struggle. I was halfway done drowning before the big fellow done foiled me."

Walter slapped him. "Call him by his name. Ezra it is. And hear me. I will not allow another man to die needlessly. You are coming with us."

Runaway wept. "Git. Be on your way. Youins with no mercy in your hearts, let me be."

He cratered over to his knees and began crawling toward the

creek. "Hush your crying," Ezra said and slung him over his shoulder.

June and Walter filled the jugs and ran to catch up. A huge canon blast echoed from the north, followed by blasts and more blasts from east and west. Ezra began trotting. June hooked arms with Walter and hurried him along.

"You see how I protected our secret?" Walter panted in her ear.

"You did," she said. "Still, you have us taking him to our…I must tell you what we did."

"What?"

"After you departed, Ezra and I went back to our hideaway and hid the treasure you left us in a most ingenious place."

Walter breathed so heavily she slowed her gait. "Good," he said.

"You have infused our shared secrets with your transcendence, with an immortal saving grace," she said.

Walter collapsed to his knees and drank from his water jug.

"I have thought that very thing myself," he said.

She yanked him to his feet and pulled him along.

"After we hid the diary—the Muses had us dedicate the hideaway as a sanctum to them. The treasure you gave us now serves as a holy relic. We swore to the Muses that only us three secret-keepers would ever enter their secret sanctum."

"You don't want to hide him there?"

"I do," she said. "But he needs more to truly save him. You see how the death melancholy grips him, like it gripped you. The Fates, having witnessed your courageous return to rescue us, now offer us the chance to use our sacred secrets to save him."

"Tell our secrets to this stranger?"

She gripped his hand. "If you share our story with him—use the power you and the Muses have given it—you can rescue his soul. We'll add to our oath, to grant you and Ezra and I the right to share our story once each—to save one fortunate soul of our choosing."

Walter halted her and took her by the shoulders. "I will save him! But first we must make sure he comprehends us, that we can trust him. He must swear to the new oath. Promise to pass the story down to only one lucky soul, like him."

"And you will be the first teller of our story," she said. "The first to use it to restore a lost soul."

"Stop your yapping and come on!" Ezra yelled. He laid the runaway out near the entrance. June roused him to his feet with water and light kisses. "We'll give you food and drink and hide you well," she said. "But not before you swear that you'll never reveal this sacred place."

"I have not the foggiest who you all are, or where I am, ma'am, but I do promise. For since I am not dead, I would be grateful not to be captured, and for a bit to eat, and then to sleep."

Runaway crawled in behind Ezra, followed by June and Walt. Ezra lit candles. Runaway was taken by the sureness and comforts of the hideaway. June and Ezra had been paying regular visits since their dedication and amassing blankets, wine and books.

June got Runaway settled on blankets under her shelf, his back against the cave wall.

"Excuse, us, sir, while we confer," Walter said.

"Gladly, if you sir, will spare me a little more of that brandy."

"Short sips, my friend," Walter said. "We need to make it last. Say, I keep wondering if we might have met. Do I look at all familiar to you?"

"Can't say that you do," Runaway said. "You wasn't in the army, was you? You look too old."

Walter huddled Ezra and June against the other side of the cave. He'd told his mother he was traveling to Vermont to visit friends and relatives, he whispered, and had even made false entries in his diary to that effect, so he would always recall the details of his subterfuge and be able to refute any possible gossip.

"I have abandoned the hospitals. But I can save this poor man. You two will be my witnesses."

He looked at June, who whispered in Ezra's ear. Ezra smiled. "I like your idea," he said to Walter, "so long as we're convinced our secrets are safe with this pathetic fellow. And June and me are more than mere witnesses."

"You know you are," Walter nodded and clasped Ezra's shoulder.

June kneeled over Runaway and fed him bits of meat and fish between gulps of water and sips of brandy.

"My dear, exhausted man," she said, "before you sleep, do you have the strength to tell us of yourself?"

"Confession lightens the soul, don't it? I come from the eastern edge of the Tennessee piedmont, not far from the mountains, where my family has a small farm. No plantation, no slaves, cared not a whit about any of that. I did not volunteer, and I avoided conscription—they got younger men first and as you can see, I ain't no spring chicken. But after the Gettysburg shellacking, some recruiters for Major General Nathan Bedford Forrest, in cahoots with the local hooligans, the home guard, forced me to join Forrest. I suspect some gambling debts I never paid up from my days in Memphis was the reason. Forrest was a big-time slave trader there, and two men, who I believe to this day cheated me in cards, worked for him, two men I left town without paying.

"I didn't have no horse, so I was an infantry man—they needed more of them to go along with the cavalry Forrest had put together. It was mostly Tennessee men. Some of us hated Forrest, but many—a lot of them from western Tennessee—slave country—loved him. They called him the Wizard, and bragged that he was still trading slaves, like they hoped to do again. Their favorite story was how he butchered a slave with an axe after the poor fellow didn't drain a mud puddle Forrest was displeased to walk around.

"The cavalry always got to the battles first, and when we infantry arrived, I hung back as much as I could without being branded a coward. Desertion was always on my mind, but Forrest was known for enjoying rounding up and executing deserters, so my hope was to stick it out without killing or being killed.

"Then come Fort Pillow, way over the other side of Tennessee, up on a bluff overlooking the Mississippi.

"One of the men from those parts, a decent fellow, told me there was lots of bad blood, even among the whites. Tennessee was last to leave the Union, and the first brought back under Union control, so them that wanted to keep their slaves, or just hated colored, came as well to hate the whites who stuck with the Union and took over the fort. Called them Tennessee Tories.

"After the Union troops made the fort their stronghold, local slaves run away and joined the Union army, so Pillow was defended by coloreds as well as regular Union. The Union commander promised coloreds protection, so scads of runaway slaves worked at the fort and lived there with their families.

"That fort was their one and only haven. The locals who used to own them was intent on hunting them down, and when they could catch them outside the fort, they would lynch them. When we got within about six miles of the fort, a lot of them slave owners, soldiers in the local Rebel army and the home guard—joined up with us. I got to feeling very uneasy when the regulars started whooping it up and drinking with them locals, talking about killing the coloreds they'd been itching for so long to get their hands on.

"That night, the idea of sneaking off crossed my mind. I should have tried. I might have got away. But I was too fearful of what that damned Forrest would do to me if I got caught and brought back to face him. I'd been witness to that, captured deserters, some of them young boys begging him and balling their eyes out as he made them dig their own graves before he shot them point blank between the eyes, one after another.

"I'd done some bad in my life, like most men, I reckon. I did buy and sell two slaves one time in Memphis—that was the money I gambled away. But I went back home and worked the farm, and we was poor, but content.

"If I'd found the courage to run away that night, my life might still be worth living. Fort Pillow was well defended, and I was relieved that next day when it appeared to be a standoff. But old Forrest, so full of himself, wouldn't settle for no stand-off. He kept riding around, ordering the poor men hunkered down by Union fire to advance closer and closer. He got two horses killed out from under him. I still wonder why one of them Union sharpshooters didn't shoot him instead of them horses. I believe that would have ended it right there, for it appeared to his troops that Fort Pillow could not be taken. I believe it was the devil himself who kept Forest from getting shot.

"Sure enough though, with Forrest whipping up his troops around all sides of the fort, by late afternoon them men was so close up under that high bluff that the Union soldiers couldn't shoot down on them no more. There was a Union gunboat, too, but Forrest had positioned his men so the boats' guns couldn't shoot on them neither, and our sharpshooters had the boat moving away to get out of their range. The front lines stormed the parapets. I was able to hang back until the rest of us was ordered to enter the already breached fort. Word had already spread that the Union commander and his solders had thrown down their arms and surrendered when the fort got overrun. So I foolishly hoped, when I finally entered the fortifications, that we'd just be rounding up prisoners.

"I could hear it before I saw it. Some of our men keep yelling, 'No quarter! No quarter!" I heard pleadings and then ferocious screams. I can't forget the screams—I never imagined man could make such distressing cries. But I understood when I saw through the doorway into one the cabins the Union had been using as their hospital.

"The pitiful begging and the woeful screams coming from the wounded and sick colored solders wasn't enough to drown out the hellish laughter of the Rebels as they held those men down and nailed their arms and legs to the cabin floors. They doused them with kerosene, and splattered it on the floors and the walls and set it afire, and ran out whooping and hollering and nailed the door shut from the outside just in case any of them poor men ripped their arms and legs off the nails and tried to get out.

"'They done surrendered!' I shouted. 'This is ungodly!' Two of our boys looked at me, eyes ablaze. The grins left their faces, and for a second, I thought they'd help me. But then come the excited screams of their blood-hungry comrades—'We found more niggers! Bring more nails and kerosene!'—and they run off to join them.

"Through the door of the next cabin I saw them drag the wounded colored solders out of their beds as they raised their arms raised and pleaded, 'We done surrendered! We done surrendered!' Two or three our fellows sat on their chests, while others nailed their hands and arms to the thick plank floors with them long, terrible nails. Oh Jesus, how those poor men screamed. Then they doused them—poured that kerosene on their heads and even into their mouths—laughing and hollering as those most suffering men screamed in agony and watched them pour that kerosene on the floors and the walls and set it afire.

"I stood frozen as the flames lickety-split made those tortured folks crackle. Over the screams I heard more clearly that I can believe possible the deep bellowing of words, one at time, like a slow, never-ending drum beat, each word carrying such vengeance as I never knew could be. 'You Rebels are damned to hell for eternity. You will never forget my voice! My...agony...will be over soooooon. But in hell, you will burnnnnnn...forever!'

"Lord have mercy on me, I can still hear him. It gives me the chills. I ran from that voice in panic, for I knew he spoke truth—I would be damned for eternity for what I'd had seen, for doing nothing for them burning men nailed to the floor like Jesus to the cross. I ran from those cabins to the top of the long slope that led down to the river bank.

"Colored men, some in uniform, some not, and their wives and children, were trapped on the river bank. Some screamed and ran in circles. Some stood still with their hands raised over their heads, saying over and over, 'We surrender! We surrender!' Some kneeled and begged for their lives.

"Our boys mocked their begging. One evil boy I can't forget said this to a man and his wife and two little children: 'I bet you all would be grateful to be my slaves now, wouldn't you niggers! Ain't you still happy you ran away?' He laughed and laughed. He started with the children, so their pappy and mammy would have to watch. He shot each one, with the very rifle the colored daddy had handed to him before he threw up his hands in surrender.

"Between killings, Forrest's men jabbered and chuckled about the particulars of the dying, how some, when shot, twitched with eyes wide open, while others closed their eyes and didn't twitch at all."

"Other men, women and children—some of them already wounded and bleeding—when they saw there would be no mercy, they crawled out into the river, and the Rebels taunted them— 'Can't you swim, nigger?'—and then slowly took aim and shot them, again and again, until they went still and sunk, or rolled over dead and floated down river.

"The wounded lay groaning and bleeding on the river bank, some begging for mercy with whatever voice they could still muster. Others lay helplessly quiet, still living. I did get one group of three of our men, who was reloading their rifles, to walk away and leave them be. It probably didn't matter none, since most those who did survive the massacre died in a forced march to Confederate prisons. I couldn't sleep that night. I got one local to share whiskey with me, in hopes that would help. But I couldn't get the sights and the screams and the pleas out of my mind's eye, much less the words declaring my eternal damnation. Forrest got us out of there the next day before the locals or anyone else showed up to find them charred bodies nailed to the floor, and all them other bodies, some wounded but not yet dead, carelessly buried in the trenches, arms and legs left sticking out. I considered myself lucky—I see now I was born a fool—for instead of being sent to guard the prisoners on their death march, I was among those of us dispatched back east.

"That was April 13. Forrest was a clever, conniving man. I look forward to meeting him in hell, where I will piss on him as we both burn for eternity. He knew from his more loyal men that some of us from east Tennessee didn't have slaves or hate coloreds and was shocked by what we'd seen. I believe he figured there was a chance we'd cause trouble if we ever got asked about it. So on his wont he reassigned us, ordered two of his trusted officers to take us east to join the troops in Virginia. He threatened us before we left, told us if we dared to desert, he could guarantee he would find us sooner or later, didn't matter if the war ended, and watch us dig our own graves.

"We was delivered to central Virginia in time to be thrown in the Battle of the Wilderness. It was a much bigger battle than Fort Pillow—butchering on a much grander scale."

Runaway finished off the brandy. June fetched a fresh jug of water and a cloth. She lifted his feet into her lap and began washing them. Ezra stood and picked up a jug of wine and handed it to him. "It ain't brandy, brother, but it's damn good wine."

"Thank you kindly, Ezra" Runaway said. "Miss, if I may, I need to get a little more comfortable."

He scooted further from the cave wall and propped a folded blanket under his head and lay almost flat.

"I want to finish my story, so you all know all the reasons I ain't fit for living and am prepared to begin serving my time in hell, though I admit at this very moment I ain't in quite as much of a hurry to die as I was a little bit ago.

"We was in the rifle pits in the middle of a thick pine and oak scrub forest, so many trees and such damn thick undergrowth, full of brambles, that you could hardly make your way through it. They started coming at us, and once the firing started, the smoke hung heavier and heavier. You couldn't see nobody till they was right on you, so both sides was loading and firing helter-skelter like men possessed. And then, I reckon from muzzle flashes, the ground itself started burning, and them tress started catching fire and falling. I already knew I was going to hell when I died. But hell had come to me, to the living, right here on God's Earth.

"The battle line run for miles, and when parts of it got overrun, men from both sides was mixed together in the exploding, flaming forest and the fighting turned even more chaotic. Wounded men fell to the ground and caught fire, screaming just as terrible as the burnt men at Fort Pillow. One man, shot in the leg, leaned over to try to stench the bleeding. A burning pine fell on his back, crushing him to the ground. 'Help me! Help me,' he hollered. But there's no help to be had in hell. His uniform caught on fire and he turned right quick into pure flames that screamed on and on like the devil was in there poking him.

"I had a sword one of Forrest's men had picked off a wounded Federal officer and given me when we'd entered Fort Pillow. The trench I was in got overrun. I dropped my gun and pulled my sword, ready to skedaddle. I turned and a Union boy—so young looking—come right at my backside. I jumped out of the trench wildly swinging my sword and cut his head right off. I'd shot at men before. I never aimed good, though I might've nicked a few who were left to die. I ain't saying this was my first killing. But I'd never imagined the eyes of a fellow the instant he knode I'd killed him stone dead. Those still living pale blue eyes looked right into mine right before his head toppled off and he heaped to the ground.

"'Yeeeeee hawwwwww!'" the Rebel fellow next to me screamed, a crazy grin on his face. 'Let's whack more heads off! We won't never get to do this again. This is the last good time we'll ever have.'

"A sword come out of the front of his throat. The fed who'd driven it through him eyed me as his pulled it back out. That's when I ran.

"Usins on both sides had turned into bushwhacking devils. I heard blood-hungry screams and saw bayonets thrust through men trying to reload. I saw a man get his neck almost severed through, his eyes blinking in surprise as his head dangled on his chest, the Federal man who killed him hollering in delight, 'die Rebels die!' I seen men on both sides enjoying the killing as much as Forrest's men enjoyed slaughtering the colored. I zigzagged through the slaughtering and the trees on fire and run right through flames shooting up from the ground. I tripped over a body and ripped off my burning hot shoes.

"I got a ways from the worst bedlam but could still hear shooting and screaming and see heavy smoke up ahead. I come into a little clearing with a small stream. Two dead Rebels lay there side by side, one with half his head missing, the other with a big bloody hole in his gut. A third one lay face down nearer the stream, the blood running out from under his body turning the water redder than the clay dirt.

"I saw through the haze blue uniforms coming my way. I flung myself down next to that bleeding face-down man and right quick stuck my hand into his gut and smeared thick blood all over my right side and played dead.

"They come through the brush into the clearing. I had my cap tilted over the side of my face so I could peek out if I dared open my right eye. It was a Union officer and two young boys following him. They didn't have no weapons and was all holding their hands out to the side, like they was looking for someone to surrender to. The officer looked frightened to death, twisting his head back and forth when I saw the right arm of the face-down man moving very slowly. The blast from his revolver blew off half of that officer's head and sent them two who was following him screaming and running. I stayed right still, and that little stream turned even brighter red and that poor bleeding Rebel next to me begun moaning and pleading, 'Don't leave me to die here.' I kept on pretending dead and told myself he was not talking to me and there was nothing I could do for him no how. Shells started landing. I prayed for one of them to land square on me and blow me to smithereens rather than leave me to a slow death like him.

"A shell landed just the other side of the stream. It shook the very earth and deafened me and covered me half in dirt. When I opened my eyes, looking at me from under the blown-up ground just beyond the stream was a grinning, bony face, small patches of flesh above each eye socket. The devil himself was rising up out of the ground. I jumped up and ran and damn near tripped on a Union captain missing his head and yanked his boots off and kept running.

"I got a ways away from the shelling and stopped and put on them nice boots. A small bunch of Confederates run by in the same general direction I was headed. I followed them. We reached a road and joined a much bigger bunch in retreat. We passed a jumble of bloody dead men and I grabbed me a rifle. The company I fell in with ended up under the command of Jubal Early.

"We eventually come all the way up the Shenandoah Valley. Last night I finally got the chance not even my cowardly self would pass up. They was looking for volunteers to scout the defense for today's battle. I pretended I was all fired up, so they picked me and four others to come down the creek valley. Them other boys stopped when we got near that fort back yonder overlooking the creek and saw all the trees has been felled to block the creek valley. I told them I'd sneak a closer look. As soon as I left them, I threw my rifle to the side and got down in the water and crawled down that cooling creek, damn near swimming in a few places, but mostly climbing over all them boulders and rocks. I tuckered out right where you found me, finally at peace, knowing I would not fight today, or ever again, believing I could drown myself in my sleep before either side found me."

Runaway took another slug from the wine jug. June kneeled over and washed his forehead and kissed it and looked at Walter.

"I was a poet before the war," Walter said. "I came to Washington in 1862 and found a new calling. I volunteered in the hospitals, and most every day and night I nursed and befriended wounded and dying soldiers. I saw much death and sadness, but what broke me was the same truth you witnessed, that some men savor and cherish the killing. That truth and those men tormented me so that I could no longer visit the hospitals.

"So I am a runaway, like you, but even more cowardly. For I did not run from battle. I deserted my soldiers in the hospitals, all those who counted on me for earthy and spiritual comforts, who now suffer and die alone.

"Like you, I came to the creek—almost the same spot—exhausted, my spirit broken, my soul barren, my very will to live vanquished, shrouded in the darkest melancholy, anxious to welcome death.

"Like you, my fate all of a sudden changed. For these two people found me by the creek side, as we found you this morning. And they convinced me to allow them to restore me, not only my body, but my soul. Like you, I had surrendered to a painful sorrow I believed would never end. To my astonishment, they cured my melancholy. They have studied it, its causes and cures, and with their fellowship and love and caring, they drove it out of me.

"I swear to you, I am no longer haunted by the death and agony I saw, or by the glee that some men take in killing. I am once again a poet, my dear sir, and in years to come you will know me."

"I thought you all just come upon each other this morning," Runaway said.

"Ah yes," Walter said. "I have revealed part of our secret, which we wish to share with you. But before we do, before we welcome you into our secret fellowship, and before we drive out the misery and anguish and heartbreak that war and killing has set upon you, we must know that you will honor us and our secrets. You must swear to our oath."

"You all are a strange bunch," Runaway said. "Very kind-hearted. But I must ask, what evil have you all done that you have need to keep secret? For I am already full up of evil, and wish to have no more to do with it."

June unbuttoned his torn, filthy shirt and began washing his chest. "We make it sound mystifying," she said. "But it's simple. We are kind and gentle people. Me and Ezra, the brave man who saved you from drowning and carried you here, both love poetry, and were blessed to help this brave poet. I don't believe we are one bit evil, though we are free-thinking in our ways." She smiled and kissed his forehead, "Our secret is simply that were care deeply for one another. And that we happily keep each other's company."

Ezra stood. "You fret about being found by Jubal Early's men. What you think they'd do to me if they get past Fort DeRussy and find us? A former slave, a runaway to them, keeping company with a white woman. The Union soldiers could conscript me. I have not the stomach for killing. That I know. We've done no evil. Unless white and coloreds having a fondness for each other, and helping each other out, like the three of us do, is evil."

"I know true evil," Runaway said. "Ain't anything you just said nowhere near it. I kindly accept your offer, and I swear to you not to say nothing, ever, about any of you. I know in my bones what I seen and what I done—and not done. Evil will always claim me, all for its own. Knowing that, I don't have not the slightest notion how you all might fix me up. But since I've proved myself too coward to find a way to die, have at it."

Walter stood. "My name is Walter. This is June. You know Ezra. I am honored to be the one who will tell you our story in full. But first you must sleep. Ezra and I will take a peek outside."

"When I finish bathing you, you will swear to our oath," June said. "Then I'll read you poetry as you drift off to sleep."

Runaway grinned. "I don't know no poetry, but I look forward to it nonetheless."

Ezra knew Walter, to undergo another crawling in and out, had desires other than taking a look about, for which there was no immediate need. Ezra knew too, as Walter did, that June wished to be alone with Runaway.

"I need to relieve myself," Walter said. "Do you have that need?"

"I do," Ezra said.

They could still hear the steady, farther away far rumbling of artillery. But they neither saw nor heard any sign of anyone, for the steepness of the hill the hideaway perched upon was far from any path.

"They say this is a last gasp by Lee and the Rebels," Walter said. "Assuming the Feds beat 'em back, do you envision staying here, after the war?"

"I can't see leaving here," Ezra said.

"The birthplace of your freedom," Walter said.

"It is," Ezra said. "But that would not hold me here, on its own. This place nurtures my body and soul. The creek. Its music. The simple beauty of the little hills and valleys, how they unroll one into the next. The open fields—no longer the grounds of my servitude.

Enough woods to shelter me unseen. The stands of towering trees. The birds. The springs. The brooklets they birth every spring. The critters who wander here, never without purpose. The gallant fox, the keen chipmunk, the unflinching hawk. What I aim to find out is if I can be as free and homelike as there are, in this refuge that receives me. I will not say how lucky I feel, for I know all things end. But yes, I plan to stay."

"And June," Walter said. "Will she stay?"

"I believe she will, unless she stops believing in poetry and the Muses and the immortal John Keats and Walter Whitman."

"I can see she wants to be here with you," Walter said. "Would you ever leave her a short while, long enough to come visit or take a journey with someone, perhaps a poet you profess to love and honor?"

"She and I do care mightily for each other, as we do for you. I count on you and me always being close in our souls. I welcome our brotherly affection, and your kind visits. But I will not be leaving here to go wandering with you, or visit you, though I'm sure you'd be a fine mate, and a friendly host, too."

"Then I must visit you," Walter said, and took Ezra's hand as they made their way back up to the entrance to sit until they were sure June had Runaway well asleep.

Exhibit C:

July 14, 1864

This hot sunny day I write by candlelight in the cool air of the hideaway. Runaway sits quietly nearby, his eyes closed in rest. He and I have spent many wonderful hours together over the previous days, just the two of us.

I'm trusting you with our secret, I told him, which could destroy what survives of the poet who wrote Leaves of Grass, because I cherish you, like I cherish all the men who have suffered and will always suffer from this war, which I am recording and describing, and will continue to record and describe until the day I die.

I revealed to him what I have not told June or Ezra—that on occasion I still suffer stiff bouts of melancholy. I thanked him for allowing us to restore him, and told him my hope that rescuing and befriending him and restoring him to health and happiness would help me escape my remaining woefulness and further recover from the war.

I lay bare my torment from abandoning the soldiers in the hospitals. I said I could no longer save them, or even save myself without June and Ezra's help. But I do believe with all my soul, I beseeched him, that fate smiles on the four of us, and that he has completed and made whole our secret fellowship, which we both can count on to steel our souls against the ravages of heartbreak and never-ending sorrow.

I never asked him his name, and he never volunteered it, a reflection, I believe, of the unique, strange closeness between us rather than a desire for concealment. I could feel in my first private conversations that he comprehended me, and wished for us to become comrades and confidants.

I don't know by what means June treated his melancholy, but I read to him from my Leaves. Between readings, I divulged my most fervent beliefs and hopes.

I described the oneness of the body and the soul, and lay bare my belief in love among comrades and close relationships of men.

I confessed how in several of my poems I wrote lustfully of men, but how I would no more, for what is the import of that, I asked him, compared to what he and all the others have been through in this war. He voiced full agreement with my sentiment. Indiscretions men commit in younger years need not haunt them in later years, he said, and that truth would be to the benefit of both of us.

I asked him how he considered the men who find so much joy and relish in killing.

I believe that was the devil coming out in men, he replied. It turns out some men are near pure devil and jump at the chance to savor hell on Earth. The lesser devils in others show themselves only when trapped in the Earthly hells men create for themselves.

He has evil in him like all of us, he said, and thanked God it wasn't his nature for it to show itself as strongly in him as it did in those men.

I never inquired after his mention of slave trading. Runaway I believe does know the power of hatred and evil more so than most. He told me he saw the true depth and nature of that particular Southern evil rooted in hatred of coloreds in the face of Nathan Bedford Forrest. When his men said they could not take Fort Pillow, his white face turned dark bronze. Runaway swore that was the devil making himself seen in the face of Forrest.

I told him my new mission as a man and a poet was to convey the war. I shared with him my regret that Leaves had never struck a chord with ordinary folks like him. I told him of my plans for a book of war poems and went so far as to mention my hope of being thought of as the Good Gray Poet. He offered me some heartfelt advice on that notion. He told me, You will reach folks like me and mine if we could read about the war, neither sugar-coated nor blaming men for what they done in battle, yet not glossing over the terribleness of it.

Today was our last visit. I must return to New York, and after his departure, I will walk from here to the train station. I read him several more of my favorite passages. At least now there is at one ordinary down-to-earth fellow, far from New York or Boston, who professes to like Leaves and promises to buy it.

June pounded on the rocks above us, the signal that she was waiting outside to take Runaway to the shack. He thanked me profusely. The worst of his melancholy has been lifted, he told me, and he greatly treasures our secret fellowship and believes he can now live a useful, contented life. He assured me he would keep his sacred vow, and would choose most thoughtfully the single inheritor of our saving secrets.

I said this to him: I see in you all the courage and valor of all soldiers—all those I comforted, the hundreds I saw die, and the many I abandoned. I will think of you fondly and never forget you, for to rescue and restore you has further relieved my troubled soul and will inspire me always.

I showed him affection only in words—I never kissed him or held him, even as we parted. But I love him mightily.

As he departed up the trail to catch up with June, I climbed atop our hideaway, to keep him in view a few moments longer, and chanted to him in my best barbaric yawp the words I saved for that moment:

I depart as air....I shake my white locks in the runaway sun
I effuse my flesh in eddies and drift it in lacy jags.
I bequeath myself to the dirt to grow from the grass I love,
If you want me again look for me under your bootsoles.

You will hardly know who I am or what I mean,
But I shall be good health to you nevertheless,
And filter and fibre your blood.
Failing to fetch me at first keep encouraged,
Missing me one place search another,
I stop some where waiting for you.

Walt Whitman

Early's men never pierced the defenses of Washington. Runaway said they lost whatever small chance they had the day of his rescue. Early delayed the attack July 11, and the Union forces re-enforced the city as Early and his officers spend late Monday afternoon and evening drinking the best wine from the wine cellar in the finest house they could find, the Blair mansion in Silver Spring.

The next day, another very hot and humid one, hundreds of men on both sides were killed in heavy skirmishing between the Union and Rebel lines. The Rebel line sent out its sharpshooters to probe the Union line and see if they could break through down Rock Creek valley. Several hundred Rebels advanced through the trees to fences and farmhouses toward the creek near Fort DeRussy.

The Confederate skirmishers took good aim and shot and killed dozens of Union infantry. More Union men were killed when they were ordered to advance on the Rebels. But the Union advance was lethal nonetheless. It was accompanied by deadly and ripping artillery that blew up the trees and an old farm house where the Rebels took cover and sliced them into smithereens, leaving dozens and dozens of Rebel sharpshooters dead, or wishing they were dead.

The battle never fully formed—it was though the men knew they could still kill each other but no longer saw much point to it. The war was decided, although the fighting would continue until the next spring. And even if the Rebels had broken through the line, they could not have held their position—they would have been engulfed by thousands of more Union troops still pouring into Washington.

Early waited for nightfall that day to withdraw the same way he came, and Union forces only half-heartedly pursued his exhausted, beleaguered troops.

Walt Whitman left to return to New York on Thursday, July 14. June and Runaway reached the shack without incident, but Ezra, returning from the creek, had spotted some Union soldiers, so as soon as it got dark, they hurried back to Hideaway. They stayed there several more days, the three of them, supplied by Ezra with food and drink and more books of poetry.

After Rock Creek valley returned to normal, Runaway did stay with June and Ezra in their shack. He found work at a mill on the creek and took his own place to live, not too far off. June, on three occasions, came to read him poetry, but came no more after September.

After Lee surrendered the following April and other Confederate generals followed suit, Runaway came to say goodbye. He gave June a long, tender hug. He shook Ezra's hand and said a moist-eyed thank you and told him that he would forever be amazed by Ezra carrying him on his back that day, all the way from the creek to Hideaway. June and Ezra walked with him on his way leaving and watched him wade across the creek, headed back home.

One secret Ezra never did reveal to June—the full comfort he found in his E+J. At the time of the carving, he believed her rebellious infatuation with him and the creek and even the Muses could end any day; part of him awoke every morning amazed she'd stayed another night; if she did leave, he would still have John, and he and John would always have their perch, attested to by his carving.

But June and Ezra never did part. They concealed their intimacy, but never their friendship, and spent the rest of many happy years in the big house June's daddy built for her and her sister.

26

COWBOY PACED AND LEANED against the wall for short stints but remained standing the whole time he told the story of Whitman's return, then held out each page of Exhibit C for me to peruse and read aloud.

"Ezra was my great, great grandfather. The story came down to me through my own Pops. Just like I would pass it on to my boy. My only child. I looked forward to it from the day he was born. Even more than seeing him graduate high school and college, or getting married and having kids. Because you can't count on those things. Those are your hopes. Whereas I could count on passing the story to my boy, bringing him right here, giving him the oath, right in the very spot where Pops gave it to me, then starting the story and watching the astonishment come to his eyes.

"Sam Ezra was a fine boy, smart too. Kind-hearted and strong and proud, the best son you could ever hope for. When he was a youngster, other parents would ask me, does he ever get excited, show what a good time's he's having? He was a shy, deep-thinking boy, but when it was just the two of us, we would talk and laugh, on and on, that best kind of talking that floats along on its own and takes no effort. It he'd been struggling and needed it, I would've told him the story, no matter how young he was. But he was going great guns. So I waited. Like my Pops waited. So he'd be more grown-up, and the miracle of the story and the duty that comes with it would take even stronger hold of him. He graduated high school right across the park, same as me. Did better than me in school. Went off to college, down in Virginia. Was doing good there, too. Dean's list.

"Remember when going after Saddam became inevitable? Sam Ezra came home for the weekend. He was a junior. I heard him coming up the steps and opened the door and he told me, his smile so proud—'I'm joining up.' He wanted to do his part, like his grandfather, a cargo pilot in World War II, and, in his kindly eyes, like me, for he said I'd done my duty, too, being a D.C. fire captain.

"Sam Ezra was the last one to jump too quick into things. He'd done just what I taught him, he told me—to take a step back, think things through, and try to do the next right thing. Grandpa enlisted to fight Hitler, he said. Saddam is the Hitler of my generation, just as crazy and dangerous, threatening the world with his weapons of mass destruction, even nukes he might attack us with. We've got to take him down.

"I must have looked doubtful.

"'I've made up my mind, Pops,' he said.

"I didn't buy any of that Saddam malarkey. He would never attack us. It was all warmongering by the top dogs who'd never fought themselves but thought it made them look more manly being quick on the draw to send others to die.

"I could see that Sam Ezra had become his own man, made up his own mind, based on his own view of the world, not mine. As it should be.

"I gave him a strong hug and said how proud I was and how proud his grandfather would be. That's when the impulse hit me like lightning. Take him into the park right now and tell him the story! I'd never worried about when the passing-on would take place. The moment would present itself. Let the play come to you, that's what Pops always told me.

"I should have followed that impulse. But I hesitated for a split second and thought this: If I tell him right now, make it first order of business right after he tells me he's going off to war, he might think I'm telling him now because his own daddy doubts he'll make it back home.

"That notion shot fear through me more than running into a blazing house. I wouldn't take the chance that even for the briefest second I might make my boy think his daddy envisioned him dying over there. Then a second terror struck me—that I was in fact considering my boy's death. I know that's normal, who wouldn't worry about that, but right then it seemed the worst thing, that he might sense the thoughts of his death I'd let get hold of me.

"I told myself that I knew, with all my heart and soul, that he would be fine. Him not coming back was an evil notion, one I would not abide. I assured myself it was simply not the time to tell him. It was only an impulse. And we all know sometimes it's better to let an impulse pass.

"We finished our long hug. That's how fast all those thoughts tore through me. I patted him on both shoulders and told him again how proud I was, what a fine son I had, and I grabbed us beers and told him to have a seat and tell me all about signing up and what comes next while I cooked us supper."

Cowboy picked his bottle off the shelf and took two gulps of bourbon and kept the bottle. I stood up to be more respectful, for the worst terribleness for any loving parent is to outlive their offspring.

"If I 'd plunged ahead, if I hadn't spooked myself with that fearful double-thinking, if I'd just blurted out, 'Son, the time has come,' I would have known, right away, that my instinct was right. I would have told him he was brave and all grown-up and more than ready to me to pass him the family mantle, our legacy.

"One time I wondered this: If I had plunged ahead, if he'd known of his own, rich heritage, a purpose so worthy, a sacred oath to fulfill, maybe it would've made a difference in what he did over there. Maybe it would have saved him somehow. I've never let myself wonder that again—I do not wonder that now, I only mention it, and I will never speak of it again.

"It was 4 o'clock on a Friday when that solemn fellow came to my door and told me Sam Ezra was dead. Blown to bits in Iraq, nothing really left of him, though they would ship home a casket.

"True sadness was a mean lesson for people like me, foolish enough to think I already knew sadness from losing Sam Ezra's mother. I sat dead still in my chair in the living room and was slow to cry because I knew instantly the sorrow would never end. My boy's doom mocked me. The wickedness of the killing of him and all the others soaked bitterly into my soul. I've never believed in the devil per se, but I could feel evil savoring the delight it took in the taking away of my boy, and I knew the pleasure evil took in watching my just beginning torment.

"You two believe such deep sorrow in the Rock Creek story originates in Keats and his sorrow-stricken knight.

"But Walt Whitman's sorrow was born of the particular tragedies of war. He loved those boys he nursed like sons, and he knew best the agony of my woe—the sorrow of those whose sons die in war.

"All night I went back and from between wailing and crying softly. I finally fell asleep, I don't know how long, until a horrid dream woke me, a vision that would not cease even upon my waking. I watched myself stand in the twilight and tell the Rock Creek story to his casket, unable to take my eyes off what was left of my boy. I tried to clear my mind and sat down and slapped myself in the face over and over, but the vision still seized me."

I glanced at Louise up in the back of her lair. The agony etched in her candle-lit face made her look very old. I bit my lip as hard as I could. Please let that be the worst moment of his story.

"I jumped out of my chair and tried to wail but couldn't get out a sound. My heart pounded such I could hardly breath. I hoped a fatal stroke right then and there would fell me. I began twisting my head around like a madman to shake the vision. Out of the corner of my eye I spotted the original family *Leaves of Grass* in the spot where it always was in the bookcase. I lunged at it and opened it and Walt

Whitman looked at me and showed me through his eyes what he saw when he created our story. For the first time I felt how much he loved Ezra and Runaway and June. How dearly he desired the salvation he found here to be theirs. How he infused the story with salvation, the very salvation I'd denied my own boy.

"I fell to my knees. 'My boy never knew. I never told him,' I wailed like a madman, confessed over and over.

"I was curled up on the floor when I woke up in pitch dark, but in the distance, clear as day, I saw Sam Ezra and me sitting on the rock right outside here, the one shaped like a lopsided couch, looking off across the little gorge and hearing the faint water below. The vision crackled once like TVs used to and I saw myself beginning to tell him the story.

"I told it in the easy talking way him and me always had and stretched out the build-up to that moment when my Sam Ezra realized the true nature of this occasion, that his daddy was passing on his family's amazing secret—the same one his great, great, great granddaddy Ezra told his boy—and the gleam popped into his eyes.

"Some people live their whole lives without ever getting that gleam. Not my boy. I watched it fill his eyes. Pure affirmation is the term I've settled on, after all these years. His eyes filled with the pure affirmation that life can be more than you could ever imagine, with joys you could never anticipate, like your daddy revealing a secret legacy that is your family's pride and joy.

"The gleam stayed strong and constant and I found just the right words and the perfect cadence and the story kept rolling off my tongue and there is not one iota of doubt that I am rising to the occasion—the story is speaking through me in a gentle, soft undertone, as clear and easily heard as the breaking waves and distant voices when you close your eyes at the seashore.

"There came this moment when the light and the sound turned themselves up and my boy and I traded unspoken things through each other's eyes, things beyond saying.

"The vision turned cloudy. It had run out. I opened my eyes, but I would not allow what me and my boy saw in each other's eyes to be lost. I kept it strongly felt and finely seen. In my hands I still clutched my *Leaves*. I remember the exact words I vowed to Walter.

'The devil of sadness will never take away the vision you've given me. I promise you that.' The hair on my neck stood up. I waited for sorrow to mock me. It dared not. I studied every detail of that concrete picture in my mind's eye of me and Sam Ezra gazing into each other's eyes. Profound relief washed over me, like never before or since. Religious people call it grace."

Cowboy wiped his eyes with his sleeve. Louise looked at least a decade younger. I touched unnoticed tears nestled in my mustache.

"There come those moments in life when despair holds us to a private accounting," he said. "When life's undeniable truth demands its due, that there is no more or no less to it that what we can find in it, right then. Find nothing, and despair will drown you for eternity.

"I never brought my boy to this secret place, and I never told him the story. But I did see, as clear and true as I stand here right now, the gleam in Sam Ezra's eyes, a sight that will comfort me the rest of my life."

I promised myself to re-read *The Varieties of Religious Experience* and hoped Cowboy would prove William James correct—mystical experiences can and do remain with some people for the rest of their lives.

"Not until then, until my vision, did I truly understand our story, the true essence of it, the power Walt Whitman gave it.

"Walt Whitman was a pragmatic and wise man. He is the greatest poet because he is the most giving and most passionate poet. His generosity of spirit flowed in his great affection for men and woman and all living things. He gave himself so fully in his poetry that to read him and to know him is to give yourself over to him as completely as he gives himself to you. So fully did he give of himself to Ezra and to June and to Runaway, that when I speak his verse, I can see through his eyes his visions of those three, his hopes for them, his great love for them, with which he infuses our story.

"That's why I can still see that gleam come to my boy's eyes. The power Walter created in the story gave me that vision, and because I could see…"

He couldn't go on. He teared up and tilted his head back and began to blink, like he could cast his tears to heaven. I wanted to touch his face, to will him on, for I was certain this was the first time he'd ever told his full-blown, unabridged story, even to Louise. He must finish. He must gather himself for what with all my might I hoped would be his crowning moment—the closing lines of his story of salvation.

"...because I could see the gleam in his eyes, I knew I was forgiven. Forgiven by Walt Whitman, and forgiven by the story, for never passing it on to my own boy. No matter how tragic my mistake, the love and salvation bequeathed by Walt Whitman had been granted to me."

He sniffled and gathered himself again and his face became rife with gratitude that spread over me and Louise as well, in our case a profound thankfulness that his story and his ending rung true to him and steeled his most fervent hope: that when darkness descended, he could replenish his gleam-in-the-eye vision, rekindle the redemption it brought to his soul.

I envied him greatly for that, and for whatever blend of wisdom and gumption and belief compelled him onward.

"The final treasure, please" he said. Louise fetched it from their trove and handed him an aged *Leaves*.

"This is the one." He opened it to the picture of Walt Whitman. "Read what my great grandfather, Ezra's son, wrote."

The picture of Walt Whitman was smaller than I had expected. Below it, printed in neat capital letters, was this (Exhibit D), which I read aloud:

OUR FAMILY HELPED MAKE THIS MAN IMMORTAL. WALT WHITMAN AND HIS WORDS LIVE IN OUR VERY SOULS AND PROVIDE US SALVATION. HE IS THE GREATEST POET AND THE GREATEST LOVER OF ALL MANKIND. HE PASSED TODAY BUT LIVES FOREVER. MARCH 26, 1892.

Below that was the signature of Ernest Benjamin.

Cowboy spread his arms and broke into preacher/fire captain mode: "Walt Whitman found salvation here with Ezra and June and Runaway, and by saving Runaway and discovering a deep friendship with Ezra, he was able to reinvigorate himself and go on to become the immortal Good Gray Poet.

"He's the only one in your so-called Rock Creek Canon whose soul and immortality were at stake. That's why the story is, first, foremost and forevermore, a Walt Whitman story. Not a Keats story, not a June story, not a Vincent Millay story."

His quick shift from a self-created miracle of grace to a humdinger of a closing argument on how he wanted me to tell the story unsettled me. I said I needed another break and was through the tight turn in the tunnel before anymore could be said.

27

THE NEAR-FULL MOON lit up the quartz specks in the sitting
rock where Cowboy had traveled to in his saving-grace vision. A
high breeze showed itself in the grounded stirrings of the shadows of treetops. Many hills away, the outside world peeked into
the forest from a high tower and winked its red light. I recalled line
by line the look on Cowboy's face when he told of Walt Whitman
forgiving him and imagined the great pleasure Grandpa would take
in Cowboy finding his keen eye in his moment of greatest need.

I'd just turned fourteen. That spring Daddy had lost his job and
his drinking had worsened and Mom sent him packing. After school
got out, two days before I began my summer dishwashing job, she
dropped me off to spend the night on the "farm."

"What's the one thing you're never gonna forget" Grandpa
asked every time I took my half seat worth of stoop. I quoted him
verbatim.

"Of all the foolishness in life, there's only two true sins for a keen eye: looking but not seeing, and listening but not hearing."

That earned me a slap on the back and my first taste of hard liquor.

The last time I saw him, the summer before I left for college, he was close to dying. Memaw, already losing her marbles, had to help him out to his stoop. He'd grown pale and even more scrawny, his eyes all runny and gooey. He was out of Jim Beam. He told Memaw and mother to go inside and turn up the radio so he and I could have a private talk.

He bummed a cigarette and sniffled and wiped his eyes.

"Remember this. All them stories you can see with your keen eye are alive. As alive as the people they're inside of. Sometimes more so. Them stories inside folks—told or untold—that's what people are made of. That's the true richness in otherins." That was by far the largest of the three groups into which Grandpa divided the world, the other two being "usins" and "youins."

"I'll remember, Grandpa" I said. "Mom says you're not long for this world."

"That's right," he smiled, "and I'll be grateful when I take my last breath. For I've been lucky, lucky like you are. So don't be sad when they tell you I'm gone. Be happy for me."

I didn't know what to say. I put my arm around him and told him I'd miss him.

He took a long drag and blew smoke rings for me one last time.

"I got one last piece of advice for you," he said. "Before you get so old you can't do for yourself, make sure you got somebody around you can count on to get you liquor and smokes."

I studied the blinking red light and lit a cigarette in his honor. Those with whom he could not share his wisdom considered him a lazy, alcoholic, daydreaming ne're-do-well. It's true he liked nothing better than sitting and watching. And he did like stories more than people. I did not want that said of me.

Louise appeared out of nowhere.

"The story's come so alive," she said. "Don't you feel it? It's so potent. It's taking me over, like *Leaves* took June her first time."

She sighed and bounced on her toes and pointed wordlessly to the moon.

"I guess it's pretty wild and untamed, the way it's stirring you up."

She sat next to me. "You think I'm daffy." She couldn't stay still. She stood and recommenced jiggling. "Do you ever get ecstatic? Like Walter when he ate calamus? I'm working up to that, imagining how wonderful your tell will be."

"Why do you think that?"

"Because of what Beatrice told Dante. 'Thou shouldst know that all take delight in the measure of the depth to which their sight can penetrate the truth, in which all intellect finds rest. From thus it may be seen, beatitude itself is based on the act of seeing.'"

"You beatify me," she said. "As in gladden me. As in me make me feel glorified."

"Blessed are the meek," I said. "Tell me your story—your downfall that brought you home to Aunty."

"Do you believe the story offers salvation?" she asked.

"From Keats' death pale warrior, or Dylan's twisted reach of crazy sorrow?"

"I believe it does," she said. "But that doesn't mean I'm totally daffy. Just lucky. Which I never forget. I live a pampered life. But I never take the story for granted. Or my freedom to dedicate myself to our canon."

"You never moved away from Aunty's?"

She ignored my question.

"I knew Cowboy would make a strong case for what he wants you to write."

"Starring Walt Whitman," I said

"With Ezra the other major character," she said. "June in a minor role. Keats too. Vincent out all together. The very three who are my salvation. When I tell you Vincent's story, imagine her and Keats together. The super-seductress and the pent-up, breast-worshipping, love poet."

"What you're telling me is to take to heart your Rock Creek Canon."

She burst out in laughter and flung your arms in the air.

"Yes! Embrace the canon! The very heart and soul of the story."

She dropped her arms. She looked at her hands like she didn't know what to do with them. I stood and lit another cigarette. She made a V with her first two fingers. I carefully placed it there. She took a long, 1930-movie-godess drag. I sat back down. She followed suit. Her pouted lips funneled a tiny smoke stream. Then came the rings. I jabbed my finger through the last one as it cleared my forehead.

"You know you're part of it now—the story—with the rest of us," she said. "Give it a chance. Let the canon speak to you. Accept your salvation."

I bumped lightly against her shoulder. "I bet you were wayward in your youth, like me."

She bumped back. "I'm ecstatic, by nature. Like June. Like Walt Whitman in the throne. Like Vincent Millay. Like I bet you like to be sometimes."

I didn't bite.

"I do crave my flights of delight," she said. "But those who reach for ecstasy are prone to plummet. My only salvation is that my raptures keep pace with my dives, though I do try to temper myself. Sort of."

"I do know about the sort-of part," I said.

"It's hard to resist. Particularly in truly fine moments. Like right now, with you so close and me envisioning you, in all your glory, writing the tell, in all its glory."

"The best stories tell themselves," I said. "Unruly ones like this, even more so."

"You are the perfect choice," she laughed. "I hope this is a dream come true for you."

She stood and held out a hand and pulled me up. She stepped closer and put her hands lightly on my chest, so I could more closely observe her cavalcade of hints and grins and smiles. I could spot each and every ingredient: her budding excitement and hankering for more of it, her overflowing river of wonder at what might come next, both cascading into the full blossom of her most pure and wonderfully alive expression—uncontained playfulness and pent-up wildness that broke free and pranced at me arm-in-arm.

She kissed me.

"I see the gleam coming into your eyes" she said. "I feel embers rekindle in me, bursting into flames."

My own ancient embers made my face feel hot. Her fingers pressed and let up on my chest, like paws of a purring cat.

"What do you imagine, when I say the story will tell itself?" I asked, keeping her close.

She took my shoulders and braced me like she was sending me on a mission of danger.

"I imagine the thrill the story feels. I envision Proust's Russian princess, who sought what she called, famously, 'That penetration by a writer of a woman's most intimate feelings.'"

"Virginia Woolf said Proust's prose saturated her with pleasure, with intense vibration," I said.

"Your tell will do that to me," she said. "Saturate me. You know I have June's blood in me. Wander off into the woods with me."

She grabbed my hand. We were two or three steps on our way when Cowboy shouted.

"Hello? ...Hello?" came from somewhere up above. I wondered if he'd been watching. She closed her eyes and squeezed my hand and let go and dashed away.

"Down here," I said. "We were just on our way in."

"Bullshit," he said, striding up hands on hips. "She's wrapping you around her little finger, just like she does those three pie-eyed Zooer poets."

I bought time by throwing him some most fitting Shakespeare: "O she doth teach the torches to burn bright. It seems she hangs upon the cheek at night."

"She's hanging a spell on you is what I'd say. I hope you got more sense than to let her sweet talk you into twisting the story into something it's not. You get it, right? That no matter what Louise believes, it wasn't June's doings that made Walt bounce back?"

"It wasn't?"

"Oh Jesus. How long since a woman paid you any mind?

It's better to never chance an answer to a rhetorical question.

"Then tell me what it was," I said

"It was Ezra and Runaway. Like Pops told me. Ezra was Walter's hero—not June. First Ezra bucked him up by shaming him. Then he helped Walter get through June's ceremony. Walter loved and cherished Ezra for the rest of their lives. Because Ezra proved him-self the kind of man Walter dreamed men would be. Proved he had a heart of gold when he helped Walter save Runaway. Ezra made possible Walt's final salvation—saving Runaway.

"The understanding and affection Walter and Runaway found for each other finished the job of getting Walter through his rough patch. Read again what Walter left us. He said Runaway 'does know evil'—he knew Runaway could well have chopped off twenty heads, not one. But Runaway sought redemption. He'd had his fill of war and killing. Just like Walt had."

I lit up a cigarette to have along with his sermon.

"Walt did more than give Runaway the story. He laid bare his soul to him. Read him *Leaves of Grass*. That's why Runaway came to greatly admire and love Walter. Their secret fellowship—that's what topped off Walter's restoration. Not what June did at the creek, assuming that even happened. Hell, even if it did, it's just back-story. What mattered far more to Walt was him and his hero Ezra saving one last soldier—one who didn't relish killing. One he came to love."

"What about the canon?"

"If you throw that cockamamie Rock Creek Canon into what you write, fine, as long you make Walt and Ezra and Runaway the heart of the story."

"What about June and all the conjuring of the Muses she did?" I said. "The spirits and her and Keats are what got Walter to his proudest moment—firing into the sky."

"All that airy, fairy, hocus-pocus?" he said. "As if June discovered this place and made it magical? No one has ever been more a part of this place, knew it better or been closer to it than my great, great granddaddy. Sure, June loved it too. But Ezra is the greatest lover this park ever had. Every step he took beyond the short distance he strayed as a slave was newly taken territory. He loved this place before he ever knew June—explored every nook and cranny—discovered every secret."

"He discovered Hideaway?"

"Yep. Crawled in there after he saw a fox come out.

"Let me straighten you out on the Good Gray Poet, too. Walter wasn't a free-love pervert poet. He was a heartfelt patriot who so loved his country he served for years in hospitals. He didn't take on that so-called 'personae.' It was all true.

168

"One last thing. Louise loves that psychedelic twist. She did that kind of stuff when she was young. You too, probably.

"Now listen up. All kinds of people have raptures, revelations, epiphanies, trances, whatever, that have nothing to do with psychedelic drugs.

"Walter willed himself to find the inspiration for the new kind of poetry he envisioned. His own imagination and trances brought on his dream-like state and his visions. His epiphanies were real, his very own."

"I'll be honest," I said. "The first time I read *Leaves*—a paperback of the original 1855 edition—I scribbled in three or four different places: 'Was WW on acid???'"

Cowboy spit and shook his head in disgust.

"So she does have you thinking just like her."

My stomach bubbled. I dragged us to more placid, well-plowed ground. "You're the one who's got me thinking. About how the war dead haunted Emily just as much as Walter. Listen to her.

My triumph lasted till the Drums
Had left the Dead alone
And then I dropped my Victory
And chastened stole along
To where the finished Faces
Conclusion turned on me
And then I hated Glory
And wished myself were They.

"Not bad," Cowboy said. "But nothing near *When Lilacs Last in the Dooryard Bloom'd*—the finest American poem ever."

"Among them, for sure," I said. "But Emily gets as much pathos in eight lines as he does in—how many hundreds of lines is 'Lilacs?'"

"Doesn't matter," he said. "You agreed. She'll never stand on stage or anywhere else near Walter. Time to go back in. One round to go. I wouldn't even bother with this part. But Louise loves it."

28

THIS MIGHT BE THE night. Vincent pressed against the thigh of Lydia, smiled longingly up into her handsome face and wanted to gobble her up. She couldn't. Not yet. On the other side of her sat Lydia's husband.

Vincent nestled between June's great niece and Alfred in the back seat of a swanky, pale green Packard Twin Six Limousine. It was Wednesday, January 16, 1924. Vincent would turn thirty-two February 22.

Immensely popular, widely read and critically acclaimed, she had packed D.A.R. Hall for her 4:30 reading, a stop on her tour in the wake of her fourth volume of poetry, *The Harp-Weaver and Other Poems.* The year before she'd become the first woman to win the Pulitzer Prize for Poetry.

To be headed for after-dinner cocktails rather than returning alone to her room at the Sheraton elated her, even if her long-held fantasy failed to pan out.

"I knew the first time I laid eyes on the beautiful you that you were a troublemaker," Lydia smiled.

"Ha!" Vincent laughed. "You've always been the powerhouse. I was only the performer. But together, oh boy, did we get our way."

"Imagine Vincent in full regalia, in white satin, a train ten feet long, leading the Pageant of Athena parade through the Vassar campus," Lydia said. "Oh, how they swooned when she took her throne and recited. What a spell she cast on us younger Vassar women. I lost track of all the ones you bedded."

"You mean the ones who liked to play the man?" Vincent laughed. "Don't be jealous, Alfred. Lydia and I were best friends, and I mean best, but somehow we never took the full plunge."

"But we did dally all night long with our poets," Lydia sighed.

"Lydia was my oasis," Vincent said. "She enchanted me my first visit to her room." She put her head on Lydia's shoulder. "You made such unhurried love to poetry. To John Keats. Rollicking on the floor in North Hall, just you and me and Keats."

"Splendid!" Alfred said. "Now I can forever imagine Lydia indulging in her apparently not-so-guarded secret obsession—a literary ménage á trois with you and Keats."

"Where are we?" Vincent said. "How'd we end up on a dark road in the forest squeezed between a rock face and a raucous creek?"

"You've been kidnapped," Lydia said.

They turned right up a hill and left up a gently curved driveway through a wrought-iron gate and crunched to a stop in an expanse of fine white gravel. Across a large brick patio and down a slope of lawn a single bulb on a rusty pole lit a stone bridge over a brook. A newly built cottage perched on the wooded hillside.

"I must be dreaming," Vincent said. "My still-dazzling, best-ever college mate and her debonair husband lure me with a promise of delectable martinis to their country manor. Turns out I've been kidnapped, taken on a moony night to an enchanted forest with a fairy-tale bridge and a gingerbread house on stilts."

A valet threw open the double doors to the grand brick mansion. "Tonight, we'll look after ourselves, thank you, Stevens," Alfred said. "We'll see you tomorrow."

"Then the master dismisses the staff so he and his sweetie can put me under their full spell."

"That's what we're hoping," Lydia said.

Alfred led them to the great room. He helped Vincent out of her coat and pulled out the middle of three, high-backed chairs on one side of a long, oak table with a lamp in the middle, the only light besides the snapping flames in the humongous fireplace.

Dainty Vincent, renown for her voluptuous shape, ignored him. The fire pulled her closer and flickered her golden red hair crimson and glistened her green eyes.

She peeled a silk scarf off her shoulders and fluttered it back and forth. Blond-haired Alfred's pale blue eyes revolted in a blinking fit when he tried to stop staring at her poppy-colored mouth, set off by the lush, Irish paleness of her long neck rising out of an emerald gown.

Tall, pretty Lydia, with striking black hair and blue-grayish eyes, bounced on her toes. "You're falling into a trance, dear," she said. "Go concoct your wonderful martinis." His face reddened and he headed briskly to the kitchen.

"My god, Vincent," Lydia said. "You've become even more captivating."

"Don't be silly," Vincent said. "I was never a natural beauty like you, that true loveliness of yours than age makes even more alluring." She glided to Lydia, tossed the scarf around her neck, then floated to the well-pillowed couch, threw her arms atop the cushions and stretched out her legs. They admired each other in silence and savored being in the room alone until Alfred, like a proud butler, sauntered in carrying a silver tray crowded with a full pitcher and three martini glasses. He handed out drinks and sat on the far side of the table.

"To an evening that's already enchanted me," Vincent toasted and drank and made a show of smacking her lips. "Would you mind terribly if I take my shoes off and put my feet up?"

"Get as comfortable as you like," Lydia said, and nestled at the other end of the couch.

Vincent flipped a shoe in the air. Alfred catapulted from his chair and fetched it. She kicked-flung her other shoe into a summersault. He rushed to retrieve it and stood flummoxed, a shoe in each hand, a lost look on his face. He took three carefully considered steps, squatted in front of Vincent and positioned the shoes just so.

Vincent reconnoitered long ways and pressed her toes into Lydia's thigh. Lydia jostled in her slinky dress and Alfred retreated to the other side of the table.

"Why you staying so far away, Alfred," Vincent said. He didn't move. "Cat got your tongue? Don't be a wet blanket. Come over here with us."

"You can relax dear," Lydia said to him, shimmying her bottom deeper into the couch.

"I'm giving him the heebie-jeebies," Vincent snickered.

"It does stun me to be in your actual presence," he said. "It's a dizzying delight, and leaves me damn near speechless."

"A toast to our long-awaited reunion," Lydia said. "We have much to tell you. And much to ask."

"Me first," Vincent said. "How'd you end up here?"

"I never told you?" Lydia said.

"Sweetie, when we spend all those nights schmoozing in college, we had better things to do than talk about family history."

"It's a rather strange story, like most things about my family," Lydia said. "My great grandparents lived in New York. My great aunt June finished her schooling and was too rambunctious for proper New York society."

Vincent nested her toes further into Lydia. "Wild like you," she said.

"My great grandfather Samuel happily put up with June's poetry obsession, but not her wild life. A business acquaintance of his lived with his family in a grand old farmhouse in the woods here, further up the creek valley. Arrangements were made. June could pursue her poetic studies in a more appropriate, less tempting pastoral setting—she was sent to board with them.

"When the Civil War dragged on, great grandfather's acquaintance moved his family to Europe. The day they left, he took June to catch the train back home. But he didn't see to it that she actually left on the train. She came back across town and moved into a servant's shack near the farmhouse. Never mentioned in her letters home that her hosts had moved away. Family lore has it that she was a devotee of John Keats and befriended Walt Whitman."

"Not yet, dear," Alfred said.

"Hush Alfred. After the war ended, June confessed in a letter. The family had vamoosed years before, but she was safe and sound and living happily in what she described as a fine cottage near the farmhouse. Samuel fumed. He was set to go himself to drag June back to New York and marry her off to a handpicked blueblood. But June, like you and me, knew how to get her way. She convinced her mother Vivian to intervene. Then June's younger sister, Emma Louise—my grandmother—mysteriously decided she, too, wanted to shun society life and escape her watchful parents.

"Vivian made Samuel buy this property and build this Tutor Revival house, complete with half timbering and diamond-paned windows.

"Emma Louise lived here with June and married and gave birth, in this house, to my mother, Ella. June never left here and never married. I was born here. Daddy wanted to move us all back to New York. My mother would have none of it, not until old age. Worked out charmingly. Alfred and I married in London, honeymooned in Paris, toured Greece for months, and then lived in Rome. When Mother and Daddy moved back to New York, we moved back here and had our precious Alberta, sleeping soundly, I hope, upstairs."

"Now it's your turn," Alfred said.

"Strong-willed woman, like your family," Vincent said. "But poor. When father was between jobs and lost money playing cards, mother declared him frivolous and unworthy of her and their three daughters and sent him on his way. She never doubted it was better for us to make it on our own, no matter what, than to settle for what others expected her and her girls to be content with. It was us against the world. In a small town in Maine. Us against the men, who distained mother and me because we didn't know our proper places. Boy, did that irk her. She'd go right back at them, fiercely ambitious for her girls, especially me, the oldest. I learned young, as she did, that I'd have to exert every bit of my will to lift myself, body and soul, above our situation."

"I see it in your poetry," Alfred said. "And in you."

"Mother pushed us relentlessly—she did everything relentlessly. Schooled us in sewing and handcrafts and music and theater. Best of all, bless her, mother gave me poetry. She recited to me. Taught me to read poetry when I was five. As a child I read her entire library—all of Shakespeare, Tennyson, Milton, Wordsworth, Keats, Shelley and Coleridge."

Alfred topped off their martinis, his eyes never leaving Vincent, and held up his glass. "To poetry and strong and very beautiful women."

"Beauty and strength come and go," Vincent said. "Poetry I've always had, ever since it vanquished me that afternoon. I took mother's gargantuan copy of Shakespeare to the attic, the only place I'd be left alone. I opened it, randomly. *Romeo and Juliet*, Act 5, scene 3, when Romeo returns to the tomb."

She recited in her deep, almost-English-sounding stage voice.

Ah, dear Juliet,
Why are thou yet so fair? shall I believe
That unsubstantial death is amorous,
And that the lean abhorred monster keeps
Thee here in dark to be his paramour?
For fear of that, I still will stay with thee;
And never from this palace of dim night
Depart again. Here, here will I remain
With worms that are thy chamber-maids; O, here
Will I set up my everlasting rest,
And shake the yoke of inauspicious stars
From his world-wearied flesh. Eyes, look your last!
Arms, take your last embrace! and, lips, O you
The doors of breath, seal with a righteous kiss
A dateless bargain to engrossing death!

"That passage downright pierced me. Especially the word 'paramour.' Knocked the wind out of me. Left me giddy, itchy all over. An unearthly happiness opened suddenly outward like a door. I stood in this very tangible radiance, on the edge of this bottomless abyss in which every color of ecstasy moved like a cloud, now drifting closer, now drawn inexorably away, and a wind from unthinkable depths puffing out my pinafore and the tops of my slippers sticking out very black and conspicuous into the air above the void."

The fire popped. Vincent and Lydia sipped in unison. "Touched by the Muses," Lydia said.

"After that, nothing could ever confine my soul," Vincent said. "And nothing could ever fulfill me like poetry, which will be the case until my dying day."

Alfred managed to tear his eyes from the pink creeping down the curve of Vincent's neck. He cocked his eyebrows at Lydia. She stroked Vincent's leg. "I promised Alfred we'd sit at the table. He's spent days arranging and rearranging books and poetry magazines for our get-together. Would you mind?"

Vincent moaned and sashayed to the table. Alfred steered her to the middle seat.

"I should have known," Alfred said. "Touched by the Muses indeed. The divinities of poetry live in you. You're a daemon."

"Touched by something," Vincent laughed. "'My soul is too big for the rest of me.' That's what I wrote in my diary when I was in high school. Then I wrote this verse:

Give her to me who was created mine!
Just as she is; half pixie, half divine!

"That Halloween I sewed a witch costume. That night I decided I had no interest in pleasing the Camden boys. I wouldn't let them kiss me. Other girls succumbed to their fate—pick out one of those boys to please. Not me. I would never surrender. For I had poetry. 'I met my fate and everything is satisfactorily settled.' So I told my diary when I got home. That night I began to imagine the perfect lover who would come to me. I poured my heart out to him. I wrote to him by candlelight. I held séances for him. I lit candles. I kept Sir Walter Raleigh's Demonology and Witchcraft next to my bed."

"So that's how you learned to cast your spells," Lydia smiled.

"My god are all gods," Vincent said. "My soul is as deathless as god's soul. For there is no degree in eternity."

"I'm serious when I tell you you're a daemon," Alfred said. "And there is more I must confess. My misconceptions of you, banished, thankfully, by your latest sonnets:

Euclid alone has looked on Beauty bare.
Let all who prate of Beauty hold their peace,
And lay them prone upon the earth and cease
To ponder on themselves, the while they stare
At nothing, intricately drawn nowhere
In shapes of shifting lineage;

Vincent interrupted to recite the rest:

let geese
Gabble and hiss, but heroes seek release
From dusty bondage into luminous air.
O blinding hour, O holy, terrible day,
When first the shaft into his vision shone
Of light anatomized! Euclid alone
Has looked on beauty bare. Fortunate they
Who, though only once and far away,
Have heard her massive sandal set on stone.

Alfred licked gin from his lips and tasted grace in the dust kicked up by Aphrodite.

"You're so direct and acute, so hard and austere," he said. "Your satirical intelligence is so sharp, yet you refuse to sacrifice lyricism to irony. You transcend irony, rather than simply stand your poetry in it. Your freedom and abandon and detachment infuse new life into the sonnet, restored by you to its proper place, the highest poetic realm.

"That's a confession?" Vincent said.

"You are so much more than the rebellious woman who writes wonderful and hugely popular poetry. I never should have doubted that you are a pure poet. In the way Keats and Whitman are. All that matters to you is poetry.

"No wonder you are so serious, so stern, so impassioned. I make

177

bold to tell you: It is so strong in you, it strains me to feel it in person. I know all about your brilliance, your beauty, your reputation for gaiety and wild living. But I find nothing casual or relaxed about you. Your granite strength and intensity and courage. The strain of being a pure poet. Almost a grimness. Like New England flint. Hardened by life, sharpened by your love and need for poetry."

Vincent's pushed back from the table. She flared her nostrils and drilled her eyes into his.

"What'd you expect? The aging, bewitching seductress of Greenwich Village, to whom poetry is a simple dalliance?"

He swallowed and stammered.

"Of course you didn't," she laughed.

Lydia toasted Edna. "A belated congratulations on your marriage. I've met Eugen, a wonderful man, who adores poetry and strong woman."

"We're a rare breed," Alfred said. "Known for living happily ever after."

"This is only my second night away and how I miss him," Vincent said. "I will not tour again without him. I detest tours. Don't tell anyone, but I'm truly very shy. And now I know why. I'm made of granite. So that's why I'm so high strung."

"Since Alfred has jumped the gun, let me finish our confession," Lydia said.

"Let's see," Vincent said. "He believes I'm half divine and have something in common with Keats and Whitman—something that makes him nervous. You gonna top that?"

"You bet I am," Lydia grinned. "At Vassar, I was much more smitten with Keats and poetry than even you knew. And I've become more so, much more so. We follow you and your work very closely—and we'd be doing that even if I didn't know you.

"We keep up with all the poets, on the lookout for the ones who could become ...immortal. Last fall we went back and forth—should we really go ahead with this? I saw you were coming to read at the Susan B. Anthony dedication in November. Frankly, we were very curious how you were faring. You hadn't written poetry in Europe, and you'd been very ill before your surgery. Then we saw you, and heard you."

"Take up the song, forget the epitaph," Alfred interrupted.

"Not your turn, Alfred," Lydia said. "We were thrilled. By your strong voice. By your poetry. To see you feeling so much better. Your admirers insisted you hold court. We retreated to the corner and whispered like school children and vowed to plunge ahead. We caught you as you left and made you promise you'd come back to Washington to visit us."

"You were rather insistent," Vincent said.

"Jump to the good part, darling," Alfred said.

"We have something we very much want to tell you. And things," she winced, "we very much want to ask you."

"How intriguing," Vincent said.

"I fear you'll find it more odd than intriguing," Lydia said. "We want to reveal, just to you, our hidden literary passions. And to talk candidly, with you, of your work, your literary reputation, your place in the canon."

"My oh my," Vincent said. "We'll talk candidly, of course. And since Alfred sees that I'm a solitary, grim New Englander, he knows that deep in my cold heart I'm extremely private and detest all that hoo-ha in the newspapers. So we'll also talk privately. Every word to be held in the strictest confidence, n'est-ce pas?"

"We want that very much too," Alfred said. "In fact, what we tell you tonight can go no further, ever."

"We insist on that," Lydia. "As do you."

"I love secrets," Vincent said. "And secret literary affairs, better yet. Less of a strain, wouldn't you agree, Alfred, than all those supposedly secret love affairs of mine you've heard all about? Now stop teasing me. Both of you. Drop your knickers!"

"Off they come," Lydia said. "Alfred and I are more than poetry lovers. Our true passion is our secret affair with Keats and Whitman. We indulge our fetish right here at this table. Thus these piles you see in front of us."

"Will the evening end with them scattered on the floor?" Vincent laughed.

Lydia grinned at her and plowed on. "We spend our most pleasurable days right here, reading Keats and Whitman aloud, or reciting them over lunch and wine. With dessert and coffee—or more wine some days—we pore over everything new we can find written about their poetry and their lives. If it's warm enough we walk to our favorite place, a wonderful rock in the creek, where the water makes music that perfectly accompanies their poetry.

"Then, in the tranquility of the late afternoon, we put our books aside and speculate about the mysteries of their poetry and their lives and shriek with glee when we discover little epiphanies, just like you and I did at Vassar. And after dinner, if it's not too cold, we take our poetic musings out under the moonlight."

"How utterly romantic," Vincent said. "A love affair with a secret canon, to which man and wife bring such passions to bear. You two dropping your knickers is getting me—I won't say it. But I will tell you, I do still carry a torch…for Keats, a torch you ignited those long nights way back when."

She rose and approached the fire to recite:

Ode on a Grecian Urn

Thou still unravish'd bride of quietness,
  Thou foster-child of silence and slow time,
Sylvan historian, who canst thus express
  A flowery tale more sweetly than our rhyme:
What leaf-fring'd legend haunts thy shape
  Of deities or mortals, or of both,
    In Tempe or the dales of Arcady?
  What men or God are these? What maidens loth?
What mad pursuit? What struggles to escape?
  What pipes and Timbrels? What wild ecstasy?

"I will stop right there. I must hear more of your confession."

Lydia sighed. "To hear you recite Keats. Oh my, I didn't imagine how exquisite that pleasure would remain. It makes me—giddy."

"You've got Lydia swooning," Alfred smiled. "I'd better get some hors d'oeuvres for us to nibble on, so we don't get too zozzled too quick."

"And a fresh batch of martinis, too," Lydia said, struck by how much she wanted to be alone with Vincent. The second he left the room Lydia ran to her and took her hands. "You must think us batty, our obsession. But what a grand time we have with it. It's our life's inspiration, second only to our lovely Alberta. Even more batty, we find that keeping our obsession hidden—our own little secret—makes it is yet more satisfying."

"Secret affairs are like that," Vincent said.

"Not only do we fancy keeping our canon secret, we intend to pass the secret on to Alberta. It sounds so silly. But Alfred and I adore the idea of this strange, private family tradition."

"You're making me jealous," Vincent said. "Eugen and I should find a place in the country and come up with a grand secret."

"We loved *Second April* when it came out in '21. And then *Harp-Weaver and Other Poems*—it's the others I love most. That convinced us. You are one of the great ones. Alfred spilled those beans already. The sonnets—the most austere ones—are what put him over the top. He prefers the ones not about love. He worries that your detractors, to deny you your proper standing, will typecast you as a sentimental female love poet."

"They would like to deny me much more than that."

They swung their held hands between them like young girls.

"We see that," Lydia said. "Those dismayed gentleman critics. When your work is too brave and revealing for them, they call you flippant. When it's too sincere and straightforward for their fuddy-duddy tastes, they call you sentimental."

"Sentimental? Oh boy," said Vincent. "That there's irony."

"You've still reaching new heights. Oh, dear Vincent, how I hope you can keep doing that. I can't wait to see what you do next."

"I'm with you on that."

"Still, I keep insisting to Alfred, your lyric love poetry should never ever be overlooked. You're a master."

She lowered her voice.

"I'm breaking the promise Alfred and I made to take turns reciting you. But I wanted to be alone with you for this one."

Alfred overheard and stopped short of turning the corner.

"Since the first time I read this, right after Thanksgiving, as soon as I got my hands on *Harp-Weaver and Other Poems*, I've been thinking of you, so anxious to see you.

What lips my lips have kissed, and where, and why,
I have forgotten, and what arms have lain
Under my head till morning; but the rain
Is full of ghosts tonight, that tap and sigh
Upon the glass and listen for reply,
And in my heart there stirs a quiet pain
For unremembered lads that not again
Will turn to me at midnight with a cry.
Thus in winter stands the lonely tree,
Nor knows what birds have vanished one by one,
Yet knows its boughs more silent than before:
I cannot say what loves have come and gone,
I only know that summer sang in me
A little while, that in me sings no more.

Lydia squeezed Vincent's hands and tumbled further into her eyes and teared up. Vincent embraced her and whispered. "I must tell you, while we're alone, you still stir me so. Do I still stir you?"

"Kiss me," Lydia whispered. "Like we always wanted to."

Vincent took her by the shoulders and they began a slow, luxurious kiss. Alfred's curiosity, inflamed by his not having heard a peep since Lydia finished reciting, propelled him around the corner, sporting a pitcher sloshing in one hand and a sloppy cheese and cracker plate gripped by the other. Vincent saw him first and brushed her lips across Lydia's cheek and gently re-hugged her. "I'm comforting my sweetie, all weepy from reciting my poem of lost love," she said.

"Did you get to the best part, Lydia dear?" he asked.

"We're on the verge," she giggled, then took one step back and grasped Vincent's hands. "My dear, we want very much to invite you into our little clandestine family canon. We want to expand the Rock Creek Canon, as we call it, to include Keats, Whitman, *and* Edna St. Vincent Millay. These stack of books and papers, it's more than Keats and Whitman. It's you, too."

Edna grinned like a naughty elf. "Now I'm sure I'm dreaming. I'm filled to the brim with pleasure and warmth, and my luscious bearcat sweetie and her handsome beau just dropped their knickers and broke out their secret poetic draught. It stirs me deep, for it's the same one Keats lusted for—

O, for a draught of vintage! that hath been
  Cool'd a long age in the deep-delved earth,
Tasting of flora and the country green,
  Dance, and Provencal song, and sunburnt mirth!

"You give me a generous whiff, but hesitate to offer me a swig. You say you *want* to invite me into your canon, but first you need to ask me things. But I ask first, why me?"

"The brilliance of your work, of course" Alfred said.

"Plus you'd be a perfect canon mate," Lydia said. "It's uncanny. Keats and Whitman and you—all renegades, rebel poets who stormed the gates."

"I learned a great lesson from Keats," Vincent said. "He was on his great tear, writing his best stuff as he managed for months to stay away from what's her name."

"Fanny Brawne," Alfred said.

"Yeah—her. He finished 'To Autumn' and was working on *The Fall of Hyperion* and composed that amazing passage—the most powerful Keats—where the priestess Moneta—keeper of the defeated Titans, sole priestess of Hyperion's desolate despair—parts her veils to show herself to our intrepid poet, who has dared to enter her forsaken lair.

Then saw I a wane face,
Not pin'd by human sorrows, but bright-blanched
By an immortal sickness which kills not;
It works a constant change, which happy death
Can put no end to; deathwards progressing
To no death was that visage...

"It still chills me. It was beyond anything Keats had ever done. Away from Fanny what's-her-name, he composes those stunning lines for an epic that would surpass even his great odes. Talk about reaching a new peak. But bless his young yearning heart, he's overcome by his hots for her. He stops writing and returns to London to see her. She drives him mad with desire. He can't have her unless he marries her. Which he can't. Because he's broke and homeless. He suffers a nervous breakdown. His great run is over. Never again would he work on his great epic. In fact, he writes no more poetry at all. Zilch. His tuberculosis worsens. He goes to Rome and dies.

"Keats lesson number one. Never let head-over-heels love distract from your poetry."

"Yes, he did go back to her and vow to drop poetry and somehow make money," Alfred said. "But what you're leaving out is that his crazy love for her helped fuel his great run. Madly enthralled by her, his only escape was to write, sometimes in a fever, like I've heard you do."

"You are a real smarty pants, aren't you?" Vincent said. "Once I believed no man or woman could ever truly touch my soul. Then this lovely man I'd exchanged many wonderful letters with, whom I'd dreamed of meeting, came to see me just before he got shipped off to the war. I was wrong—I did love him, madly. That was as close I ever came to Keats' soul-crushing heartbreak. I didn't write desperate love letters like Keats did. I wrote poetry. One sonnet after another, including the golden vessel one."

"Arthur Ficke," Alfred said.

"Don't ever mention his name again," Vincent said.

Lydia threw off her shoes and cleared her throat and stood tiptoe at the end of the table.

Into the golden vessel of great song
Let us pour all our passion; breast to breast
Let other lovers lie, in love and rest;
Not we,—articulate, so, but with the tongue
Of all the world: the churning blood, the long
Shuddering quiet, the desperate hot palms pressed
Sharply together upon the escaping guest,
The common soul, unguarded, and grown strong.
Longing alone is singer to the lute;
Let still on nettles in the open sigh
The minstrel, that in slumber is as mute

As any man, and love be far and high,
That else forsakes the topmost branch, a fruit
Found on the ground by every passer-by.

"You recite me beautifully," Vincent said.

"I told you you'd do wonderfully," Alfred said. "Though you are breaking our promise to recite snippets rather than entire poems."

"It would be a sin to stop in the middle of that one," Vincent said. "Keats lesson number two. Technique. As he told Shelley: 'Load every rift with ore.' I latched onto that one, too. That's why I prefer sonnets. Overload 'em with Keatsian ore, then use my New England flint, sharpened with my strained grimness—eh, Alfred? —to chisel 'em down to the hardest, shiny granite."

She drank.

"Keats does have flint and iron in him, like you," Alfred said.

Vincent snickered. "You think I'm being too flinty hard tonight? When I'm feeling healthier and better than I've felt in years? When I'm getting slowly plastered but not yet too lit. When I'm with such beautiful, adoring, poetry-loving company? Does it surprise you that shy, flinty me is yapping away so?"

"Yap on, please?" Lydia said. "You're making me dreamy."

"I'll tell you one Walt Whitman story, never ever to be repeated. When I say I believed at one point that no man could ever hurt me, that's what I *thought* I'd learned from an older fellow I was mad about when I was at Vassar. What I actually learned is that in matters of love it's always better to be the wanted—not the wantor."

"You never told me about your love affairs," Lydia said. "Other than that girl in Maine, before you came to Vassar, you rascal, when you discovered you could cast a spell with your touch, make a girl absolutely crave you."

"We'd better skip that one," Vincent said. "Would be too much for Alfred, don't you think?"

"I'm sure it would be," Lydia said.

"Damn it!" said Alfred. "You must tell me later, Lydia."

"This fellow was much older than me, very mysterious, went under an assumed name," Vincent said. "A sad and very sensitive soul. The initial spell I cast on him wore off quickly. He wouldn't see me for months and months. Told me in letters that we'd have to be content with spiritual love. How satisfying can that be? Sent me love poems, but still wouldn't see me. I tried to make him jealous by writing back about my Vassar seductions. No luck. Said he found those beautiful, like Sappho would.

"Playing hard to get made me more determined, since meanwhile I'm charming everybody I set my sights on. I pleaded with him to see me one more time. He finally relented and I went to his apartment and nestled at his feet like I'd done before when he liked me being his snuggle pup. He read a little of his own poetry to me. Didn't do much for me. Then he asked me whether I liked Walt Whitman. I knew Whitman only from a high school textbook with a picture of the Old Gray Poet, or whatever his moniker was, and below it that god awful "Captain! My Captain!" poem. Talk about sentimental.

"My old fellow, is his silk robe in his favorite chair with only a reading lamp on, opens up *Leaves of Grass* and tells me there's nothing that can match taking flight with Whitman. I'm dubious and begin to fret that I'm in for a long listen because my friend has had a snoot full and doesn't even offer me a drink. So I'm antsy twice over."

"Then I hear those opening lines and all of a sudden don't give a hoot about hooch or how long he'll go on reading. Whitman stuns me. His audacity. His ecstasy. His lines of free verse are like nothing I've ever heard. How did he ever come up with that stuff? He was a newspaper hack and a pulp novelist—a lousy one. Yet I'm bedazzled by the beauty of his yawping. Talk about touched by the Muses. I want some of whatever they gave him. And I'm embarrassed for myself. How could I be such a sap to have figured him for a sad old man who best poem was about a dead president?

"Then my fellow jumps to 'The Sleepers.' I'm astounded by the blatant sexuality. People find me scandalous? How did he ever get away with that? He pretends he's a woman! Turns into a flying peeping Tom!

"My fellow sees I'm getting bright-eyed and says wait until you hear the *Children of Adam* and *Calamus* poems. I've never memorized any Whitman—free verse is tough. He reads me that part that says something about love juice and I can't believe my ears.

"Wait!" Alfred said. "We can make use of our piles."

"Splendid," Vincent said and drank and winked at Lydia.

"Only if you find it quickly," Lydia said, matching Vincent's sips and winking back.

"Got it!" he said:

Love-thoughts, love juice, love-odor, love yielding, love-
Climbers, and the climbing sap,
Arms and hands of love, lips of love, phallic thumb of love,
breasts of love, bellies press'd and glued together with
love

"You think I could get away with that?" Vincent said. "Next my fellow reads the one about the oak growing in Louisiana. Beautiful verse but also, I can't help thinking, very phallic."

"Hold on," Alfred said. "Here:

. . . its look, rude, unbending, lusty, made me think of myself. . .

"That's it," Vincent said. "I can tell from my friend's voice that he's getting wound up, like he did years before when we'd get all lovey-dovey. And damn if I'm not getting kind of tingly myself and wondering whether he's working up to something—maybe a grand finale, for we'd never gone beyond petting.

"Then he closes the book and tells me a story.

"In the published version of his poem about New Orleans, Whitman says all he can remember is the time he spent with a woman he met there who loved him. My mysterious fellow says he knows a professor at Columbia, a Whitman scholar, who found the original manuscript of the poem. Turns out in the original version, it wasn't a woman, it was a man."

"Ye gods," Alfred said. "Your friend knew Emory Holloway."

"Hush," Lydia said.

"So my fellow says to me, 'Dear child, this is our last visit. I'm going away, likely to die. I do love you, the way a father loves a child. I have not meant to be cruel, but I must be discrete, like

Whitman in his time. You see, Walt Whitman speaks to me, like Sappho to you. Do you understand?'

"It dawns on me what a dumbbell I've been. The few times we'd fooled around smooching, he insisted we do it in the dark, and I realize he'd been pretending, imagining me to be a girlish young fellow. That's why we never got past necking. Isn't that a hoot? All that time trying to seduce him. Now I did learn from years of chasing him that it's always better to be the sought-after than the seeker. But I learned, too, that it's damn hard to get a fellow to go for you when he prefers men."

"I know a story about that very thing," Lydia said. "It is damn hard, but not impossible. So what did you say to your old fellow?"

"I thanked him for opening my eyes to a great poet, then said we were two ships that passed in the night—he preferred his own sex, while I'd been zigzagging and come to prefer the opposite sex, except for special occasions. I didn't mention that last part.

"The next day I read *Leaves* of the Grass and couldn't have agreed less with him that Whitman was discrete. Maybe he tempered himself when he was older, for the sake of reaching more readers. If that's a crime, lock me up. Why do you think I look like a chaste librarian on my book covers? I don't claim to know Whitman well, but I do know only a great poet could write *Leaves of Grass*."

"A pure poet," Lydia said.

"To my favorite Whitman line," Vincent raised her glass. "'Whatever satisfies the soul is truth.'"

"To tonight," Alfred toasted. "To being waylaid by beauty." He put down his empty glass and stepped toward the fire and turned and faced them.

> I should not so have ventured forth alone
> At dusk upon this unfrequented road.
> I am waylaid by beauty. Who will walk
> Between me and the crying of the frogs?
> Oh, savage Beauty, suffer me to pass
> That am a timid woman, on her way
> From one house to another!

"That," he said, "is a proper Millay sonnet snippet."

"Ha!" said Vincent. "Two lines short of the entire poem. And how the modernists hate those exclamation marks. Too innocent and straightforward. At least there aren't any elisions in it. Those infuriate them. Too simple and o'er used by us romantics.

"Before I take my turn reciting, I'll tell you what your two are tip-toeing around. You worry that if you induct me, I might fizzle out, end up a forgotten nobody."

Lydia turned stricken and put her face in her hands.

"What is it?" Vincent said.

"We do fret about your future standing. But not because of our little canon. Because your poetry, your standing, should never diminish. You should be immortal, read long after we've all gone, like Keats and Whitman."

"I do hanker for immortality. What poet doesn't. When they wheeled me in for my operation—it was much more serious than we let on to the newspapers—I told a dear friend, 'Well, if I die now, I shall be immortal.' That may have been my best shot," she laughed. "You know, *femme fatale*, tragic death at a young age, etcetera.

"But I refuse to worry about my place in the canon. The canonists, I only hope, can never dictate whose poetry is read. I don't expect them to treat me kindly. My hunch is the gatekeepers will say I fall short as a 'pure poet,' to use your phrase, and will try to confine my reputation to my rebellious-woman persona, the loose floozy of the Village. When my defenders point to my body of work—and there will be lots more of it, I promise you—my detractors will say I was driven by money and fame more than poetic vision. As though being poor and hustling to make a living means your poetry isn't as pure. As though the passions of poetry must be coddled, can't exist as purely in those whose must deal with mundane realities, like paying the rent."

"Who could ever say that?" Alfred said. "Keats and Whitman were never free from that struggle."

"When I got to the Village after Vassar, I had fifty dollars. I couldn't leave my sister Norma and mother behind—all for one and one for all. I told Norma, it's going to be hard, baby. But we'll make it. She came first. Couldn't pay the gas bill in our third-floor walk-up. Got so cold the violets on the windowsill froze."

"You poor girl," Lydia said. "I wish you'd called me."

"*Renascence and Other Poems* came out in December. I knew I'd never get a penny from that. Mother came, and we moved to Charlton Street. We fell behind on the rent and got evicted just before Christmas. I had to make some money. I wrote and wrote and wrote and got some poems published in magazines and sold fiction under a fake name and we scraped by, Mother and Norma working any odd jobs they could find."

"Then you began your great Keats-like run," Lydia said. "You wrote all the poems that went into *A Few Figs from Thistles*. Then from summer '19 to summer '20, you churned out everything in *Second April*, and half of what's in *The Harp Weaver and Other Poems*."

"Worked around the clock," Vincent said. "Finished my play, too."

"You were a wreck by the end though," Lydia said. "You took the *Vanity Fair* job in Paris. What we heard and read about you sparked our worries. You seemed driven to take lovers, to scorch the candle at both ends. Worse yet, you stopped writing poetry."

"After my Keats-like run—I love that you call it that—I did come apart," Vincent said. "I chased Eros frantically and caught him, over and over. In Paris. All over Europe. I repeated at a faster, crazier clip my days in the Village. It wrecked me. I had to stop. I met an amazing man and got married. Then I got over that dreadful surgery and began to work again. Finished my first new sonnet just last August. Composed it all in my head and dictated it to a friend.

Lydia recited:

I see so clearly now my similar years
Repeat each other, shod in rusty black
Like one hack following another hack
In meaningless procession, dry of tears,
Driven empty…

"So sublime and revealing," Alfred said.

"Eugen is the farthest you can find from a tradition-bound man," Vincent said. "He's a free thinker, a true admirer of strong woman.

He worships me."

"So we've heard," Lydia said.

"I've had two dreams come true since my European collapse. A wonderful, grown-up man with the means to care for me loves me and wants nothing more than for me to write poetry."

She paused and sipped.

"And the second one?" Alfred said.

Her smile turned mischievous. "He denies me nothing. Including my freedom to love whomever I want, whenever I please. Lydia won't believe this, but I honestly haven't thought about that. Until tonight."

Alfred's eyes refused to stop widening. Lydia's breath caught and made her gulp.

"But so far at least, you two are bringing forth more the poet in me than my out-of-practice Eros chaser. God, how I love that you call me a pure poet! Pure and flinty!"

She threw down the rest of her drink and let go a raucous laugh.

A tug of war broke out in Alfred. Aspiring lust yanked full bore while his ever-dutiful love for Lydia and sense of propriety dug in their heels. He wished he could read Lydia's mind. He wondered if Vincent could so inflame her that he could go along for the ride, indulge in what would be the wildest adventure of their life. He downed his drink.

Lydia's bemused smile gave cover while her mind spilled forth still potent Vassar memories of Vincent's legendary coyness and seductiveness—she'd slept with a score of women and could've bedded many more, including her. She desperately hoped Vincent's declaration of poet trumping seductress would turn out to be a gambit, a clever way to put the idea of a forever secret wild night back in play after their tasty kiss.

"So your seductress is off duty, at least for the moment," she said. "No doubt she could wreak havoc."

"You think so?" Vincent said. "At Vassar you epitomized what I was still learning: always be the wanted, never the wantor. That's why I was always...reluctant." She winked openly at Lydia.

"You better stop being so tantalizing, both of you" Alfred said. "I endeavor to think about pure poets rather than my fantasies, which, at the insistence of these martinis, I readily admit both excite and frighten me, for I've been told, Vincent, that men who see you in the buff can never get over it."

"You blaming that on me?" she laughed. "Here's another secret you damn well better keep. I was a virgin until I was twenty-six, when I decided I could partake just like men do. Why must some men, once you've made love, go head over heels and believe they possess you and must have you again and again? I shun those weak and demanding ones. But those wise enough to share passion and not insist on trying to possess me? We're lifelong friends.

"Now listen to this one, and remember it if you can, for it could be years before I'm satisfied with it enough to publish it.

> *Women have loved before as I love now;*
> *At least, in lively chronicles of the past—*
> *Of Irish water by a Cornish prow*
> *Or Trojan waters by a Spartan mast*
> *Much to their cost invaded—here and there,*
> *Hunting the amorous line, skimming the rest,*
> *I find some women bearing as I bear*
> *Love like a burning city in the breast.*
> *I think however of all alive*
> *I only in such utter, ancient way*
> *Do suffer love; in me alone survive*
> *The unregenerate passions of a day*
> *When treacherous queens, with death upon the thread,*
> *Heedless and willful, took their knights to bed.*

"You've begun another great run, haven't you!" Lydia said.

"I sure hope so." Vincent said. "But here's the real question about that. Having lovers has so inspired me, if I'm over that, how will I stay inflamed? So far, so good. Don't get me wrong. I'm glad Eugen insists on an open marriage, for I still believe one must surely be either undiscerning or frightened to love only one person, when the world is so full of gracious and noble spirits."

Lydia's desire brought her out of her chair, stood her up to wander off down the hall to the master bedroom and see if Vincent would follow and Alfred would stay put. She gripped the sides of the table.

Vincent read her mind. "The trick for us so-called romantics in these so-called Roaring Twenties is to figure out how to hit the brakes," she said. "Old habits die hard. Recklessness is exhilarating. Liquor rouses up that heady sense that we're free, that anything can happen. Which tonight proves true. But passions are not inexhaustible. It's tempting to think you can indulge them all, spark them with liquor and other things to get those heightened sensations of life."

"We love our flights of wild fun," Lydia said. "That's one reason we worry so about yours."

"We've learned to fear them," Alfred said. "That's how much we love them."

Vincent smiled at Lydia. "I recall in minute detail the great allure wild nights hold for you. I can't help it. You know how I can pull up a memory and study it for minutes like a photograph. I wish you could see what I see right now."

Fresh pink spotted Lydia from cheeks to chest.

"My god," Alfred said. "You're a daemon with an eidetic memory. I shall make every attempt to dissuade myself from imagining what brings such blush to my beloved. But I am weak." He rolled his eyes.

"You two do slay me," Vincent said.

"My dearest Vincent," Lydia smiled, "unless you object, we hereby officially expand the Rock Creek Canon to Keats, Whitman, and Millay. Not a provisional expansion, mind you. For all time. And not that you need inspiration, but our silly, selfish hope is that your inclusion in our little group might in some small way buttress, even kindle your future poetry. For we believe our canon is blessed by the Muses."

"This dream just keeps getting better," Vincent laughed. Her face turned serious. She blinked away tears. "I'm more honored than I've ever been. Truthfully, this is much better than the Pulitzer Prize."

"Alfred and I promised each other we would ask one more thing of you. Will you write something for us, to give to us, something to...bear witness to your induction into our secret canon? We'd love something for Alberta, when she's grown up enough to inherit the family secret. What a thrill it would be if you'd write a little something for us."

"I'd love to," Vincent said. "Now that's some concrete inspiration—an assignment. I'll do it right away. Oh, what fun, to write something that will be kept secret forever. We'll never speak directly of it again, or of this night."

"To our clandestine canon and our untellable evening," Lydia toasted.

"Now that's not to say we can't flirt among ourselves with our secret. Eugen and I will have a party for you two. In New York. Think of the fun! We can make obscure references to our immortal Rock Creek canon, to our forever under-wraps trio—our poetic ménage á trois. And when we wink at one another, we'll pretend we think no one is watching, but we'll make sure someone is. Our trick at Vassar—remember?—to make the other girls jealous? We'll be just as silly. And it'll be even more fun."

She finished her martini and stood, grabbed her scarf and threw it around her neck.

"When you've still having a wonderful time, that's the time to leave. Before I drink more and begin kissing both of you, since I do count you both foremost among those gracious and noble spirits I say should be loved."

Lydia and Alfred knew they should all move quickly. Alfred fetched her coat and roused the driver, and they heard the car start up.

"I have your address, Lydia. I will mail you my testament. Now walk with me to the car. All of us arm in arm."

"How can we ever thank you?" Lydia said. "This is our dream come true."

"I thank you both for an indescribably marvelous night—I do hope I haven't been dreaming. Now each of you, kiss me on my cheek."

She hurried into the back seat and rolled the window down and threw them kiss after kiss as the car pulled off.

Lydia and Albert walked slowly inside and stared into the fire.

"It does seem like a dream," Alfred said.

"But it's not a dream. We did it. She'll send us something

wonderful. We'll add it to the treasures. We'll have her in the canon for all time. It's brilliant. Expand the canon without using up your single tell."

"You could have seduced her, I think," Alfred said. "Or visa versa."

"I wasn't sure, and I didn't want the end of her monogamy to be pinned on me, though I wouldn't bet on it lasting."

"So you chose discretion, the better part of valor."

"I did," she smiled, "partly because I wasn't sure you'd leave us be."

"We'll never know," he grinned, and drained the pitcher in their glasses, "To tonight. To our success—recruiting a pure poet to keep our Rock Creek fellows company."

"And to our hope that Vincent ain't done yet," Lydia said. "And most of all, to saving our secret for Alberta."

Three days later they received Vincent's testimonial, handwritten on stationary from the Sheraton with a note attached (Exhibit E).

Dearest Lydia and Alfred,

I worked on the enclosed like a ditch-digger, starting as soon as I got back to my room and writing through the next afternoon. I hope it suits.

I'll never forget one moment in our evening of secrets. I'll mail you an invite to the party I promised. Remember—no mentions of the RCC, only hints and winks.

Love,
Vincent

January 18, 1924
Testimonial to the Rock Creek Canon

This testimonial comprises extemporaneous (after midnight) lines of free verse (free in every sense) and two unperfected sonnets. All are dedicated to Lydia, Alfred, and Alberta, and to the two pure poetic souls whom I join, to linger immortal in Rock Creek forest.

Calling Upon Keats and Whitman (With Very Free Verse)

I call upon you John and Walt, familiarly no less
For I join you for all time

In these woods, this leaved temple of immortality
Where you return from flights of prowess
You are taken aback by my arrival, I've no doubt,
This scared girl from village Maine
Poor, austere, over-indulging, chasing Muses
Through mooned woods until straight out

Struck by this divine poetic afflatus, this Aeolian harp
Draws me dancing after you
I too an ecstatic mix: woman, man, creature
Gypsy soul, singer of forbidden songs
Insatiable, pursuing you Walt
Laying with you pond side, praising calamus
Digesting each other until we summersault
Beyond this universe to the ones 'ere you go
To effuse yourself, as you like to say
Unpack your o'er flowing visions
You mine from streets and sky.

I return to find you John, in endless mellow autumn
Where you grieve no more, love melancholy
O'er come by our poetic dream come true
You awoke and indeed it was truth
The salve of your earthbound heartbreak

I embrace you, embarrass you, plead
Take me to Moneta!
Through your vale of soulmaking
On your leap from writ in water to immortality
Every rift loaded with ever-living ore,
But I need still seek crucibles of pureness
To assure me I stay forever.
I say to both of you, your poetic blood
Runs widespread, forward through the ages.
I claim it; a hearty dose—
Lust for beauty, thirst for ecstasy
I love madly too, but like you,
None more than the Muses.

And I too ecstatic to be touched
By none as much as poesy.
Let us sing deathless songs!
Rejoice in our rhythmic movements
From over-clothed blindness
To naked vision.
Our intimacy is inevitable—
In the canonical sense.

Two unperfected sonnets—

I.

If I die solvent—that is to say,
In full possession of my critical mind,
Not having cast, to keep the woods at bay
In this dark wood—till all be flung behind—
Wit, courage, honour, pride, oblivion
Of the red eyeball and the yellow tooth;
Nor sweat nor howl nor break into a run
When loping Death's upon me in hot sooth;
'Twill be that in my honoured hands I bear
That under no condition to be spilled
Till my blood spills and hardens in the air:
An earthen grail, a humble vessel filled
To its low brim with water from that brink
Where Keats and Whitman learned to drink.

II.

I dreamed I moved among the Elysian fields,
In converse with sweet women long since dead;
And out of blossoms which that meadow yields
I wore a garland for your living head.
Danae, that was the vessel for a day

Of golden Jove, I saw, and at her side,
Whom Jove the Bull desired and bore away,
Europa stood, and the swan's featherless bride.
All these were mortal women, yet all these
Above the ground had had a god for guest;
Freely I walked beside them and at ease,
Addressing them, by them again addressed,
And marveling nothing, for remembering you,
Wherefore I was among them well I know.

As Lydia predicted, Vincent did partake of her freedom, though not until four years later, in 1928, when she chose to ignore Keats lesson number one and fell madly in love with a much younger man. But poetry remained her true love. His long-running and eventually successful attempts to break off the affair inspired what some regard as her finest sonnets and best poetry collection, *Fatal Interview*. In 1931, at the height of the depression, it sold 50,000 copies within months of publication.

29

LOUISE PROUDLY PULLED EXHIBIT E from a metal lock box kept in a separate storage bin and held it in front of me. It was written in long hand, small, straight up-and-down writing, each page sealed in plastic in a zippered leather binder. She read aloud Vincent's note, her dedication and each of the three poems.

"The last two were later published as is," she said. "This first one, of course, never was and never will be."

"Edna is no doubt a fine poet," Cowboy said. "And I get a big kick out of Lydia and Alfred, how clever they were, despite being so smitten. But since she never learned the story, she's not truly part of it, or of your so-called canon, for that matter."

Louise feigned a calm smile. "Vincent not in the story? Not in the canon? You can't be serious."

Cowboy stood and stretched.

"We're talking about the first and only written tell," he said. "So Lydia and Alfred and Edna have a fun night, get juiced on martinis and Edna goes back to her room and, lit on gin, writes some inspired things. You're saying she and her three poems should stand in the story alongside Ezra and June? And Walt and Runaway? And Keats?—I'm sure Jack will get a lot of him in there. I'd say Edna deserves a footnote, at most."

Louise sucked in two long breaths, enough to spew fire. "You know full well how determined I am to see Vincent fully restored to her rightful place. How for years I've worked the literary establishment, the publishers, the bloggers, anyone who gives a damn about poetry. How hard I've fought to reclaim the contested ground taken from her by her distracters—beating back, among others, the very charge Vincent predicted—ironically leveled by a young, hot-shot female striver climbing the literati ladder—that Vincent's poetry was less than pure because she strove to make a living and succeeded. You, more than anyone, know how hard I've fought, in every way imaginable, for every inch of greatness Vincent has reclaimed, including funding the restoration of Steepletop."

She unclenched and re-clenched her fists. She held up her right arm. It quivered. She'd stopped herself from slapping him. Her eyes veered from anger to sadness and back to anger, if not contempt.

"And after all these years, you want to steal away her night of unsung glory, the night she came into our story. How dare you speak of her as an interloper, a footnote. My dynasty inducted her into the Rock Creek Canon, ninety-plus years ago. And rightfully so!"

Cowboy played for time by over-savoring a bourbon swig. He gave the slightest nod and surrendered, but not before taking a nasty parting shot.

"If Jack buys all that and puts her in, she's in. Fine. But she's not top-drawer material in your canon. Not in the same class as Walter, or even Keats, your two heavyweights. She'll be riding their coattails."

Louise let her arm drop and even managed a faint smile.

"I simply can't fathom why you're not proud to have her. America's greatest love poet. To this day one of its very finest sonneteers. Among the very last poets to be widely known and loved who could pack halls with devoted readers."

She eased us the rest of the way back to bonhomie by stretching her arms in the air and doing toe-touches.

"Vincent belongs with Walter and John. They love her company," she said. "That first sonnet is an exquisite tribute to them—her humble vessel filled by them. Imagine the fun the three of them are having."

She grabbed Cowboy by the shoulders and kissed him hard and quick on the lips.

"That's what Vincent does to Walter!" she said. "And imagine her and Keats." Her smile amped up to full bloom.

Cowboy turned his hands palms up. "You see what I'm up against with your two? There's the story I know. Then there's the wild, wound-up one you two conjure up, dragging in all your favorites like they're here at the same time, together, a gang of vagabonds—unruly, time-traveling poets come to highjack the story."

Louise giggled and applauded. "That is a perfect description! Why you're every bit as poetic as Alfred, when you put your mind to it."

She amazed me. How could she be so lively, not dead tired. I jumped to my feet and rode her wakeful surge. "What's most amazing is that our vagabonds live in their own, actual real-life canon that births its own members, its agents of canonical influence, who, in the case of Vincent, go on to expand the originating story that spawns the canon in the first place. That's beyond meta-fiction."

"Got no clue what your highfalutin mumbo-jumbo means," Cowboy chuckled. "All I'm saying is the story doesn't need all the razzmatazz you two whip into it. My no-magic-spells, no time-traveling, non-Twilight Zone version is plenty amazing."

He squatted down to his bottle, took a short pull, then rose up revived, spread his arms and voiced his hero.

> *You shall no longer take things at second or third hand...nor*
> *   look through the eyes of the dead...nor feed on the specters*
> *   in books,*
> *You shall not look through my eyes either, nor take things from me,*
> *You shall listen to all sides and filter them for yourself.*

You are asking me questions, and I hear you;
I answer that I cannot answer...you must find out for yourself.

"That is to say, my dear professor, that you'll decide for yourself how the story is written. This is the last thing I'll say about that. It's Walter's story. He birthed it when he created the first treasures, including the oath, and then, in order to save Runaway, jiggered the oath to allow the single tell, so the story could live on, which is the only reason the three of us are here. Period."

He put his hand to his mouth and half-heartedly stifled a burp that nonetheless enveloped me in bourbon vapors.

"Break time," I blurted, and sprung up into the tunnel. I shimmied through it without incident, relieved myself, then nestled in among the rocks below the entrance and lit a cigarette. She came out first again and stood over me.

"How splendid was that?" she said. "The story and the canon are coming through us, building to a crescendo. I meant every word I said to Cowboy. But what matters most to me is that the Muses and the poets speak to you. Hear them, and your tell will be whatever it's meant to be. I'll help you anyway I can."

"I'd rather work somewhere besides Cowboy's basement," I said.

"You'll work at my place," she said. "I've got all the Keats and Whitman and Vincent poetry. You can reread whatever you need to. I'll read and recite whatever you want. I'll even brew you coffee and feed you lunch. We'll start in the morning."

I was too uneasy to properly express my gratitude. A worry nagged at me: what if the story is one of those never meant to be written down, like wild animals who can never be tamed.

She kissed me on my forehead and disappeared. To keep awake I lit another cigarette. Three drags in Cowboy cleared his throat.

"That was a fun time, huh" he said. "I got Louise good and riled up, and even got you spouting your fancy-pants professor talk."

I figured he'd be staying for Louise's slumber party. "I'm heading back," I said.

"Me too," he said. "Wait while I tuck her in."

30

THE DEAD NIGHT SILENCE broke only once. I swear it was the cry of a departing nightingale. From the open flats along the creek Cowboy saw a shooting star. I missed it. I asked him to tell me about Louise's youthful downfall. She'd told him about it only once, years ago, he said. He gave me the zippered-lip and made me promise never to repeat him.

"The three of them, her and her two fellows, all wannabe poets, were young and foolish enough to believe they'd found nirvana, their own separate universe, centered in Louise's elegant apartment, staying up for days, powered by who knows what kind of drugs, scribbling poems and wandering the park in the dead of night. Taking days to recover, then repeating themselves. That went on for months, the clock ticking down on all of them.

"The fellow she was intimate with snapped first. After another run of sleepless days and nights, they finally crashed. 'Burnt to a crisp' she said, all inspiration spent, nothing left to say, beyond exhaustion. They pulled the dark curtains and collapsed in her big bed. Louise and the other fellow went dead to sleep. But her lover boy was beyond sleep, couldn't shut himself down. He got up and anguished alone in the living next room all night. At some point he convinced himself he'd heard unmistakable sounds of love-making. He barged in and jostled them from a dead sleep—he was certain they were only pretending—and screamed at both of them for betraying him. She and the other fellow were astounded, couldn't believe the state he'd worked himself into. They denied again and again that anything had happened, and did their best to calm him, to convince him he'd imagined it, or been dreaming, that he just needed to sleep, and when he woke up, he'd realize how crazy he'd been acting and all would be back to normal. Their denials and advice only further enraged him, and he stormed out as Louise, semi-unhinged, wailed for him to stop, to stay, to come to his senses.

"They waited all that day and night for him to return. Louise's friend gave up and went home, but she wouldn't leave for fear she might miss the return of her lover, his senses regained. But his delusion of betrayal only grew worse, obsessing him, fueling him as he wandered the streets and the park for days on end. The first time Louise emerged from her apartment she spotted him huddled in a door way across the street, a big back pack strapped on. Though he looked like a tormented, insane homeless man, she was still hugely relieved to see him, and began to cross the street, but he gave her such a hateful stare she stopped short, and he fled, looking at her as though she were a monster.

"That's the moment she realized her worst fear was true. Their months of crazy living had done him in, pushed him over the edge. He'd gone mad.

"She didn't see him again for weeks, until he began to follow her, always at a distance, always wearing a backpack, looking more and more haggard and homeless. Every time she turned around and stopped, he'd run away, but one time she caught up with him and pleaded with him to come with her, to let her help him. He looked at her with a terrible mix of hatred and horror and shoved her away and kept running.

"Weeks passed with no sign of him. One day she was walking up Connecticut Avenue from Dupont Circle, waiting to cross the street, when he rushed her like a coked-up madman and screamed in her face, "Betrayer! Betrayer!" over and over.

"She shoved him away and held him by the shoulders against a building. She'd never betrayed him, she said. That was pure madness. He'd lost his mind. He needed help. She would not abide his insanity. If he came with her, she'd help him. If not, he'd better never bother her again, and if he ever did, she'd call the police and get him committed."

Cowboy touched my arm and stopped walking. "I've never forgotten how she described what happened next. His whole body quivered. He couldn't stop shaking. She saw in his eyes that he knew, if only for an instant, that what she'd said was true. He had lost his mind. Then that look of horrid hatred again filled his eyes, and he spat at her and skulked away, clutching his arms, trying to stop shaking. Louise was so distraught she couldn't go back and be alone in her apartment. She went straight to Aunty's house."

"What happened to him?"

"A lost soul to this day they say. There's some crazy talk that he disappeared into the park and lives hidden away like a hermit. Never mention him. Not to her. Not to William. Not to Zach. Not to anyone. It's my one absolute rule for the park. Maybe the only one. Never, ever speak of him."

He zipped his lips one last time and laid his most intent stare on me. I nodded.

I'd found, like you can in every place, if you dig deep enough, a story forbidden to be spoken.

"What happened with Esther?" I asked

"That was some years later. She was killed in a car wreck. Not too far from here. She'd spent the night before with Louise, at the playhouse.

"Louise was stunned, but stoic. Eli was heartbroken. He dedicated himself and the Zoo Crew to the everlasting memory of Esther. He hung onto the house and eventually bought it, somehow. I suspect

Louise helped him. He never did become a writer. He never did have another girlfriend. But he kept his vow. The Zoo Crew is still going strong, and Esther is still their mythical princess."

"When did you meet Louise?"

"Not too long after she lost Esther."

"How'd you find her?"

"She found me. Pure luck. I didn't often go to Hideaway. I knew the manuscripts by heart. But when I got to feeling real low, I'd go there and pull them out and hold them, the pages and the words so exquisite to the touch. I'd close my eyes and thank Walter and I could see that gleam in my boy's eyes. I'd just started putting the manuscripts away when a woman's voice comes bellowing down the tunnel. 'Helloooooo. Don't be alarmed, whoever you are. I know what's in here. I'm part of it. Like you, I hope.' Her voice and what she said made me smile before I ever saw her. I'll never forget that moment. I've come to believe that I knew what she looked like before I saw because her voice was so alive and so comforting. Then I saw her face, that excited smile she still has. She let me take her hands and help her down, both of us thrilled to find another secret-keeper."

We crossed a bridge.

"So your immediate predecessors, your dad and her Aunty, didn't know each other?"

"Never met," he said. "Our lines separated after Ezra and June. You see, Ezra had fathered his boy down in Carolina, before he came up here."

"Earnest Benjamin," I said.

"Yep. When Earnest B.'s mother died down in Carolina after the Civil War, years after Ezra had skedaddled up here, somebody dropped Earnest B. at The Kingdom of The Happy Land. I kid you not. Founded by freed slaves who came from as far away as Mississippi, picking up others on the way, inspired by their dream of a haven in the empty mountain wilderness they'd heard of at the border of the Carolinas. They made it there, and their dream came true when the wife of a dead Confederate colonel deeded them two hundred acres. Earnest B. never left there, never came up here, as far as we know."

"You figure Ezra must have traveled down there and tracked

down his boy and passed him the story," I said.

"Must have. Don't know when that was, but I do know that Earnest B. passed the story to his boy, John Ezra, my granddaddy, who eventually came north and settled here and brought the *Leaves* inscribed by his daddy."

"You're saying you knew nothing of Louise's family, and their story?"

"I knew June. She was in our story too. But I'd never heard of Lydia and Alfred or seen what Edna left them. That was kept in the Louise's family's house, like my family's *Leaves* was kept at our house. It wasn't until Louise and I sorted out what we wanted to do with the story that we agreed to put the Edna manuscript and Earnest B.'s *Leaves* with the other treasures.

"My bet is that Ezra took Earnest B. that original *Leaves* and gave it to him when he passed him the story. Earnest B. inscribed it years later, as you saw, upon Walter's death. Then at some point Earnest B. passed the story and the *Leaves* to John Ezra, who ended up moving up here."

"Then you and Louise crossed paths and compared stories," I said, "Thus began the great debate."

"Yep. Which has kept us happily together with plenty to talk about all these years," he said.

"But now you've both got to give up your original family versions, and live with the reconciled one that I swore I'd write down."

"So far, so good, I'd say."

"That's not what I'd say."

The trail leveled near the eastern ridge top. Cowboy stopped and sipped studiously on his last inch of bourbon.

"You swear not to repeat this to Louise?"

For the umpteenth time I swore silence.

"In the official written tell, give her everything she wants— muses, canons, Edna—the whole kit and caboodle."

True love. I was happy for them. I knew she wasn't interested in me, not in that way. She was fond of me, quite fond. Mostly because I'd agreed to do what they wanted. But also, I like to think, because she could tell I'd see the story as something much more important than the two of us.

"You're a thoughtful fellow," I said. "Pretty good story-teller, too."

"Thanks for doing that for her," he said, pretending I'd agreed. "Now you can knock the tell right out."

Since we walked side by side, he couldn't see the grin that came on my face. In the twenty-plus years I'd been working on my Keats masterpiece, I've never gotten beyond the second page.

We hopped rock to rock across a wide, low-running stream, crossed an empty road and began slogging up the last hill to home.

"Soon as you're done, we'll have a big celebration," he said. "A long-awaited and momentous occasion."

I envisioned my line-drawn rendition of the Immortal Dinner, which I'd unpinned from my apartment wall, from right above the keyboard, where I could study it meticulously while I failed to write. It resided carefully rolled up in Beauty's trunk inside *Flaming June*, that magical Victorian painting of a young, sleeping woman.

Cowboy said goodnight and headed off to the front of his row-house, up the street from the trailhead. The basement entrance was around back, up the alley from the sitting rock, where I sat and smoked, too riled up for bed. My mind began spinning on its own and landed on a boyhood Christmas Eve. Dear Mom slapped down two slices of Wonder Bread and lathered them with Bluebonnet margarine and spoonfuls of sugar. I endeavored always to never say anything that might hurt her feelings, so I smiled apologetically before pointing to the mold splotching the crust and beyond. "It'll scrape off," she smiled back. "A little mold never killed anybody." We finished our dessert in high spirits, listening to Christmas carols on the radio and admiring our tinsel-laden tree.

The manuscripts sure looked authentic. The accounts Louise and Cowboy told of how the story was passed down to each of them hung together and, more important, rang true to me as they told them. By god, their tale could be true; the manuscripts could be the real thing.

Temptation is the faithful sidekick of good luck. I could go early in the morning and hide in woods and watch for Louise to leave Hideaway. I could retrieve the manuscripts, get them properly authenticated and be credited with a great literary discovery, an absolute bombshell.

I couldn't betray Cowboy and Louise.

I wouldn't steal the manuscripts. I'd give them back. The two of them could still auction them off and cash in. I didn't covet money. But my name forever cemented in literary history?

I couldn't break the solemn oath I swore to Cowboy and Louise and to the Muses and to John Keats himself.

It wouldn't be the first promise I'd ever broken. Cowboy and Louise and the Muses might never forgive me, but my friend John might. His mortal self was never holier-than-thou and always forgiving, even of those who cheated him out of money.

It would make me an untrustworthy scoundrel.

It would be for the sake of literary scholarship.

It would be an act of pure selfishness, all for thirty seconds of fame and a shot, maybe, at a cushy professorship.

It'd be for the sake of an amazing story. I could envision the headline in *The New York Times*, front page, right below the fold: "Heard of Walt Whitman? Thank This Unlikely Pair of Lovers."

I imagined the disappointment in William's face.

I would never double-cross William.

December 28, 1817. The Immortal Dinner is hosted by Benjamin Robert Haydon. He stands in front of his humongous painting, 'Christ's Entry into Jerusalem,' years in the making, still unfinished.

A small crowd gathers round. There is balding William Wordsworth, the famous poet, and bird-chested Charles Lamb, renown essayist and poet. And there's John Keats, only twenty-two, hardly known at all. Hayden has recently completed the portion of the painting of the crowd welcoming Christ. There, among the crowd, are the faces of Wordsworth, Lamb and Keats, all greatly honored to see themselves in Haydon's masterpiece. John's eyes light up. He is very proud of me for resisting temptation. He tips his glass and drinks to me.

I heeled out my cigarette and buried the butt and strode to my basement quarters to rest in peace.

31

I SAT IN THE END seat next to the aisle in the fourth row of my high school auditorium. I faced Haydon's actual apartment, not a stage set. The unfinished painting hung on the back wall, the hugeness of it much more impressive in person. In the foreground I counted seven happy fellows who stood drinking around a long, rectangular dinner table; three others stood nearby and smiled at them.

Dinner had not yet been served and never would be. The mood rose as rambunctious celebration and palpable awe flew from the rising chatter spiked with embraces and fervent handshakes. Heads turned nonstop, for all present were keenly interested in everyone else's every word, all made giddy by the discovery that actual immortality far surpassed their dreams of immortality. Soon all partook in a single conversation about their amazement that immortality could be ever so lively and jointly celebrated. A light blue mist of euphoria drifted over them toward me.

Keats slung down wine and said while he had always fancied himself a true dreamer, he was now certain, for who else ever dared dream of this aesthetic heaven where great spirits converse.

Wordsworth, seated aside the standing throng, said he had never bothered to imagine what immortality would be like, for he knew it was unfathomable even to those assured of it. No one knew what to say to that.

"To the Muses," toasted Keats, "who bring us to greet each other at journey's end."

I held a mason jar full of fresh gin and tonic and toasted with them. The taste of gin and the realization that their celebration had just begun filled me with great pleasure. I startled myself with a loud chuckle and to my relief realized they could neither hear me nor see me, though I sat only twenty-five feet away. Perfect. Nothing was expected of me.

"Let's thank this good fellow for opening our eyes," Hayden boomed, and raised his glass to Walt Whitman.

Keats stepped forward. "To our messenger from the Muses, whose arrival from the future revealed that we dream not in death of a dinner party we once had, but live on, in true immortality."

All raised glasses. Whitman, no longer standoffish, told them the indescribable pleasure he felt in their company, an infinite contentment so unlike the short-lived pleasures of life. I wondered why Emily wasn't there. Blessed relief washed over me. She was there, happily hidden off-stage.

Whitman asked Wordsworth to recite what he believed to be his finest work. A rare smile came to his craggily face as he looked at Keats and Lamb. He would be honored to recite, he said, but be was loathe to cut short their lively conversation, for he had always treasured their talk, despite his dour manner when he was a mortal.

He raised his glass to Keats. "I never doubted you had the mind to be an immortal poet. But I didn't think you'd have time. For when we passed each other on Hampstead Heath that morning, years before you died, I knew your illness had fatal hold of you. I salute you, and I thank the Muses. To John Keats, who lived just long enough to compose the world's greatest odes."

John smiled in embarrassment. "Certainly no greater than yours," he quietly said, then roused the crowd by shouting: "To Haydon! For there's no finer setting for our eternity that his dinner party!"

"To my immortal dinner!" Haydon shouted.

Lamb told Whitman how wonderful it was to be there, if only as a guest who must soon depart. "Unlike your immortal fellows, I don't know who you are, and I never will," he said. "Still, I am touched, immensely so, to be able to congratulate you in person."

"You are a fine, gracious fellow," Whitman replied. "Are you by chance Lamb?" Lamb smiled and nodded yes. Whitman's white hair and long beard turned intensely beautiful and glistened in the mist as he embraced Lamb.

Edna Vincent Millay, in a slinky green dress, entered stage right and filled me with great desire, an unsettling urge to run to her and ask her to go off alone with me. Everyone stopped talking and watched her. I stood. She spotted Keats. "She will not be going anywhere with me," I declared out loud and plunked back down and savored my gin.

She announced to the hushed room that her first desire as an immortal was to touch the face that cloistered the beautiful mind of John Keats. She put her hands on his cheeks and pressed his face against her chest. He stood comfortably, unembarrassed, the small stature that plagued him in mortal life redeemed in cushy delight, and willed the dream to slow. Something caught Millay's eye in the window at the far end of the room. A pinch of worry twirled into the mist like a smidgen of black ink in still water.

There is an odd-looking fellow leaning on the post box outside, she said, cradling Keats' face to her with both hands.

I could see him. His big black hat and long hair looked familiar. His left forearm was propped on the oversized mailbox. His loose-hanging hand perturbed me. It was too long in the wrist and the tips of his long fingers appeared to be missing.

Keats didn't move. Neither did Millay. No one said a word. Haydon strode over to them to break the spell. He didn't recognize Millay, for like Lamb, he was only a guest and would not be staying. He put his hand on John's shoulder and jolted the dream out of its slowness.

"John, there is a fellow just arrived named Roberto who wants to meet you," he said, and led Keats by the arm to a slight man with curly hair and big ears who wore rounded eye glasses and dressed in blue jeans and a polyester shirt.

"When I was kid in Mexico City, I stole an anthology of English poetry and read your Grecian urn poem," Roberto said. "Years afterwards, when, like you, I knew I was dying, I imagined your timeless urn to be a portal to the abyss."

"The abyss of immortality!" Keats smiled. "That's why you're here. That's why we know who you are, Roberto Bolaño. That's why we celebrate your very words: 'I had a vision of torrential grace, burnished like the dreams of heroes.'"

Bliss that I could taste with my eyes filled Roberto's taunt face. It shivered up and down my spine and I repeated out loud: "Torrential grace, burnished like the dreams of heroes."

Millay eyed Roberto but made a beeline for Whitman.

Keats glanced knowingly at me and grinned, the only moment any of them took notice of me. "Roberto!" Keats said. "There is another fine image of yours with which we celebrate our immortality."

The room fell silent. Millay halted her advance on Whitman.

"Tell me," Roberto said.

"'The heroes setting out for immortality, armed only with their writings,'" Keats boomed. "That's us. We made it, didn't we! To Roberto," he exclaimed, and raised his glass.

They all toasted and drank, then for no apparent reason went quiet and absolutely still. I wondered if they'd reached the end of time, the moment they would vanish into forever, but Keats began chanting Roberto's line, the first line of an epic Homeric hymn they would be composing for eternity. The others joined in and repeated it: "Setting out for immortality/armed only with their writings."

A thick, bluish tear that I could see as though I was looking thought a microscope emerged from the corner of Roberto's right eye. I felt it on my face. It slid down to a vein over my right cheek bone and made my face grow immense. The vein soaked up the tear. It would be part of me forever. I touched its slight remains with my fingertip and put the nectar of immortal words on my tongue and vowed to never forget how sweet it tasted.

Millay put her left hand on Walter's chest and whispered in his ear. He grinned as he'd never grinned before. I longed to know what she said, to see what she'd do next, but my eyes were drawn back to the odd fellow leaning on the mailbox who still gazed in the window.

32

I WOKE UP AWASH in the heavy cream that kept the dream's wonders vivid and madly uncapped my bedside pen and scribbled frantically on the blank back pages of Annie Dillard's *Pilgrim at Tinker Creek*. I made myself write single words and short phrases and with my heart still pounding rushed back though my jottings and added details so keenly felt they still lingered. Finished, I stopped for a moment of profound gratitude for whatever state of grace had granted me my singular success in dream recordation.

I reread my notes and added a few more now vaporizing details. I gasped. I thought I might faint. I rushed to the stacks of plastic crates shoved against the wall. I dug through the first crate of books, writers of both poetry and novels. No luck. I dumped out the second and third crates and fell to my hands and knees and shoved several Bolaños to the side and spread books with both hands until I found the rest.

My Brautigans were all nested together. I flipped through the one I wanted and found the italicized passages and earmarked the pages. I underlined the last line of the final one. I dumped the clothes from my canvas bag, stuffed it with my evidence, pulled on my pants and shirt, slung the bag over my shoulder and marched out the door.

Louise had unlocked the gate for me. She leaned over the porch railing in her silky housecoat, the same rich green as Vincent's dream dress.

I heaved my bag on the table and caught my breath. "I wrote down my dream the instant I woke up." I sat and not once lifting my eyes from my scribbles retold it without a hitch.

I held up a paperback. Across the top in big, red letters was the name Richard Brautigan. Below it, in smaller black letters, were three underlined books titles: *A Confederate General from Big Sur*, *Dreaming of Babylon*, and *The Hawkline Monster*. A picture of the man in black, his left elbow resting on a mailbox, the fingers of his left hand oddly disfigured, took up most of the cover.

"Leaning on the mailbox," she said.

"Yep, that's him." I said. "You ever read *Confederate General*?"

"No. I only read one Brautigan," she said. "A very strange one. Something about watermelon."

"*In Watermelon Sugar*," I said. "Brautigan was a destitute Beat poet in the late 1950s. *Confederate General* was his first novel, in 1964, before *Trout Fishing in America* made him a sensation in 1967. It sold four million copies. Got him labeled forever as a hippie writer. *Watermelon Sugar* came after that.

"In *Confederate General*, the narrator goes with his crazy friend to Big Sur. It's based on Brautigan's real life—he visited a friend who lived in Big Sur in a primitive shack. The narrator, Jesse, is Brautigan. His friend, called Lee Mellon in the book, claims one of his ancestors was a confederate general. Before they leave San Francisco for Big Sur, Jesse and Lee Mellon get drunk and go to the library and search through a book with all the Rebel generals. No General Mellon."

I sat down with the book in front of me and flipped it open to the first italicized passage.

"Read this," I said. "Brautigan throws in the italicized passages at the end of the regular chapters to create a separate narrative. Flashbacks to the Civil War. All about a particular fellow in the Battle of Wilderness. I dog-eared them."

She paraphrased as she read. "Private Augustus Mellon, thirty-seven-year-old former slave trader, ran for his life in the Wilderness. Ran barefooted through a spring. Saw two dead solders lying next to each other."

She flipped to the next flashback. "He saw Union solders coming through a thicket. He dove forward onto the ground and pretended he was dead. The Union soldiers were so scared that they didn't see him. They had thrown their guns away and were looking for a Confederate to surrender to."

She turned to the next marked passage and read. Her turn to gasp. "He found a Union captain lying headless. He took his boots!" She flipped to the next earmark. "Then he was up and moving."

She reread the last passage, the last part of which I'd underlined, out loud.

Augustus Mellon stumbled into a clearing that had a deluxe muscle building course of artillery at one end of it, and then a furious assault by Texas Troops, Hood's old boys against the Union army, and General Robert E. Lee tried to get into it, but those Texans won't allow it, and then the 8th Big Sur Volunteer Heavy Root Eaters arrived and one of them offered Traveller (Lee's horse) a limpet to eat, and Private Augustus Mellon had a new pair of boots, and then the 8th Big Sur Volunteer Heavy Root Eaters began dancing in a circle, the general and his horse in the middle, while all around them waged the American Civil War, the last good time this country ever had.

"I can't believe it," she said.

"Go ahead," I grinned. "Say what you can't believe."

"Brautigan told Runaway's story!"

"Yep," I said. "Brautigan inherited the secret story from his friend, Lee Mellon. The narrator of the novel, Brautigan, mentions that Lee Mellon lived in Virginia. Whatever his real name, the story worked its way down to him from Runaway, his great grandfather, I figure, who, as Brautigan knew from his friend, was a private, not a general."

"My god," she stammered. "You've found the missing Whitman line."

"Yep. But Brautigan didn't reveal most of your secret story—only Runaway's snippet, disguised as fiction."

"So only those who already know the secret story would recognize it," she said.

"That's right," I said. "So it didn't count as using up his single tell. I'm sure of that."

"Imagine the fun Brautigan had putting the clues in," she said. "Playing dead, stealing boots off a headless man."

"He saved my favorite clue for last," I said.

"'The last good time...'" she said.

"'this country ever had,'" I added. "Brautigan finished *Confederate General* in 1964, one hundred years after Ezra and Walt and June saved Runaway. He put in the Runaway story to commemorate the hundredth anniversary."

"Rather than giving us a private testimonial and poetry, like Edna, he left us a canon treasure hidden in his own novel," she gleamed. "I believe you've discovered a new member of the Rock Creek Canon.

"I've expanded the canon by two," I said. "Don't forget Roberto."

Her face squinted up.

"For being in the dream?"

"But why was he in the dream?"

"Tell me."

"After I read *Savage Detectives*, his breakout novel that was translated into English in 2007, I read everything else he wrote and everything I could find written about him. He was a ravenous reader. He read famous poets, obscure poets, dime-store gumshoe novels, the classics, science fiction. He liked to brag that he'd read everything, even bits of paper he'd find in the street. He loved to critique writers and wrote scads of essays and literary history in addition to his novels.

"He was broke, a twenty-four-year-old vagabond, dead set on being a poet, when he left Mexico City for Madrid. The first book he bought was the complete poems of Jorge Luis Borges. He stayed up all night reading it."

"Like Keats stayed up all night studying Chapman's Homer," she said. "Which inspired him to write a brilliant sonnet and give up a medical career to be a poet."

"Indeed. And Bolaño, like Keats, never forgot how he felt after his discovery that night—he said later he was certain that there was nothing else that would have changed the crazy life he'd been living. Only Borges. Who, Roberto wrote, had intelligence, bravery and despair—the only things that keep poetry alive.

"Borges became his hero, his life-long inspiration and strongest influence. Guess who was Borges' biggest influence and inspiration."

"Keats?"

"You knew."

"Wild guess."

"When Borges was a child, his father read him Keats. Borges called it was most significant literary encounter of his life. Said he felt something momentous happening, not only to his intellect, but to his whole being, to his flesh and blood. Hearing Keats, Borges said, provided him the revelation that poetry and language would be his life's passion.

"So Keats did for Borges what Borges did for Bolaño," I said. "You can see it plain as day in Borges. He became like Keats' chameleon poet. Giving himself over so completely to his imagination, his fantastical inventiveness, his famous *Ficciones*. It flowed from Keats, through Borges, to Bolaño."

"Direct descendants of Keats," she said. "I have to read them both."

"There's more," I said. I gathered all my Bolaños in front of me and opened *Between Parentheses*, a collection of his non-fiction, to an earmarked page and read her this:

It's true that all American poets must—for better or for worse, sooner or later—face up to Whitman. And yet Borges's poetry is the most Whitmanian of all. Whitman's themes are always present in his verse...a response to Whitman unmatched by any other contemporary response, a dialogue and monologue with history, an honest tribute to English verse.

"So Walter came to Roberto, too, the same way Keats came to him—through Borges," she said.

"Yep. And Roberto, in his poetry, pays homage to Whitman," I said, and thumbed through *Tres*, a book of Bolaño poetry.

I dreamt I was eighteen and saw my best friend making love to Walt Whitman.

"Fascinating," she said.

"There's more," I said. "Bolaño is also connected to Brautigan. The clues are everywhere. Roberto loved to make lists. In his novel *Woes of the True Policeman* there are lists of superlatives, like in a high school year book, in a chapter entitled, 'Notes from a Class in Contemporary Literature: The Role of the Poet.'" I read to her. "'Most fun: Borges and Nicanor Parra. Others: Richard Brautigan, Gary Snyder.'

"So Bolaño knew of Brautigan and read him," I said. "Roberto was a broke, drop-out poet. Like Brautigan. Roberto couldn't scratch out a living from poetry. Like Brautigan. So he turned to novels and wrote a renowned one based on himself and his drop-out friends. Like Brautigan."

I picked up Roberto Bolaño *The Last Interview and Other Conversations*.

"Hold onto your seat," I smiled. "Here's the truly telltale evidence—the ultimate clue. From Roberto's last interview. He knew he was close to dying. He was asked whose novels are most important to him. He names a few, and then he says this:

Other books I will not name are the tip of a lone spear I had the good fortune to be handed, to carry in secret. They were stories of war and fish, and they too were the tip of a still invisible literary spear.

A squint hardened her twinkling eyes. I'd turned the tables. Now she was the one reluctant to believe.

"A double clue that leaves no doubt," I said. "'Stories of war and fish' is a clear reference to Brautigan's two best novels—*Confederate General* and *Trout Fishing in America*—which are 'the tip of a still invisible literary spear,' one that Bolaño tells us— on his death bed no less—he'd had the 'good fortune to be handed and carried in secret.'"

The squint refused to give. She cocked her head at me.

"Come on," I said. "He couldn't have been more clear that he inherited the story. Unless he flat-out revealed our secret."

"He'd never do that," she smiled. "He was a secret-keeper."

"Yes indeed," I said. "Brautigan told him the story and Brautigan and Bolaño became secret brothers in arms. You can see it in

Roberto's early novels, way back in 1980. *Antwerp* is a strange, fractured, anti-literary narrative, like the two Brautigan novels, the stories of war and fish. *Antwerp* even has short, little numbered chapters, like Brautigan.

"So you agree Roberto should be in the canon too?" I said.

"You heard Keats tell Roberto he's immortal," she smiled. "Keats was telling you that Roberto belongs in the Rock Creek Canon."

"I don't want to hit Cowboy with any of this, until I finish the tell," I said. "He might have trouble adding them to the canon, even though they're in Walt's line of secret-keepers."

A frown shadowed her face before she before she could grin it away. "I bet he'll be fine with it. He just wants you to be done. But yes, wait until then to tell him."

She took my hands and pulled me to my feet and hugged me.

"My hero," she said. "The secret keeper with the canon-expanding dream. The Muses truly do favor you. I can feel them radiating inside you."

The brown-blue concoction of super-aliveness made her eyes as sumptuous and promising as those of the one and only woman who ever fell in love with me.

"Do tell," I said, and gave her a little squeeze.

She stepped away, her palm on my chest. "No distractions," she said. "Time for you to get started."

She got a big pot of coffee brewing, then plunked down her laptop in front of me and raised the lid. She brought me cup after cup. I banged away until I joined her on the porch for my first smoke break. No breaks, she told me—I could smoke inside. A while later she brought me a plate full of scrambled eggs and set it down without saying a word. The hours vanished. The words mounted. The story took voice. I was anxious to see William. I didn't feel like talking to Cowboy and left well before cocktail hour so I wouldn't pass him on the trail.

33

I glided smiling down William's driveway, a bouquet of 7-11 corndogs-on-a stick in one hand and a bottle of cold white wine in the other. I must have been beaming.

"They told you the story, didn't they!" William said.

"Even better than that," I said and told him of my discovery. "Now I'm Louise's hero."

"Congratulations on joining the club," he grinned.

"There's more," I said as we crunched and swigged. "They showed me their secret hideaway. I not only heard the story. Cowboy told me about his son, and Louise told me about Esther and Eli. Why didn't Cowboy and Louise pick Eli instead to record their story?"

"Eli has his own park story, along with me and the Zoo Crewers. We got our own secrets, our own hidden places."

222

"Show me," I said.

At dusk we took the trail back beyond Cowboy's and headed south and ended up on a street that went past a huge, locked gate to the zoo. Below us another road curved sharply right before disappearing into a tunnel. William pointed to a sheer, vine-covered bank, hundreds of feet high, houses clinging its edge. He called it the Zoo Cliff, the demarcation line between a neighborhood called Lanier Heights and the beginning of the vast woodlands that surround the zoo and extend miles north through the park.

He told me the history of the Zoo Crew, how in the late nineteen seventies the earliest Crewers, not yet a named tribe, a wild bunch of would-be musicians and poets loosely centered around the New Wave scene, forayed to the north and discovered a mostly unclaimed, enchanting territory rife with well-hidden spots ideal for partying and more private endeavors, like love-making and drug-dealing.

We walked up a road that climbed around the topside of the cliff. We zigzagged steep, short streets of a hill and down a set of steps into a canyon of nineteen-fiftyish, mid-rise high apartment buildings and stopped in front of the lone stand-alone house they surrounded. The Zoo Crew house, William proclaimed, aka the House of the Rising Sun. Its ornately wrought-iron embellished porches and balconies make it look like it landed from old New Orleans, its name forever enshrined the first night Eli and Esther and the first Crewers watched the sun rise from the roof.

The street dead-ended and we climbed a long stairway out of the canyon. The streets leveled out. We stopped in front of a row-house where Esther had once lived, where Louise would fetch her. William pointed to our feet. "E+L", etched in the sidewalk long ago, had been recently re-chiseled and deep-coated with silver spray paint.

We crossed a street to a playground where Esther often walked with either Eli or Louise, one or the other, never the three of them. Esther preferred their separate company. William pointed to a withered one-time community garden where Louise and Esther grew vegetables and she and Eli grew reefer that never failed to disappear before its proper harvest time. William folded back an opening cut in a chain link fence and we climbed through and entered the deep woods that circle the zoo. Certain Crewers, he explained, carry wire-cutters and dutifully maintain the critical snips for unfettered travel between the zoo property and the park.

"Nobody will ever need to write down the Zoo Crew story," he said. "It's already recorded and sanctified. We're entering sacred ground, home to the very first Zooer sites."

He pointed to a poplar tree. E+E, inside a heart, was carved at eye level.

"There's eight more of these as you work your way north. Zach and his chosen acolytes have them mapped. But this one, this is the very first one. Eli's first carving, soon after he met Esther. They stopped here on their way to her favorite spot when she took him there for the first time."

He had me lay hands on it, each hand just covering an E. "It feels fresh," I said.

"The Zooers are zealots about making sure they never disappear."

"Preserving the sacred Zoo Crew markings."

"That's right," he said. "Protecting their heritage."

A ways further, on the opposite side of an even fatter poplar, he showed me the very first E+L, not in a heart, but in a circle. "Carved by Esther and Louise," he said. "With a Swiss Army knife Louise had had since childhood and bequeathed to Esther for this first carving. Esther chose this tree and carved the L. Louise took the knife and carved the E. Esther took it back and carved the + and the circle. Crewers have mapped and preserved eight more of these, too."

At our next stop William unbagged the wine. We drained it and he declared, his voice its tangiest and his eyes their keenest, that we stood on the most sacred Zoo Crew ground, Esther's favorite hidden place, known only to him and Louise and Eli. Esther brought Eli and Louise, separately and secretly, to her most sacrosanct ground, where she and Eli made love for the first time, and where she and Louise lounged together after carving their first E + L and vowed to be best friends for life.

"Where Louise almost told Esther the secret story," I said.

"She told you about waiting too long, huh?"

"Told me they were at Esther's favorite spot when she denied a strong urge to tell her."

We looped round back toward Cowboy's, through another peeled-back fence opening, and stopped at Esther's hideaway, the bridge vault where she'd invited Louise that day they first met. Flowers withered at the foot of the green metal door.

"Eli will bring fresh ones tonight," he said. "In the dead of every night, between three and four, he takes the same walk, the one we just took, and ends up here. Louise wanders down here on occasion, too, roundabout midnight. She never leaves anything. She's got her own shrine to Esther, the last place she and Esther went together that afternoon, just an hour or two before the accident. It's farther up the park, way up in the rocks on the ridge over Soapstone Valley, private, not part of the tour."

In the silence on the rest of the walk back, I pondered how William was so much more than the irrepressible, good-hearted, erudite man of poetry and simple pleasures that I'd come to greatly admire. I walked with a man of great gumption who, denied access to one renown park secret, had become lord, keeper and champion of another hidden legacy, just as rich and mysterious and celebrated as the one claimed but withheld from him by his friends Cowboy and Louise.

From that night on, William and I spent every evening together, breaking bread and taking long walks. He was my guide to that enchanted, never-ending labyrinth of woods and neighborhoods. He showed me how to disappear from the city anywhere along the miles of the park's ubiquitous boundaries and reemerge elsewhere, in a different another part of town, unseen on the entire journey if you so wished, avoiding all roads and marked trails that slice up the park, staying within the silent swaths of woodlands, spotted only by deer and owls and nighthawks and a limping fox and, very occasionally, by like-minded misfits on their secret ways to their own elsewheres.

Our walks and his peerless Zoo Crew tours revealed to me, even more than Whitman's secret story, the true nature of the park, its inner soul of secluded hills and valleys and secret nooks and crannies and sacred spots and markings unperturbed and unspoiled to this day.

During those evenings of our heyday we swapped stories about everything except his own past.

Poetry was our favorite pastime. We read out loud and memorized and practiced reciting our favorite John Keats and Langston Hughes. I read him poems by Bolaño and Brautigan, and despite their strangeness, he took a fancy to several, particularly "Resurrection," in which Bolaño says poetry is braver than anyone and slips into dreams like a diver into a lake.

Over dinner one night we rated the relative pleasures of Whitman, Keats, Hughes and Dickinson. He'd come to like Emily. He declared her "soulful and sassy" as well as "satisfying to the soul," but ultimately less pleasing to his ear than Keats or Whitman and less inspiring than Hughes.

That night for our after-dinner stroll we checked in on Black Beauty, still safe in her spot near Cowboy's place. We leaned the seats as far back as they would go and sipped our wine and listened to my Dickinson CD. I don't know if William saw my eyes made misty by the beautiful voice of the Latina poet whose story I recounted for him, but he did ask me to replay the last poem she ever recorded for me.

I died for beauty, but was scarce
Adjusted in the tomb,
When one who died for truth was lain
In an adjoining room.

He questioned softly why I failed?
"For beauty," I replied.
"And I for truth—the two are one;
We brethren are," he said.

And so, as kinsmen met a-night,
We talked between the rooms,
Until the moss had reached our lips,
And covered up our names."

"I declare that to be my favorite Emily," he said. "Our sly, mysterious gal got tight in eternity with young, love-starved John."

226

"Tell me your story, William" I said.

"I will tell you one thing," he said. "After mama disappeared, one of the neighbors told me that my daddy—mama never once spoke of him and I saw him only one time, when I was real little—had died right here in D.C. I wanted to visit his grave. But the city didn't have a clue where he was buried. After thirty days unclaimed, they cremate you with whoever else is ripe that day for burning. They take all the soot—you mixed together with strangers—and bury it out in Maryland. A landfill full of the unmarked ashes of dead poor people. Good thing they treat dead homeless people better now. You get your name recorded in a book, a list of the unclaimed cremated."

"If I outlive you," I said, "I would be deeply honored to bury you on a beautiful hilltop back home, looking out over the rolling apple orchards, with a proper casket and a headstone that says whatever you want on it. Let's come up with something good to carve on there right now and write it down so we remember."

"Thank you kindly," he said, "but Cowboy already promised me he'd get me cremated all by my lonesome and sprinkle my ashes in the creek."

"Where you'd live, before you came to the park?"

"I got evicted from the room I rented when I got too old and weak to work day labor. Never spend the night in a homeless shelter, friend. A big, crazy dude tried to fiddle with me while somebody else stole all my stuff. I got out of there right then, walked west all night. Wandered into the park at daybreak, found a little private spot not far from Louise's Esther shrine and took a nap in my new-found haven.

"Thank goodness for my sake," I said.

"Met Louise that very day," he said, "and Cowboy, too."

34

LOUISE TURNED STINGY WITH her distractions. I would have thought her fickle and even a bit cruel but for the occasional looks she gave me. I knew better than to hope for romance; I lusted only after her high-spirited play. Once or twice a day she checked my word count and re-corralled the books and papers I'd dug through back into five vague piles, one per canon member. As she headed back out to the porch with her own pile of selected readings, she'd shoot me a grin with lit-up eyes, which I took as a promise that I would be graced again by her most lively, wondrous self.

Every day on the dot at six Cowboy arrived for cocktails. He would unfailingly first ask about my progress, then offer one or two seemingly heartfelt, pro-Whitman remarks to maintain his façade of lobbying on behalf of his version. As he neared the end of his first drink, she invariably asked me if I'd like a stay for a bite to eat, my signal to politely decline and say I needed to be on my way to dinner at William's.

Her unrestrained, irrepressible self returned Tuesday of week two. She came inside mid-afternoon and stretched and touched her toes. "You're right, mister dream private eye," she said, and skipped twice to the end of the room into her ballerina pose, one hand in the air, the other rubbing her tummy. "I hereby verify the great influence that Whitman had on Brautigan."

"Finally, some detective work," I said. "Lonely Marlowe could use a partner."

"Your leaning-on-the-mailbox dream pal is indeed a Whitman-infused literary rebel," she said. "The aim of his poetry and novels is to set language free, to liberate words."

"That's all you got?"

She slide-stepped to the back of my chair and leaned over, close.

"*Trout Fishing in America*," she whispered in my ear, "is as anarchistic and unconventional as *Leaves of Grass*."

She pinched and wiggled my cheek. Two slow-motion stretch lunges took her to the end of the table, where she threw her hands high in the air and completed her workout with three toe touches.

"Both *Leaves* and *Trout* are held together, very loosely, by their single metaphors: leaves of grass and trout fishing."

She leaned over and eyed me, palms to table.

"In both books, the narrators see themselves as witnesses, and are obsessed with listing and cataloguing whatever they see, whatever they imagine.'

"But get this—my best evidence," she said. "Guess who Brautigan was reading when he and his honey were on the camping trip when he sat around the fire writing *Trout Fishing*?"

"I want to hear you say it."

"Walt Whitman."

"So, partner," I said, "you agree then that we can tag Brautigan a 1960s descendant of radical, wild Walter, before June and Ezra tamed him into the Good Gray Poet?"

"That's what I'm telling you, pal."

"Book him," I said.

"Will do," she saluted, and sashayed her way back out to the porch. Before I could get back to work, I fantasized joining her with a pitcher of martinis. Both of us would drink one too many and disappear into the woods. If we didn't make it back before Cowboy arrived, I'd tell him we'd been on a walk.

She went quiet again, for days. One morning I badgered her until she took me back to Hideaway. I spend all day with the manuscripts, not hiding my copying of them. She sat reading and said nothing, reinforcing my suspicion: what would it matter if I was copying them if they were going to be sold off.

The next day, presumably satisfied by my lunchtime assurances that the tell was going well and the end was near, exuberant Louise rebirthed in her full glory.

By the hand she took me up the creek to the storied rock, where we sat in warm sun facing north and dangled our bare feet. She asked if I'd had more canon dreams. When I said I'd not, she conjured up Keats and Whitman.

"What about Vincent and Richard and Roberto?" I said.

"Vincent is keeping our two newcomers busy back in the playhouse, so the four of us can have some time to ourselves," she said. "John and Walter tell me you make them giddy, the canon dreamer himself visiting their favorite spot."

That strong dose of her powerful, flamboyant, flighty-minded self spun a happy shiver up my back. Her imagination was contagious. I raised my arms and gazed into the oaks. "I say this to them. The Muses, way back when, brought June and Ezra and the two of you here to establish the original Rock Creek Canon. Hail to you, high priests of our canon, floating immortal in this creek valley. To you, John Keats, I say this: you've never been more pleased than you are today."

"John asks, why is that?" she said.

"Because when June and the Muses first brought you forth here, you were alone, without the fellowship you so crave. But not for long. Walter showed up. He was your first inkling that you might be in the come-true, Rock Creek version of your fondest dream.

"Then, sixty timeless years later, Vincent joined you and Walter here, providing you yet more reason to believe that a pure poet, among his many forgotten dreams, might dream a true dream."

"John's vision of immortality," Louise sighed.

"Yes, Johnny boy," I said, "the very dream that your mortal self told us of, when you imagined the immortals greeting each other at journey's end, no longer mere poetic egos fussing and fighting over greatness, but serene, like you, in your negative capability, in uncertainties and mysteries, and thus finding great pleasure in each other, like freed flowers budding anew with the fresh touches of the Muses."

Louise gripped my hand and closed her eyes as my voice, seemingly on its own, wended its merry way. "And today, fearless Johnny, you're flush with happy, happy bliss. More than ever. Because you see your dream comes truer yet, even more alive, with two more immortals joining you, including your dear Roberto."

Louise opened her eyes and looked up into the trees with me.

"John and Walter," she said, "here, with us, the keepers of your immortal canon, what sayeth you to each other?"

Their spirits hovered above, eyeing each other as my words flowed more easily than they ever have, before or since. "To you Walter, Johnny says he cares not how harshly you criticized his poetry. He says, 'I cherish your good company, and I savor bearing witness to your ecstatic flights, high above, where you reap the joys of my vision of pure posy heaven."

"To you John," Louise said, "Walter says he loves you dearly. He says this too: 'My only unmet desire is that our immortality won't let me go back in time, to the death bed of your mortal self, to hold you, to whisper in your ear that your dream is almost at hand.'"

"Then rejoice, Walt Whitman," I said. "Your desire was realized. For I, John Keats, assure you that the Muses, just as they did for you, did comfort me at my mortal death. They poured in my soul the vintage draught, cooled by the ageless essence of all pure poets, past and future. So that you were there with me, as I was there with you."

She squeezed my hand. Hers had turned moist. "And the Muses promise me, Walter and John," she said, "that you two high priests of Rock Creek posy will both be there, with us, to give final comfort to the keepers of your dreams."

If imagination were lightning and great poets kindling, the whole damn woods would have burst into flames. We both lay back and looked up at the sky, our hands tightly gripped. Something inside her had hardened long ago, and on this and the other most memorable moments she gave me, she had been able to undo that hardening, and I glimpsed the curious, impetuous child and the ecstatic, young woman and her present unvanquished self all wrapped in one as we rose together, hand in hand, rapt for an instant in might still could be but would not be.

"What wonders we make, the two of us," she said. She let go my hand and turned on a dime all glum and pressed her front teeth again and again into her lower lip. I wanted to watch only the changing shades of pink and red, not the sadness drowning her eyes.

"You can put your name on the tell," she said. "As you may have already guessed, no one is ever going to see it."

I couldn't hide from her the dumb surprise that overtook me.

"It's going to be hidden away, forever, with the manuscripts."

"What the hell's wrong with me?" I blurted out. "How could I ever think the two of you were going to cash in, to sell the manuscripts."

"I don't know why you'd think that," she said. The disappointment in her voice made me ashamed. "We told you we'd figured out how to set everything right, for us and for the story. What other way, besides hiding away the tell, could we keep the oath, keep the story secret?"

"Why'd you wait so long to tell me?" I said.

"Cowboy insisted I wait until you were finished."

"You though I'd back out?"

"You tell me. Why'd you want your name on it?"

I dropped my head in shame.

"You took the oath too" she said. "If you thought we were going to break it, were you going to try to stop us?"

"Nope." I swallowed and looked her in the eye. "I had my own temptations to face down."

"Before or after your dream?"

"Right before."

An all-might-still-be-well smile flashed on her face but vanished in an instant. "Tell me then. Do you intend to break the oath?"

"No," I said. "I was tempted, but I couldn't do it."

"Well, you must be disappointed how it's all turning out" she said. "You'll never be recognized. Not for recording the story. Not for discovering the missing Whitman secret-keepers. Not for anything."

"I don't care about any of that," I said. I swear it was not until I heard myself say those words that I realized they were true. "How on Earth could I ever be disappointed? I'm so lucky. I've been told an amazing story. The Muses gave me a dream that revealed the most satisfying literary discovery I could ever imagine—the expansion of the Rock Creek Canon."

She hugged me. Deservedly so, I thought, elated by the thought that I might have, finally, for once, lived up to someone's hopes.

We slowly pulled apart, smiling eyes re-entangling and hands taking to each other's shoulders. "And to top it all off," I said, "I've found three wonderful new friends, and a place I cherish."

She disguised the worry that flashed in her eyes with a half-hearted grin. Even that wouldn't stay put. She gave a quick brave smile and took my hand and pulled me across the creek barefoot. I could not figure how my fondness for my new friends and the park had spooked her so. Must be something else. When we reached the playhouse, she told me she needed to be alone and would see me in morning. On the walk to William's it came to me: She had begun grieving for the story, for banishing it forever to a cave.

35

I DID NOT MENTION Louise's disclosure to William, for I decided it would come as no surprise to him, who, unlike me, possessed enough of a keen eye to see that that Cowboy and Louise would never break the sacred oath. Arriving early, well before cocktail hour, I found him rocking briskly away in his chair perusing the "New York Review of Books," collected from the front porch since it wouldn't fit through the mail slot. I reported that I'd near wrapped up the tell and he reminded me that his lady friend was due back soon and there was a place he wanted to show me.

We took the high trail past Pulpit Rock and crossed the creek. We went under a roadway bridge, left the main trail for a deer path up a long hill. We crossed a marked trail and climbed the last bank to where the rise flattened out.

Stacked for hundreds of yards across the ridge top were

humongous sections of disembodied monuments and grand buildings, chunks of granite and marble a dozen feet wide and fifty feet long, transported somehow into the forest and laid forever to rest.

"Welcome to the Boneyard," William said. "Our city of ruins."

We walked beyond the ninety-degree corner of one tall, helter-skelter wall, around the end of an even wider, more jumbly row of immense blocks and reached the innards. We climbed over more giant chunks scattered about and entered a private sanctum in one corner of a three-sided fort of double walls, thirty feet high and a dozen feet apart. Between the piles that made these parallel walls were caverns with oddly angled, protruding sides and ceilings. We peered into one the size of a roomy tent, crossed and beamed by a jangle of twenty-foot-long marble pieces, Roman numerals carved into their ends.

A frying pan caked with furry lard sat on an old-timey, metal milk crate over a fire pit. Half-burnt sticks angled down through the open squares of the box fire. Tiny skulls and bones and empty water bottles were around it.

"The old guy who lived here all these years must have liked squirrel," William said.

A realization shot across my eyes before I could stop it.

"What?" he said. "You heard something about him?"

My tongue tied up on me enough that I think he knew I was lying.

"Nope," I said. "You know him?"

"Nope. Zach is the only one who ever saw him. A couple of summers ago Zach had been up all night and ended up here, sitting up on the wall, right down there, watching the day break. This gaunt, old guy with long, wispy gray hair and a big pack with a frame on his back walked around the corner, just like we did. The sight of him spooked the hell out of Zach—he stayed dead still and hoped the guy wouldn't notice him.

"But he fixed Zach with a terrible stare. Zach told me he felt like he was committing a terrible crime, just by looking at him. Said the guy had the most despairing eyes he's ever seen. Zach was so terrified he froze—couldn't look away. He swears the old guy—Melancholy Man, he called him—kept him locked down with that stare until he was in full tremors. Melancholy Man squinted one last, hatred look into him and disappeared, right in here, into his cozy little home. Zach swears he truly feared for his very soul, that those frightful eyes could have ripped it right out of him.

"Did the fellow wander around the park?"

"Cowboy says that in all his years in the park he's never seen Melancholy Man nor heard a word said about him. Says Zach was hallucinating, too tired out from being high as a kite all night."

"You never saw him?"

"No way. After what Zach told me I've always detoured way around the Boneyard whenever I wander up this way."

"So neither Cowboy nor Louise or nobody else has ever seen him?"

"I just told you that, fool. Cowboy made Louise promise him long ago to never wander farther north on her jaunts than Pulpit Rock. And from what Zach told me, I believe the old fellow hated being seen, that he was a hermit, hid away here. That's why nobody ever saw him except Zach. Cowboy claimed he didn't believe Zach. But Cowboy was spooked, I can tell you that. I was there when Zach told Cowboy about him. Cowboy said neither one of us better mention Melancholy Man again, ever, to anybody, or he'd ban us from the park. Don't ever tell Cowboy I told you about him."

"Where is he? Is he coming back? He's probably hiding."

"Getting spooked, huh? Don't worry. I got word yesterday from one of the brothers who is tight with a park cop. They found a dead body off the trial, halfway hidden, down a bank that leads down to a spring and a little pool, right down the hill. Must have been Melancholy Man's watering hole. They got a body bag and hauled him down to the road and threw him in the trunk. Probably slated to be incinerated. I wouldn't want to be mixed up in that batch of ashes, I tell you what.

"I'm reclaiming this territory. For Zack and the Zoo Crew. And I'm claiming these fine living quarters for you and me."

We climbed around inside like we were inspecting an apartment to rent. He pointed out two spaces on the ground where we could sleep, looked down upon by all variety of nooks and crannies and slanted granite tops he pointed out where we would keep our drink and food and books and whatever else we wanted to haul in.

"It's kind of far from supplies," he said. "But we'll have enough comings and goings between us to keep supplied and living the high life. The view isn't as good as my backyard. But we've got our own private courtyard. And with a fire, we can make our own damn coffee in the morning."

"I got to be honest with you," I said. "I'm hoping to get an extended invite from Cowboy. There's room for both of us in his basement."

I didn't know what to make of the funny look he gave me.

"It's not your place to invite me to move into Cowboy's" he said. "I'm claiming this place, and you're invited to move in and join me, even though it's not your first choice."

I thanked him kindly and told him what a fine place it could be, for him or for both of us.

36

BOLAÑO ENTHRALLED LOUISE, WAYLAID her like the crying frogs waylaid Vincent on the unfrequented road. Late the next morning she finished *Amulet* and walked in from the porch crying, her hands holding the paperback open to its back pages.

"The abandoned young poets march into the valley, singing, toward the abyss," she said.

"The ghost children," I said.

"She can't stop them," she cried. "All she can do is watch."

"She hears their song," I said.

She wiped at her tears and read:

*I hear them singing still…such a beautiful song it is…how beautiful there were …
I heard them sing and I went mad. …And that song is our amulet.*

"Wait until you read 2666," I said. She waved me off and went back outside.

A day later, I told her I really was almost done. Mid-afternoon the following day she walked in from the porch, saw me staring at the ceiling, and asked if I'd finished. "I want to read through it one more time, tonight," I said, and printed out pages. "I'll hand it over tomorrow."

She looked peeved and said she'd hoped to have it that day, in time for Cowboy's arrival. The next day would have to do, she said, and told me to meet them at the Hideaway, at four o'clock. She dropped her frown and smiled that we'd have a ceremony—the dedication of the tell—and then return to the Playhouse to celebrate."

I left before Cowboy arrived and wandered north so I wouldn't run into him and then headed west, down one of the long park fingers that reach out into the city until I reached a wide boulevard. I got a bite to eat and sat outside until dusk and walked south.

I came upon an old woman wrapped in strips of white sheets, her black face covered in white make-up. Her shopping cart was full of carefully folded white sheets. A comforting peacefulness in her face drew me toward her, and when she smiled, I sat down next to her on a stone wall near a bus stop.

"Good evening," I said. "I'd like to share something with you." I pulled my wad of remaining cash and peeled some off.

"I don't need money," she said. "I need a piano. To make my hands better."

She held them out and showed me her tangled, bent fingers.

"When I was a young girl, I performed Chopin on the stage of the Opera House at the Kennedy Center," she said. "The crowd clapped and clapped. I don't know why I never gave another concert. The woman I lived with had a beautiful piano. I kept house and cooked and played the piano. She loved to hear me play. When she died, they sold her house and gave me these all these linens. I keep them clean. All I want is a piano."

I took her right hand and caressed and stroked her fingers, one by one.

"That's a sad story," I said. "But the way you tell it is beautiful, as beautiful as you."

"Thank you," she said. "Don't be sad. I try not to ever be sad."

She kept her smile and watched me massage her hand. Her palm flattened and her fingers loosened, but as soon as I let go the fingertips curled up and retouched the bottom her hand.

"I was told a story, maybe as beautiful as yours. But no one will ever hear it again."

"Why?" she said.

"The keepers of the story made me swear to never tell it. They want the story to stay secret, silent, forever."

"Stories live their own lives," she said. "They like to be told and retold, to friends and strangers alike, like my story does. Although no one believes it."

"I believe you," I said, and began to plead her other hand.

"Will you give me a piano?"

"I don't have one," I said. "If I did, I'd take you to it right now so I could hear you play." I had to take a deep breath to pull back tears.

"Don't be sad," she said. "I play in my dreams. My hands are all better in my dreams."

"I wish I could be so lucky as you'd play in my dreams, so I could be lifted by every beautiful note."

She squeezed my hand and let go and we watched her fingers curl back up. "I promise I will," she said with a smile more knowing than Mona Lisa. I didn't speak for fear of crying. I kissed her check. We said no more and exchanged smiles as I walked away down a side street past a synagogue and veered off behind a huge apartment building into the woods. I wandered until I could make out the occasional faint running of the unseen creek and lay down in the dark on a hilltop and envisioned the face of the woman. I cried finally, as sad as I've ever been, until a vision of her parting smile lifted me to my feet. I hurried back to the copy shop I'd passed and arrived before it closed.

37

THE NEXT MORNING, I found Zach face in hands sitting across from William, slouched forward and bleary-eyed.

"He's got something to give you," William said. "And something to tell you. Right, Zach? Yo Zach. Heads up."

Zach lifted his haggard, anguished, tear-stained face and held out a white paper folded up too many times, its creases beginning to rip. "Give this to Louise," he muttered, all runny and needing a good nose blow.

"Why don't you give it to her," I said, trying to sound sympathetic but needing to know.

"Tell him," William said.

"It was just her and me and Christopher," Zach said.

"Your little, curly-haired friend?"

241

"Yep. It was perfect, our best night ever. Sitting way out on Pulpit Rock in the dead middle of night. She sipped red wine from that old wine sack and threw her head back and smiled at the moon, a beautiful goddess.

"We sat very close, touching, me on one side, Christopher on the other. She asked us if we'd compose a moon-shadow poem on the spot, like the contests Keats and his friends had. Like Vincent Millay's two boyfriends wrote poetry for her stretched out either side of her in her big bed. Instead we each recited a poem we'd written for her yesterday and she listened, glee in her eyes, mesmerized, until we finished, then looked back up to the moon and saluted it with her wine sack. 'Here's to Bacchus and to Apollo, and to the other two grantors of divine madness, Poetry and Love,' she said. 'And to my Endymions—my young moonlit poets.'

"She started reciting Keats' 'To Autumn.' She began the final verse.

Where are the songs of spring? Ay, where are they?
Think not of them, thou hast thy music too,-

"I'd never see her sad before. 'I'm stopping right there,' she said. 'Let autumn remain unfinished, in its timeless time, like the never-to-be lovers on the Grecian urn.'

"She looked down at the creek and bit her lip. 'This is the last time I'll ever see you two,' she said. 'The time has come for my valiant young poets to find a new muse.'"

"I couldn't fathom what she was telling us. I pleaded with her. How could she abandon us? She is the moon goddess of the park. The muse of the Zoo Crew. We are her poets!" Betrayal and loss mixed in his tears. I wished desperately I had a hanky to hand him.

"She said we'd always be with her, in spirit, that we were her last and most beautiful and most beloved Zoo Crew poets. But her time as Rock Creek muse was done."

"'It can't be,' I told her.

"She turned cold, her face stern. 'My dear boys,' she said, 'muses come and go. I have fulfilled my calling in the park. Now leave me be. I want a moment alone before my final departure.'

"We sat stunned. She told us again to leave and said she would not say goodbye, for she hates goodbyes as much as Keats. She quoted the last words in the last letter he ever wrote, when his death was imminent." I spoke them silently as he intoned: 'I can scarcely bid you good bye, even in a letter. I always make an awkward bow. God bless you!'

"Chris pulled me down the path, out to the trail. I stopped and turned and took my last look at her."

He wiped his face with his sleeve and stood and sniffled.

"Promise you'll give her that?"

"I do."

"She said you'd be leaving soon, too."

The last little bit of me not already hardened finally shaped up.

"If I don't see you again," I said, "remember one thing for me, will you? Don't let your heart be broken. Not by anybody. Life's too short."

William wrapped his arm around Zach's shoulders. "Go get some sleep, friend," he said. "You'll get over this. Remember, history's not over. The Zoo Crew lives on."

He trudged off.

William yanked from the fern patch our most recent half gallon of white, half full, and pulled on it longer than he should.

"You know better than to drink in the morning," I said.

"Not when I been up all night. That poor boy came here morose, in the middle of the night and woke me up. Tried my best to buck him up. Didn't do too good. You need bucking up now too?"

"Hell no," I grinned, and joined him in the rarity of a warm morning swig.

He pointed down the narrow side yard at the half-door-sized entrance to his lair, the dark dirt alcove under the front porch.

"Right after the mailman comes and finishes tromping on my ceiling, it's beddy-bye time for me. Speaking of which, I hear through the grapevine that Cowboy wants you out of his basement. Pronto. But don't worry. I still got you, brother. You can stay here until we move to the Boneyard."

"I decided last night I'm heading home," I fibbed. "I can stay with my cousin. Find work out in the apple orchards."

"You'll be telling those apple pickers all about Keats," he laughed. "Spreading the gospel. Adding them to your flock, like you did me."

"The only reason Cowboy wants me out," I said, "is because he's got his heart set on you moving in."

"You kidding?"

"No sir."

"You know I got an open invitation to the Zoo Crew house. Can move in there for the winter if I want."

"They don't need you like Cowboy does," I said. "I know you got this beautiful spot, as well as your new Boneyard digs. But if you ask me, I think you ought to do it. For Cowboy. He needs you. To keep him company. He hates living by himself anymore. I'm afraid you'll hurt his feelings if you don't move in."

"I'll always look out for Cowboy. I'll move in with him. Even though he never told me his story. My gal will be broken up. But I can still keep an eye on things for her. Hang out here when I need a break from Cowboy."

I told him what Louise and Cowboy would do with the story. I told him all about the beautiful Woman in White and what she had to say about it. He said maybe the Muses sent her. We talked on and on about that until the mailman clomped up the steps and across the front porch. I followed William up the side yard and stood and watched as he ducked under the porch and crawled on top of his sleeping bag and lay down his head.

"You be sure to drop by and let me know what happens before you skedaddle," he said. I nodded yes and kneeled to watch him curl up on a sleeping bag and tuck a dirty white pillow under his head. "You can get out of here now," he smiled. "I don't need you to tuck me in."

I strolled streets and alleys and pondered for long minutes how terribly I'd miss him, that fun-loving, lively minded man, so fine at unearthing the silliness and joy in others.

I found a well-hidden spot and sat and smoked for a long while until I saw Cowboy cross the bridge on his way to our rendezvous. I hauled my books and other belongings out of the basement and packed up Black Beauty, tucking a copy of the tell between framed *Flaming June* and the Immortal Dinner.

38

CRAZY FLICKERS SHOT UP the tunnel from the votive candles that packed the floor of Hideaway outside the circle of rocks. How Louise loved to dazzle, to set you spinning, just like June in her day. She and Cowboy sat squeezed among literally hundreds of little flames, both of them beaming, anxious for me to hand them the completed tell so it could join the other treasures carefully stacked in the middle of the circle.

I made them wait. "William asked me to give this to you."

"Who's it from?" she asked.

"He didn't say," I fibbed.

She unfolded it and showed it to us. It was a typed copy of "To Autumn."

"Read at the grave of John Keats, June 19, 2005—Forever yours, Zach," was hand-printed across the top.

She refolded it and tossed it in the circle. "How endearing," she said. "I want it to stay here, with the manuscripts and the tell."

"Of course," Cowboy said, being his most agreeable self set solely on getting the tell officially into their hands as quickly as possible.

By that point I wanted to believe I finally had them pegged: admirable and lovable, seemingly with a loose screw or two, yet crafty and sly, a most tight-knit cult of two, blessed by the Fates, true believers with good reason to be, the end of their lines, the last of two families bound through five generations by pure poets and the Muses.

The chief benefactor of their good fortune, I smiled unhurriedly at each of them and tossed the tell into the circle. "I hope this lifts a burden off you two. You deserve that. You've been so dedicated and served the story so well for so long."

"It does," she smiled. "We can finally step away. Just in time for me. Before I become a completely batty old lady, shuffling through the woods in the moonlight, reciting dead poets." She looked more worn out than I'd ever seen her.

"Now you don't need to do that anymore," Cowboy said. "Because your dreams—our dream—has finally come true. Our tells were not wasted after all. They'll will live on in the story, forever."

"They will indeed," I said. "I can promise you that."

"Praise be to the Muses," she said softly through a tired-out smile.

"The more I get to know you two," I said, "the more you remind me of Ezra and June, and Lydia and Alfred."

"Speaking of Lydia and Alfred," she said, "I'm moving into the big house. The grand room is all redone." She gave Cowboy a say-something look, the same look June gave Ezra.

"I look forward to spending many leisurely hours there, in my big new chair," he said.

"And with me at the big table, too," she said, "just like Alfred with Lydia, our poets spread out before us."

"The tell begins with Ezra," I said. I needed Cowboy first.

"Does it give Walter his proper due?" he asked.

"Very much so," I said. "He speaks for himself. As does John Keats. Walter and John become very close, just like you told me they did, right after we first met, on my lucky day."

I turned my smile to Louise. "And Vincent, my goodness, does she get her say. And you two, of course, get your say. You're both heroes in your own right. I brought the story up to date because of the discovery."

"What discovery?" he said

"You'll like this," she said.

Good to hear. I was counting on her to help me ease him along, first. I knew she'd have last say.

I told Cowboy the short version of how the Walt line lived on through Runaway and reached Brautigan and Bolaño before disappearing again. He was thrilled, though he'd never heard of either of them.

"You can study the evidence yourself," I said. "I'm leaving you all their novels and poetry. I'm driving home tonight. I need to get back, to help out my cousin. I'm all packed up and ready to go."

The happy relief in their eyes told me how greatly that eased their minds, to know that the message had gotten through and that I'd taken the high road rather than making them send me on my way. They completed our well-mannered charade by feigning surprise but saying nothing.

Going for a little ceremonial flair that he hoped would satisfy June and wrap things up in a jiffy, Cowboy lifted the tell over his head in both hands and looked straight up. "In tribute to the Muses," he declared and lowered his gaze to me. "On their behalf, I thank you. You're a good man." He stood. I remained seated. A whiff of vague concern clouded Louise's face.

"All I did was write it down" I said. "You two are its saving grace. The last of two dynasties, lovingly bound together, once again, by your secret legacy. Which the three of us brought back to life so you two could imprison it forever it in this cave."

My well-rehearsed buzz-killer turned their faces stern. He sat back down.

"So here we are, in the everlasting grave of our beloved story, celebrating its eternal entombment."

"You know how this sets everything right for us," Cowboy said, his voice icy. "It's the best we can do. We'll never break the oath. I thought Louise already set you straight on that."

247

"You want to betray us?" she said. "You want to break the oath to get your name on a big literary discovery?"

I tried to look hurt. But all I could do was admire William's brainstorm and smile.

"Oh yeah of little faith. There is a simple way to let the story live on and protect the secrets and still honor our oath."

"Tell us then, for god sakes," he said. His look told me that he hoped I had something good. Either that, or Grandpa's mythical keen eye was fooling me yet again.

"So long as the manuscripts are never found, the story can be safely disguised as fiction, an obvious and total fabrication. No one will ever believe it. You know that."

He looked at her. She stared back and pulled out Exhibit A, then read aloud. *"By writing these words, I, Walt Whitman, sanctify our vow: That every word and deed that has occurred in the short time I have diffused myself here with my two new comrades—fine comprehenders of me and my poetry—will remain forever unrevealed."*

"That's the beauty of it," I said. "Nothing would really be revealed. It would remain perfectly disguised, as a tall tale. It can't possibly be seen as anything other than made up."

Cowboy rubbed the brim of his hat between his thumb and forefinger. He was teetering. His eyes began that sparkly rotation, even more mesmerizing surrounded by the super-fidgety battalion of candlelight. If I had him, everything just might fall into place.

He looked again at her. "Just another made-up yarn," he said. "Maybe that would be okay."

She turned stone-faced, like Walter could do, and looked right through me, drifting off, I hoped, on a flight of fancy toward a happy landing. Cowboy and I stared at her and waited. Finally, he cleared his throat. She blinked rapidly. Another good sign—possibly a consultation with my friends the Muses. But her mouth, those lips my lips had kissed, if only once, couldn't shake off its frown. I played my last card.

"If the story is freed, so is the Rock Creek Canon. Think of that. Our canon, begotten of our pure poets and their ardent admirers. Walter and John brought together by Ezra and June. Then their kindred spirit Vincent, drawn in by Lydia and Alfred, joins Walter and John and reinvigorates the canon.

"Then Brautigan arrives, drawn in by Walter and Runaway, and resurrects the canon's secret legacy, in print no less. Then Bolaño, a descendant of Keats and Whitman in his own right, inherits the secrets and pays secret homage to the canon, again in print, for all to see, and bingo, your whole canon is again very much alive and well. To be known and recognized, if only as a fiction, another flight of fancy. Free to stake its rightful claim, if only in the imagination."

She closed her eyes. "Don't stop," she murmured. "Tell me more." I felt we were making love, of a literary kind.

"It is a peerless, living canon, unsurpassed in its authenticity, its audacity and its strangeness. It spans the ages, as well as three continents. It is, in my humble opinion, the singular, most sublime, canon of our time, perhaps of any time."

She opened her eyes and smiled.

"How would you do it?" Cowboy said.

"I kept an extra copy of the tell, in hopes you'd both agree. If not, I'll destroy it. The story will appear out of the blue. Written by Anonymous. Untraceable. The manuscripts are transcribed in it. Obvious flights of fictional fancy. Just like the rest of the story."

"Hold everything," Cowboy said. "Folks with nothing better to do might start poking around, just to prove how the story can't be true, or even worse, why it might be true. That would ruin everything, including our well-deserved retirement."

"I already thought of that," I said. "That's why all the names will be changed and everything about the secret places all fuzzied up so they can never be found. Just in case. Not that anybody would ever bother."

Louise reverted back to poker-faced.

"Besides us," I said to her, "the Muses and the Rock Creek poets are the only ones who'll ever know it's true. Just like when Brautigan told Runaway's story in his novel. Nobody has ever suspected that's true. Walter's secrets will be safe, the oath unbroken."

"I think Walter would like this," Cowboy said. "It'd be another fictitious fable added to his mystery. He was always doing that himself, hinting at things that never really happened, to add to his own legend."

"Like saying he made babies?" I said. He shrugged.

"But it would be a true calamity if the manuscripts ever come to light," I said. "For us and the story. We'd have broken the oath. Worse yet, the story itself, if it could be proven true by the manuscripts, would be plundered for everything it's worth by the literary establishment, especially the academics. Deconstructed. Torn asunder and reinterpreted in vicious tugs of war over literary theory and whatever fashionable academic causes are most in vogue. If we do this, you two can never ever cash in on the manuscripts."

Bless her heart, she jumped to her feet and put her hands on her hips and grinned at me. "Oh yeah of little faith," she said. "Cowboy says Walter approves. The Muses tell me they also approve, and therefore they command us, to grant the story and the canon its most fervent desire, to be set free, out into the world."

I never saw Cowboy happier. Time to make hay.

"William wants to move into your basement. I convinced him that you very much want him to, so your house won't be so empty."

"I do want him to," Cowboy said. "I've asked him before, and I was planning to ask him again before it turns cold."

"Glad to hear it," I said. "He's moving in tonight. I gave him my key."

He nodded and stood and smiled at Louise.

"Now all he needs is a little stipend and he's all set," I said. "I wish I had it to give to him."

"Let me take care of that," Louise said.

"I detest goodbyes as much as Keats," I said and stepped toward the tunnel.

"Hold on," Cowboy said. "We should take the manuscripts to the big house right now. Lock them up in the safe."

"But keep the tell here," Louise said. "For the Muses and our poets."

"Whose spirits will gather here as soon as we depart," I said. "I can see them now, jabbering away amongst themselves and taking turns toasting us."

"We'll come back tonight and read it by candlelight," she said.

"Right after dinner," he said. "We'll restock this place."

Louise tucked the manuscripts under her sweater. Cowboy retrieved his *Leaves*. They hid the tell. We all leaned over and began blowing out candles. I went out first. Louise followed. Cowboy must have wet his forefinger and thumb, for I heard the dying sizzle of the last candle.

"You best hurry home with those," I said outside.

"Not before I have a hug from my Keatsian hero" she said. Cowboy followed with a handshake and one last hearty thwack on the back.

"I almost forgot," I said. "I added four others to the Rock Creek Canon, honorary inductees, but all granted full-fledged membership and immortality by the Muses. Jorge Luis Borges, whose enshrinement is dedicated to my old friend Fernando. E.M. Forster, on behalf of Mrs. Cummings, another old friend. Langston Hughes is enshrined in honor of William. And Emily Dickinson is added in honor of me, the canon expander."

"Done," Louise said. "Fine," Cowboy shrugged, and waved me goodbye.

"One last thing. Since we're freeing the story, won't you grant me my tell? I do have someone now."

"William, I hope," Cowboy said.

"Yep."

"As long as he sticks to the oath," Louise said.

"He doesn't want to pass it on" I said. "Just wants to know for his own self."

They nodded in unison.

I told them I would remember them fondly for the rest of my days. I reminded Louise that no matter what else lay in store for us, we could rest assured we'd see the Muses and John and Walter gather round at our end, and I told Cowboy they'd certainly be there with him too. Before they could reply I turned my back and headed off. In honor of Walter, who never says goodbye because he's always waiting for you, and of John, who finds goodbyes exceedingly difficult, I threw up an arm and did not look back.

39

MY REBORN KEEN EYE, newly cocky, revealed shades of glee and sadness and kindness flashing across William's face as he directed Beauty's last glide down the driveway. I wondered what my face showed, if William could see the struggle between exhilaration and dread of another final farewell, the most bitter of all.

I told him first of how the news that he'd agreed to move in so thrilled Cowboy, who expected him that very night. I handed him Cowboy's basement key, and could see happiness light his brow like neon as he thrust it to the bottom of his pocket and patted it.

I recounted, blow by blow, how Louise and Cowboy had warmed to our plan and reminded him what a wizard he was to have come up with it. I told him how hugely relieved they were for the fate of the story to be finally lifted off their shoulders.

He smiled proudly and declared, "We did good, didn't we?"

Lastly, I told him how neither of them batted an eye when I added Langston and Emily to the official Rock Creek Canon. He uncapped the chilled bottle I'd brought him and toasted. "Welcome to my park, Emily and Langston. Now we'll get even better acquainted."

I joined him in sipping and told him the secret story. It was our finest hour.

"Cowboy ended up just like Ezra," was the first thing he said when I finished. "Happy ever after, both of them, with their favorite gal and poets."

"You're a lot like Ezra, too," I said. "Discovering the park, making it your own, making your home here, and best of all, spending your days tromping around your own little paradise, just like he did."

"And now that I know about his hideaway, I'll go there when I need to get away from Cowboy," William said.

"You'll probably run into Louise."

"Probably so."

We stepped down onto the patch of grass at hill's edge and sipped and stood side by side in our favorite spot, staring off into the park.

"Come go with me," I said. "Take a little vacation before you start looking after Cowboy. I'll show you the Blue Ridge, and I promise to bring you back soon as you want."

His face pained up in displeasure. "I don't want to go anywhere."

"You're right. Better not," I said. "Cowboy is expecting you to-night. You can't disappoint him. And you got to keep your eye on the park, now that you're the protector of not one, but both of its secrets."

He took on a most contented expression, a most distant look, as if seeing nirvana. I tried to envision it along with him, but all I could imagine was I-95 stretching long miles ahead of me.

"You're not going to turn all sad when you're all by yourself, are you?" he said.

"Hell no," I said. "How could I? I'm resurrected, friend. Thanks to Louise and Cowboy and most of all, to you. For I am content in the knowledge that we've served the story well, that it's being told as it wished to be told, that we sung best we can for the Muses, bless their hearts."

He again clasped my shoulder. This time he gave it a squeeze. Time to go.

"You and me," he said, "we'll always have the story and our Rock Creek Gang."

I climbed into Beauty and took one long, last gander at his wise, kind face and began backing out. He gave Beauty a little love pat on her hood and for an instant I believed he was having a change of heart and would hop in with me. I tapped the brake and leaned over to throw open the passenger door when he turned away and threw up a hand goodbye.